HEALING A
Highlander's
HEART

BRENNA & QUADE

KEIRA
MONTCLAIR

DEDICATION

Thanks to my beta readers for this book: Janet, Joan,
Kathy, Merry, and Annie
Your hard work is greatly appreciated.

OTHER NOVELS BY KEIRA MONTCLAIR

THE BAND OF COUSINS
HIGHLAND VENGEANCE
HIGHLAND ABDUCTION
HIGHLAND RETRIBUTION
HIGHLAND LIES

THE CLAN GRANT SERIES
#1- RESCUED BY A HIGHLANDER-Alex and Maddie
#2- HEALING A HIGHLANDER'S HEART-
Brenna and Quade
#3- LOVE LETTERS FROM LARGS-Brodie and Celestina
#4-JOURNEY TO THE HIGHLANDS-Robbie and Caralyn
#5-HIGHLAND SPARKS-Logan and Gwyneth
#6-MY DESPERATE HIGHLANDER-Micheil and Diana
#7-THE BRIGHTEST STAR IN THE HIGHLANDS-
Jennie and Aedan
#8- HIGHLAND HARMONY-Avelina and Drew

THE HIGHLAND CLAN
LOKI-Book One
TORRIAN-Book Two
LILY-Book Three
JAKE-Book Four
ASHLYN-Book Five
MOLLY-Book Six
JAMIE AND GRACIE- Book Seven

CHAPTER ONE

Late autumn, the 1200s

Her eyes flew open at the touch of the cold steel blade against her cheek.

"Do no' move, lass. I do no' want to have to cut you."

Brenna Grant jerked with a gasp.

A sharp pain perforated the right side of her face. She cringed at the sensation of warm blood trickling down her neck. *Stop! He will kill you. Do as he says.*

"Ah, lass, what did you have to go and do that for? I told you no' to move."

Lying helpless in her night clothes, she peered through the dark chamber hoping to distinguish a face or any clue as to who held the knife, but the man was out of her line of sight. Sensing his body crouched behind her pallet, she let the air out of her lungs slowly, not wanting to set him off. Who was her attacker?

"Are you the healer?" Hot breath scorched her ear. He smelled of sweat, horse, and the odor that results from days of not bathing.

"Aye." She closed her eyes before reopening them, hoping something would happen to change her situation. Her brother or his guards could charge into the room at any moment, so Brenna made the decision to do as he ordered. Alex and her other two brothers would save her, wouldn't they? Yet this invader had gotten past her brother's powerful defenses. That thought alone frightened her.

"There's a good lass. Now, we will stand up together. You will grab your plaid, shoes, and cloak, and you will leave with me. Understood? If you yell, I will slice. Verra simple. Do as I say and naught will happen to anyone else."

The knife moved to her throat and eased enough for her to nod her head. She berated herself. Why did she always have to be so honest? She should have lied and denied being the healer. Perhaps he would have left. No, it was always better to tell the truth. She couldn't risk endangering her family.

"Smart lass. Now where are your healer's herbs and poultices?"

She pointed to the left of her bed, where her satchel sat ready for any emergencies.

"Ready?"

He tugged her out of bed and dragged her over to her chest of drawers where her clothes were kept. She dressed quickly and grabbed her cloak before slipping on her shoes and picking up her satchel.

Sweat beaded on her forehead, between her breasts. "Where are you taking me?"

"You do no' need to know." He grasped her arm above the elbow, digging into the tender skin hard enough to leave bruises. "If I hear any sound from you as we leave, I will take your sister as well. Jennie is her name, if my sources are correct, aye? I have a lad waiting to grab her at my request. You'll come willingly. Agreed?"

Brenna nodded her head, cringing at the thought of anything happening to her sister. She would do anything to protect Jennie. When he eased his pressure on her arm a bit, she threw a few more essentials into her healer's sack and followed him to the door.

He clamped his fingers down on her arm again as he

led her down the dim passageway. She stumbled over something and nearly screamed. One of the guardsmen lay sprawled on the floorboards. A brief moan rose from him after the impact. She sighed, grateful he was still alive, though who knew for how long. Her brother, Alex, also her laird, would have an apoplexy when he discovered his guard had failed.

When they reached the staircase, another lad joined them. She sighed with relief. Her sister was not with him. They snuck out the back entrance and headed for the wall surrounding the keep. She almost tripped over another body near the kitchens, but her captor yanked her aside just in time. Nothing else impeded their path.

Stumbling across the back of the bailey to the wall, Brenna faltered several times attempting to keep pace with her captors. Where were they bringing her? Her brother had no enemies to her knowledge. If any neighboring clan had need of her healing skills, she would be glad to help—no threat required. Alex often sent her with an escort to tend the sick and wounded, whether they were within the clan or not.

She didn't recognize either man running alongside her. Both had blackened their faces, and their voices and clothing sparked no familiarity. They wore no plaid. All Highlanders wore their plaid; it was a matter of pride. What reason could they have for breaking with tradition?

Tumbling over a tree root, she yelped. "Slow down, please!" Her plea fell on deaf ears.

Her kidnapper caught her before she fell, pulling her tight to him. "Mind your mouth. We will not risk losing everything for you."

What could he mean? Two others awaited them at the wall. One shoved her toward a rope ladder, uttering only a single command.

"Climb."

She stared at the four warriors, gulped and stuck

her foot on the bottom loop. As she grappled for the rope, the dampness of her palm slid across the rough twine. A hand pushed her bottom. Reacting instinctively, she swung out and struck the offender in the chin with her hand.

"Do no' touch me," she whispered between clenched teeth.

The warrior started to swing back, but her kidnapper stayed his hand.

"Do no' touch her. The chief will have your arse." He turned back to her and pushed her up the ladder. "Get moving, lass. We do no' have time for games."

Chief? What chief? After her brother's marriage to Madeline MacDonald, she knew most of the lairds in the Highlands. This could not be a Highland laird forcing her against her will, could it? Her hopes dashed as realization struck. This was no amateur kidnapping.

When they dropped to the ground on the other side of the wall, her kidnapper grabbed her elbow, tugging her toward a nearby horse. He grabbed her waist with one hand and put his other hand under her foot, helping her onto the horse. He mounted behind her after hooking her satchel to the saddle, and then, digging his heels into the flanks of the beast, set off at a frantic pace. The other guards followed.

Brenna searched the area for other horses besides the three behind her—her brother's guardsmen, anyone. She saw no one. It wasn't long before even the guards who followed them disappeared from sight, leaving her alone with this stranger.

"There are no other horses, lass. And no one to save you. Your guardsmen are busy with a fire on the other side of the keep. This was well planned. Get it out of your head now."

He leaned down to whisper in her ear.

"You willnae be rescued."

CHAPTER TWO

Brenna's patience had disappeared a long time ago. Several hours had passed, and still they rode on. Her captor refused to answer her questions. He ignored her, refusing to be civil, and she could no longer tolerate it. She would annoy him until he gave her answers.

She took a deep breath, hung on for dear life, and started. "Where are we going? Where are you taking me? And I willnae stop talking until you answer me. I have three brothers and I ken how annoying incessant female blether can be, and I will continue until you respond. Or are you that heartless? You have nae feelings for anyone? You ride your horse until he foams; you barely allow me the opportunity to see to my needs. Your partners have never caught up with us. Why do we ride alone? Why have they no' caught up with us? Why can we no' stop and rest? Why cannae...?"

"Enough, woman!" His dull roar echoed in her ears.

His very loud sigh gave her hope. Had she been successful?

"You want answers; I will give them to you. You ride with me because I am the best. No one else will be able to get you where we need to be in time."

"But we ride alone. We could easily be attacked." She attempted a glance over her shoulder at him. He wasn't that ugly. He had light brown hair, brown eyes, and a strong nose. True, he still had an odor that riled her sense of smell something fierce, but he didn't appear as angry as he had before, just focused.

"No one would dare attack me. I am the best rider in the Highlands and the best swordsman, too. I am the only hope there is of getting you where you are needed in time. No one is with us because they couldnae keep up. They ride behind as protection against your clan. I have the best horse and he will do as I order. Do no' be concerned about him. He will get his reward when we arrive. I am no' normally cruel to animals. These are rare circumstances." His brown eyes met hers. "Now cease your prattle."

"Get me where? Where are we going?"

"Cease, I said!" He tugged her back against him when he bellowed.

"Fine," she muttered out the side of her mouth. He hadn't told her much, but at least he had spoken. She dared not aggravate him more, lest he slap her or do any number of vicious things, like Madeline's stepbrother, Kenneth. How her sister-in-law had survived that man's cruelty was a wonder. But Kenneth's abusive nature had eventually made him addled and wild, impossible to predict. Something told her that this man, who seemed in complete control of everything, was another type altogether.

She watched the stranger from the corner of her eye, and she was quite sure she saw the corner of his mouth twitch.

⁂

A short time later, he led his horse off the path and into the forest. She brought her hands in front of her face to protect herself from the branches that flew at her. She feared they would be catapulted from the horse. The man never slowed. Perhaps he was trying to frighten her, but she refused to concede. Though she covered her eyes with her hands, she never made a sound.

Finally, after what felt like half a day, he tugged on the reins and brought his horse up short. When Brenna pulled her hands from her eyes, a small cottage sat in front of her. Where had that come from? Her captor dismounted, grabbed her by the waist and set her on the ground.

"See to your needs, lass." He gave her a push toward the back of the cottage before snatching her healer's bag and striding inside.

The softness in his voice startled her. Behind the cottage, she noticed three other horses. So they were not alone anymore. She made quick with her business and stood outside the door.

How did he know she wouldn't run? She could. She turned in a circle, trying to determine which way she would go. Since she had no true sense of direction, she wouldn't get far. There was another reason to stay—like any healer, she could not ignore it when her skills were needed, and someone inside that cottage was undoubtedly injured or ill. She moved toward the door and was wondering whether to open it or knock first when it flew open, and her kidnapper tugged her inside.

"Over there." He pointed toward the back of the cottage near the hearth.

She stood long enough to notice the two guards on either side of the doorway. Which one was the chief?

"Stop gawking and move on over. The one on the pallet needs you. Now heal him. I will get more wood to warm the cabin." The door slammed behind him.

The guards at the door ignored her. Clearly they were not in charge. She blocked them out so she could focus on her new patient and do what needed to be done so she could return home.

As she approached the hearth, her eyes began to adjust to the gloom inside. It was still dark, but dawn would soon arrive. A man slept on the pallet, barely moving. The smell of old blood permeated the air. His shallow breathing and wet cough alerted her to how serious his ailment was. This man was close to death. Kneeling beside him, she started her assessment of his condition. Her mother's advice still held true: a healer's greatest skill was to listen and observe before deciding on a course of action.

All threats to her safety forgotten, she settled herself to the task at hand. Touching the man's shoulder, she could feel the heat of his body, a sign that his system was trying to rid itself of the poisons inside. Sweat dotted his forehead, more evidence of the fight in progress. This must be the chief of their clan, which explained the urgency. The lad was very near death.

She shook him to see if he would respond, but he did not budge. Starting her examination at his head, she noticed he had dark brown hair, sun-bronzed skin, strong cheekbones, and a straight nose. Long eyelashes settled over his skin, and even near death, he was a handsome man. She found herself wondering what color his eyes were. He breathed through his mouth, making it easier for her to ensure that he was still alive.

Folding the blanket back, she noticed his chest was barely moving. There was a rattling sound deep in his lungs that she didn't like. Adjusting the blanket a bit lower, she found the source of his problems. His belly had been ripped open.

The door flew open, and her kidnapper appeared by her side moments later. "'Twas a boar." She noticed the grim look on the faces of the guards by the door, shaking their head when the boar was mentioned.

"'Tis a deep wound," she said. "He was sick before the injury?"

His brow furrowed as he stared down at her. "How could you ken that?"

She motioned him over and pointed. "There. Do you

see the swollen part of his insides protruding from the wound? It is full of poison and could leak into his belly." Looking up at her captor, she nodded. "'Twas a good thing you can ride fast. He does no' have much longer."

"But you can help him? I did no' ride for naught, did I, lass?" His eyes searched hers with a need she understood.

"I will try. Do either of you have a name?"

"Aye, his is Quade and I am Logan. 'Tis all you need to ken. Get to work while I start the fire."

"I need water. Is there a stream nearby so you can fetch fresh water?"

"Aye, not far. I'll return with what you need."

"Be quick about it. Without water, he will surely die. Much of your body is water. My mother taught me that though it is the most basic part of us, it is the most necessary, too. He can't fight the fever without water and I must clean his wound besides." She stopped to give Logan a searching look and held her breath. She had just barked an order at her captor out of habit. Would he follow it?

"Och, lass, fine. I'll go for water." He dumped the wood in his arms on the floor, gave orders to the guards and slammed the door behind him on his way out.

She let her breath out; grateful that he didn't mind her abruptness as so many others did. She turned back to her patient. There was much to do for this man, this clan chief known as Quade. Would she be able to save him? She opened her satchel and began to pull out the tools she would need—a knife, a needle and thread, and several long strips of clean linen. She found the jar with her poultice for fever and one for healing open wounds.

Once she was prepared, she finished her assessment of the patient, noting his long, strong hands, and his flat belly on the left side. There were no open wounds besides the one she'd noted, but the wound on his right side was one of the largest she had ever seen. The cut was long, but for some unknown reason, the boar had missed his bowel. A rip there would surely have killed him. She stared at what had caught her eye before. At the very end of his bowel, a small appendage sat ripe and full of pus, ready to burst and spread its poison to the rest of the cavity. She knew she couldn't allow that to happen or he would surely die. A long time ago, her grandfather had described something similar. She had been awestruck as she listened to his experience of cutting something out of someone's belly to save his life.

And now she was witnessing the same situation. Could she cut that appendage out of his body? Would he survive without it? Somehow, she knew what needed to be done, and she prayed for the strength to do it.

Logan returned with a bucket of water and a kettle filled to the brim. He set them next to her and rekindled the fire in the hearth. He motioned to the guards by the door. "Outside. Keep wood by the door and get whatever the lass needs. She has serious work to do. No interruptions. The others should be along soon."

Brenna organized her tools and supplies. She glanced over at Logan as he continued his work near the hearth. "I may need you to hold him."

"He looks to me as if he willnae feel anything, lass. Just do it. If he awakens, he can handle it."

"How many days ago did this happen?" Brenna searched his face after he turned toward the pallet.

"The boar attacked two days ago. We were on our way to your land when Quade felt ill. We stopped so he could heave everything out of his gut again. 'Twas the third or fourth time. This time, a boar came charging out of the wood and impaled him before he could react. He was too slow with the sickness." Logan stared at his hands. "I couldnae get there fast enough."

"What happened to the boar?"

"I killed it. I sent a couple of our guards back with the meat. Our clan needs it."

"You were already coming for me when Quade fell ill? Why? I thought you kidnapped me to save him, your chief." She paused for his explanation. What else did they want with her?

"You do no' need to know. He is your primary concern. Sew him up." He headed toward the door. "I'll find us something to eat."

"Please stay, I may need you." Brenna stopped and stared at him. "Please."

He nodded and then strode to the door and to send one of the guards hunting for food. When he returned, his hands settled on his hips as he motioned his head toward the body on the pallet. "All right, lass. Get started. We do no' have much time."

Brenna grabbed the bucket and ran water over her hands. "Why the rush? Where else do we have to go?"

"Cease with the questions. I will tell you when you need to ken. Why are you doing that?" Logan grabbed the vessel from her hand and took a swig.

"I need clean hands if I am to stick them inside his body. My mother always told me dirt on the hand caused problems for healers."

"Suit yourself, but be on with it."

Before turning to her patient, she pointed to the hearth. "Place a kettle of water on the hearth. 'Tis too cold to pour on his insides and I need to wash the dirt out from the boar. The temperature of the water alone may kill him."

Shocked but pleased he did her bidding again without argument, she turned back to her patient and began her task. Closing her eyes and offering up a quick prayer for guidance, she sighed. After tying off the bowel above the damaged appendage, she started cutting.

A few hours later, she sat in a chair staring at her patient. She couldn't believe how well his surgery had gone. The appendage had come out without breaking open, and after washing the dirt out of his insides, she had given him many stitches inside without even making him flinch. Logan had left after turning a bit green while watching her put Quade's bowels back where she thought they belonged. The stitching had taken most of the morning, but she was pleased with her work.

Logan entered with a couple of roasted rabbits.

"Here, lass." He offered her one on a large stone. "Have to say you deserve it. Do no' ken how you do what you do. Did he ever awaken?"

She glanced down at her patient, handsome in his sleep. "Nay, he hasnae moved. He is a sick lad. I covered his stitches with my salve and tried to get him to drink, but I couldnae arouse him. Mayhap in a few hours." She reached for the rabbit legs, amazed by how hungry she was. "Throw your bones in the kettle with the water. I will cook some broth for him. He won't be able to eat anything else for awhile." Brenna tossed her first one in the water.

Logan strode to the hearth and grabbed the kettle. "Lass, I will see to that. Why do you no' rest a bit? You may be needed later when he awakens."

Brenna nodded and moved over to the pallet to feel her patient's forehead once more.

"Aye, I am tired."

He tossed a blanket to her. She threw it on the floor next to the pallet, not wanting to stray far from her patient. Even though it was broad daylight, she was asleep as soon as her head hit the floor.

"Curse it, Logan, what have you done to me?"

He attempted to sit but groaned and fell back on the

pallet, grabbing his right side. Before he could even process the presence of another person, the face of a lass with a glorious mass of brown curls shot up next to him.

"Hellfire, who in blazes are you?"

"Stop moving and quit your cursing! If you rip my stitches out, I willnae do them again."

Quade stared into the beautiful brown eyes of the strange lass. Saints above, she must be the healer. By instinct, he tried to get closer to her, but his side hurt too much. He had to stop and ease himself back down on the pallet.

"Arghhhh!" He bellowed his frustration, and Logan's laughter echoed through the small cottage. He peered at the shabby surroundings. He finally noticed his brother at a small table not far away. Two of his guardsmen stood by the door. Naught else was visible except the beauty next to him.

"Problem, brother? Hurting a wee bit? Why do you no' say good morning to all and quit yelling at the lassie at your side. She saved your arse, no' me." Logan threw back some ale as he chuckled.

What in blazes was Logan talking about? Were they in the Grant keep now? He didn't recall meeting the Grant laird or asking for their healer's assistance. Quade's mind cleared a bit but only when he stopped gritting his teeth from the unbelievable agony in his right side. Och, aye, he recalled now. He had stopped his horse so he could lose his insides for about the fourth time that day when a boar had burst out of the brush and run straight at him. He didn't remember much after that.

"The boar got me, Logan?" He spoke to his brother, but he couldn't stop staring at the brown-eyed beauty next to him. She brushed her hair away from her face before bolting to her feet.

"Mercy!" He could think of no other words to adequately describe the lass. If not for his need to empty his bladder, he might have been embarrassed by his reaction to her. She couldn't be the healer they had been seeking. He had heard the renowned Grant healer was young, but no one had mentioned her beauty. This wasn't something one would forget.

He reached for his side again but a lovely hand swatted him until he stopped.

"I said, do no' ruin my stitchery. I worked verra hard on you. That boar almost ripped out your insides. And a piece of your insides was full of poisons and had to be cut out of you. If you keep fussing around like a laddie, you will tear the stitches inside your body as well." She returned her hands to her hips, but then swatted him again when he did not listen.

He couldn't help himself. "Stop hitting me, woman! I am in enough pain, I do no' need more. What are you talking about, cutting out part of my belly? What did you do to me?"

"Cease your whining, Quade, and leave her be. This is the Grant healer, and she saved your sorry life."

"Och, aye! I have to pish, find me something, Logan. I cannae get up. And you," he pointed at Brenna. "Step back. A little privacy, please, to relieve myself."

She turned away from him, hands on her hips, with a look that could fry an egg. He couldn't help but smile. What a sight for sore eyes after all he had been through! When he finished, Logan helped him before turning and heading out the door. The lass moved right back to the pallet and dragged a stool with her. Groaning, he arranged himself so she didn't have to see everything but kept clear of the wound. Somehow, he knew she would be checking.

"What's your name, lass?" He gazed into her doe-like eyes. Och, he had not seen a beauty like this in years, if ever before.

"Brenna. As you know, I am Laird Grant's sister. My mother and grandfather were both healers. My mother taught me everything she kenned about healing. My brother has kept me verra busy with his guardsmen."

"Are you the healer that saved the laird's leg, the one that was hanging by no more that a piece of skin?"

"Och, there was more than one piece of skin. You are listening to exaggerations. But the answer is aye, I repaired the vessels and attached the leg as best I could."

"And he can use it?"

She nodded. "He has a bit of a limp, but 'tis still attached." Her smile lit her face from within.

His heart warmed like a laddie just looking at her. He could no' take his eyes away. "How do you do it, lass? Cutting up my insides? Many would faint at the sight. What drives you? And did you deliver your brother's lads, both of them, with a knife at your throat?"

"Nay, the addled man was gone when I finally delivered my nephews. My brother's wife had a nasty stepbrother who tried to kill both her and her bairns. My brother, thankfully, sent him away with just enough time left to deliver the twin laddies. Och, they are the sweetest ever." She paused, gazing out the window, her thoughts evident on her face. "I do what I do because I was born to do it. Like my mother and my grandpapa. 'Tis in my blood."

"What about a husband and bairns? 'Tis what most lasses wish for. No' you?"

"I take what comes each day. I am too busy to think about bairns and I have my wee nephews to love." She touched the area around the stitches tenderly with the back of her hand. "Good, 'tis no' warm yet. You are better off with the sour piece of flesh out, but you could still develop the fever from the wound."

"Brenna, I like your name. I must say I am pleased you do no' have a hairy chin or a wart on your nose like some healers I ken." He couldn't tear his eyes from her. "Since you are touching me, am I allowed to touch you, Lady Brenna?" He knew he was probably being rude, but her soft skin beckoned him.

She pulled back, blushing. "Why would you want to do that?"

"Och, aye, you have the prettiest skin I ever saw." He reached for her cheek, brushing the surface with the back of his hand. The small movement made him want to caress every inch of her soft body. The puzzled expression on her face caught him and he dropped his arm. She backed away. It had been a while, but he wasn't usually ignored by lasses, especially since he had become chief.

She sighed before returning her gaze to his belly, scrutinizing her work. "And you havenae pulled any stitches out and you arenae bleeding."

He heard that sigh and, taking it as encouragement, brushed the tender skin of her neck and ran his thumb across her bottom lip. He knew he should stay away from her, but he could not stop himself. "Seems I need to thank you for saving my life."

The door shot open and Logan dropped two dead rabbits on the small table by the hearth.

"What's wrong?" Logan said, staring at him until Quade dropped his hand from Brenna's face.

"'Tis naught wrong. I was thanking the lass for saving my life. Now that I can see the damage, I ken she had quite a bit of sewing to do.

Ducking away from him, she picked up a jar of salve and covered his wound with it, making him wince. "Are you hungry?" she asked. "Do you think you could eat some broth?"

"Only if you feed me." He gave her the most innocent stare he could muster, expecting her to call him out for his sloth, but she didn't say a word.

"Och, aye." Logan yelled over his shoulder as he left the cottage, slamming the door behind him. So his brother had noticed his infatuation. It wasn't surprising; he didn't usually miss much.

He was a bit embarrassed by his fervor, but he couldn't help it. She strode to the hearth and filled a bowl with broth. The sway of her hips almost caused more pain than pleasure, but he still couldn't avert his gaze. She pulled the stool back to the bed and sat beside him, stirring the broth to cool it. He didn't think he had ever seen a woman with so much natural beauty. She brushed a stray strand of hair away from her head, not the least bit worried about how she looked. Just as well that Logan was gone. He wanted to lose himself in the brown-eyed beauty in front of him, even though she had no idea what he was about.

"Open up." Brenna aimed the spoon at her target.

He savored every spoonful until he started to choke on the broth. With the first cough, it felt as though his insides were bursting from his body. He stared at her as if she could help.

"Guard your belly." She grabbed his hands and pushed them against his wound.

The pain made him want to scream, but he fought it.

"Hold your hands up against your injury, like this." Brenna braced his hands tight against his body, using hers as support. "It won't hurt as much."

Gasping for air, he finally cleared what he needed to and tried to ease his breathing to stop the pain. Her face was a mere inches away from his. She was so close that her sweet floral scent washed over him with each breath, igniting a different fire in him. He closed his eyes for a moment and when he opened them, she was staring at him, a perplexed expression on her face. Brenna Grant was a complete innocent when it came to male desire, without a doubt. This shocked him because she was such a beauty, but it would not stop him.

Forcing himself up on one elbow, he reached for her cheek and brushed his lips across hers briefly. He didn't care how much pain it would cost him; he had to get closer to her. She froze, but didn't pull away, so he kissed her again, deep enough to really taste her. He couldn't muffle his groan of pleasure. This time she reacted immediately, jumping back from him with confusion and concern in her eyes.

Pain seared his belly, and he fell back onto the hard pallet. What was wrong? Why did she stare at him so? He grabbed her hand and squeezed it tight as he closed his eyes and succumbed to exhaustion.

CHAPTER THREE

"How long before he can travel, lass?" Logan sat on the stool by the hearth the next morning, chewing on the bones of whatever small critter he had caught and roasted and chugging a tankard of ale.

Brenna glanced over at Quade. He hadn't awakened since the previous day, after she fed him the broth. His breathing told her he was in a deep sleep, precisely what was needed for him to heal.

"Probably a few days before he can sit upon a horse. His injury is in a bad location for riding. He could tear both the inside and outside stitches if he tries too early."

"Two days at the most. Then we need to move on."

"Two days? 'Tis no' enough time to heal properly. Bleeding on the inside can kill a man. 'Tis no need to hurry, as far as I know." She stared at her captor, daring him to argue. "Unless there really is someone else for me to heal?"

"No' for you to ken yet." He continued to chew, not too concerned with her questions.

"Why can you no' tell me what goes on? Why do you no' use your own clan healer? Why me?" Stubborn man. How she hated being at Logan's mercy. She didn't like all the stirrings in her heart brought on by this new situation or by Quade.

"We have a healer. Gunna is her name, but she is too old. She has tried. We came for you because your healing skills are legendary."

"Aye. What does that have to do with...?"

"Are you no' Elizabeth Grant's daughter, kenned as the best healer in the Highlands before her death?"

"Aye."

"Have any of your brother's guard's died from injuries since you have been the healer?"

"Nay, but..."

"Och, then you understand. And we have tried many others. Naught works. You are next..."

He stared at the hearth as if deep in thought. The room was silent for several moments. "Upon further thought," he finally said, "my plans have changed. Now that you have mended Quade, I will take you on ahead and leave the guards with him. There are enough to travel with us while leaving some behind to protect him." He tossed another bone into the kettle.

Brenna found herself shaking her head. "Nay!"

His eyelids narrowed as he peered at her. "Why nay?"

She didn't understand her own quick response to him, so she didn't have an answer. The faster she did the work he needed her to do, the faster she could go home. She should be ecstatic.

But she wasn't, and it was because she wasn't ready to leave Quade. Rubbing her fingers across her bottom lip, she thought about his kiss. He had taken her completely off guard.

And she had enjoyed it.

That's what confused her most. This wasn't her first kiss. She had been kissed once before. When she was four and ten, one of the stable lads had grabbed her and pinned her to a mound of hay. He had slobbered a wet kiss on her lips and his roving hands had touched her through her clothes. She had tried to kick and scream, but he was too large and she, too small. Fortunately, she hadn't needed to wait long before her brothers ran into the stables and lifted the lad in the air, tossing him across the paddock. Not knowing what else to do, she'd run off in mortal shock.

Her brothers had never mentioned the incident within her hearing, but word must surely have gotten around for whispering had followed her wherever she went for the next fortnight. Much to her gratitude, she never saw the lad again. His sloppy saliva had achieved one thing: She wasn't interested in intimacy with a man. She couldn't help but cringe when she thought of it, even now.

How could anyone bear to be kissed if it involved all that saliva? She had made up her mind never to marry. The fact that her brother was Laird Alexander Grant, renowned as the best swordsman in the Highlands, helped her keep her oath, since no man had ever dared to touch her or try to get close to her after that foolish stable lad.

She knew she was past the age to marry, being twenty and four summers. And when Alex and his wife, Maddie, asked her whether she wanted to marry, she always adamantly denied it, saying she was too devoted to her work as a healer.

After what had happened with Quade, she wasn't so sure anymore.

In truth, a small longing had already come to life inside her. The love she saw each day between Alex and Maddie made her wish the same for herself one day. However, the custom in the Highlands was that she would be taken away from her brother and his keep when she married. That would mean leaving her sister, Jennie, behind. She didn't think she was capable of it. Jennie had matured, but she was still young. The death of their parents had been especially difficult for her, causing her to regress into early childhood behaviors at times.

She closed her eyes, recalling the soft warmth of Quade's lips and the tingling she had felt from his touch. This was a whole new area for her to explore, and she found herself eager to discover what went on between lads and lasses. The best way to explore it would be away from her brothers.

"If you are still tired, go to sleep. I will clean up. Get some rest. It will be another long ride back to your land."

Logan's words startled her. Her eyes shot open; it embarrassed her that she'd been caught daydreaming about Quade's kiss. She didn't even know what clan they belonged to. Was Quade the laird? She had heard Logan refer to him as a chief. She knew very little about these two men, but wanted to learn more.

"So what is Quade chieftain of? Where are you from?" She peered at Logan from the corner of her eye to see if he was in a talking mood.

"We're near the Lowlands, lass, and 'tis all you need to know."

That partly explained why she didn't know them. She had never been in the Lowlands. Her brother had knowledge of the clans near there, but she had never been allowed to travel that far away from home. She reached into her sack and pulled out a roughly bound book, the worn pages held together by rope.

"What's that?" Logan jerked his head at her before he swilled more ale.

"My mother's journal. She recorded every patient she had so she could learn from each experience, and so I could learn from her, too." She handled the well-used pages with the care they deserved. Her mother's words were like a balm to her soul at times. She had chronicled more than just her knowledge as a healer in the book; she had also shared her feelings. Brenna had re-read it many times, and she rarely allowed it out of her sight or her chamber at home.

"You can read?" Logan's eyebrows quirked in surprise.

"Aye, my mother made sure we could all read and write."

"Are you planning to write about me, Lady Brenna?" Even the timbre of Quade's weak voice caused a shiver to run up her spine, contrary to the gruffness of Logan's voice. Why did something so basic as a person's voice affect her? This all made no sense to her, and she feared it would not turn out well.

She sat up tall, trying to ignore the effect he had on her, and turned to look at him. A small smile crossed his face that squeezed her heart. She hoped his smile was just for her. Would she ever know? Returning her book to her sack, she gave him her full attention.

"How bad is your pain?"

"Not so bad, today. At least, if I do no' move." He chuckled and then yelped, no doubt reminded of the steep cost of even a slight belly laugh.

She couldn't help but smile. "I can put a few drops of something into some water to help with your pain if you would like."

"Nay, I do no' like the way it makes me feel. I can bear it. Do no' concern yourself." He gazed into her eyes in an intent way that made her heart flutter in response. What did this man do to her?

"There is no reason to deal with the pain." She moved toward the pallet. Something about him tugged her closer, and she was powerless to fight it.

"Nay, your potion makes me feel like my bum is out the window." His gaze never left her as he spoke. "I do no' wish to forget anything of this day."

She swallowed before reaching up to wipe the sweat from her brow. Standing next to Quade's pallet, her heart swelled at the evidence of how much better he looked today than yesterday. What did he intend with his words? Was he trying to tell her that he was glad she had been the one to tend him? Her belly quivered as his gaze raked her from head to toe. No one had ever looked at her like that before, no one. A rush of heat began at her breasts and headed to her belly and the juncture of her thighs.

The stool behind her tipped over as Logan jumped from his seat. "Och, aye! Here we go again." He bolted out the door without any warning.

She turned and stared at the door. And what could he mean by that? These men were challenging all her conceptions of the world.

Quade grabbed her hand and started to stroke the tender skin on the inside of her wrist. She shivered as she stared at the contrast of his tan skin against her paler color, and her eyes moved to find his. Something smoldered in his gaze that she didn't recognize, a yearning for something he didn't have. What could he possibly want with her?

The door swung open with a bang, followed by a shout from Logan. "Nay, willnae allow it, brother. I'll be staying to observe." He righted the stool and sat down, crossing his arms as he faced his brother. "Do no' let me interrupt."

Brenna jerked her hand away and turned back to the hearth, more confused than ever. She took her time ladling broth into Quade's cup, allowing herself time to calm the turmoil in her blood. Now she would be an object of scrutiny for both brothers. She peered over her shoulder at Logan, who was still sitting on the stool and glaring at his brother. When she looked back at Quade, he was returning his brother's hard stare.

Stepping over to the pallet, she sat on the chair, grabbed the spoon and fed her patient.

His gaze followed her every move now, ignoring his brother, and she marveled at how green his eyes were. Why hadn't she noticed that before? They danced with a bit of gold, and the sunlight over her shoulder made them iridescent, shining with a delight she didn't comprehend. His scent breached her defenses, causing her cheeks to heat. He was so close his warmth diffused into her sensibilities as well. What else could be causing this warmth to spread through her core?

She said a quick prayer, thanking her mother for her steady hand. Otherwise, her hands would betray her heart right now.

Nay. She was not ready to leave Quade yet, not even to return home.

In the middle of the night, Logan and Brenna both jumped from their resting places on the floor. Brenna brushed the sleep from her eyes as she tried to figure out what had awakened them. Quade moaned in his sleep, and she rushed to his side.

Thrashing back and forth on the pallet, Quade alternated between moans, groans, and mutterings. She sat on the side of the blanket and gripped his hands, hoping to orient him. She couldn't allow him to continue with his tossing and turning or he would injure himself again.

Logan stood in the background, watching as she stroked Quade's arms, using soothing words to calm him. His forehead burned with the fever and his glassy eyes reflected the battle going on inside his body. Sweat dotted his chest when she pulled back the blanket to check his wound.

"Will you fetch fresh water, Logan? Water may calm the fever." She never turned away from Quade, but from the sound of the door slamming, she knew he had heeded her words and gone to the stream.

When Logan returned with a fresh basin of water, she soaked several linen strips in the cool liquid and bathed Quade's face. He rambled incessantly, but she was unable to make any sense of his words.

When his forehead cooled a bit, she brought a cup to his lips, holding his head gently to encourage him to drink.

"Quade, drink this." He didn't respond, though he did stare at her.

"Quade, please. 'Tis Brenna. Remember me? Drink

this; 'twill help you feel better."

She managed to get a small amount in his mouth and he swallowed reflexively, his eyes still on her.

Abruptly, he pushed her hand away. "Lily?"

"Quade, 'tis me, Brenna."

"Lily? 'Tis really you, Lily?" The look of anguish in his eyes was too much for her. Who was Lily and who was she to Quade? Why would thinking about her cause him such pain?

After drinking a bit more, his head fell back on the pallet.

She turned to Logan. "Who is Lily?"

Logan stared at her, and boldly declared, "Lily is his wife's name."

Brenna made her way to the stream after seeing to her needs, making sure she was out of the line of sight of Quade's guards. The ones who had been with them at her brother's keep had arrived yesterday, but she didn't see them today.

Fortunately, Quade's fever had passed overnight. A few drops of her mother's special draught had put him right back to sleep. Once asleep, Logan had helped her dress his wounds with more salve. Quade was strong. She had done all she could, and the rest was up to him.

Fever ended the life of many strong young men. The best healers were unable to understand why some recovered and some passed on from the same affliction. Was it the will to live as her mother had always suspected?

Breathing a sigh of relief, she was grateful that the worst was over for Quade. He had awakened cursing this morn, so she'd decided to leave him with Logan and take some time to herself. Apparently, Logan was no longer worried about her leaving. She snickered as her eyes searched the area. Perhaps he had good reason, since she would have absolutely no idea which way to go. Her sense of direction could send her to England as easily as it could back home.

Splashing water on her face, she chided herself for allowing a small kiss to scramble her senses. No wonder many of the lasses at her keep complained about lying, cheating men. Quade was married. How could he have kissed her? The worst part was that she'd enjoyed it. Perhaps it had been only a couple of days, but she had actually allowed herself to think about getting married and having bairns like Alex and Maddie. She'd had a difficult time falling back to sleep last night after Logan revealed the truth. Quade had come into her life only a short time ago, so she was at fault for allowing him to affect her so.

As she wrung out some of her clothes, she wondered again about a man, nay, a chief, who would so easily lie to her. If he had tried to kiss her when he was sick with fever, she could understand. But there had been no fever when he caressed her face, rubbed his thumb on her lip, and kissed her near senseless.

When she finished her ablutions, she headed back to the cottage, but stopped as shouts disrupted the peacefulness of the forest. Quade and Logan were arguing loudly enough to send critters scuttling for cover. The guards had moved to the area behind the cottage where they were roasting their meat. She crept closer to the door until she could understand the words the brothers were hurling at each other.

"You have no right to be looking at her." Logan bellowed.

"Who says I am looking at her?" Quade's voice was low, but distinctive.

"I saw how you were with her. I was just outside when you kissed her. Or do you no' remember?"

"I will look at her however I choose, and it is no concern of yours." Quade's shout didn't have quite the strength of his brother's, but his intentions were clear.

They were discussing her? Quade had admitted to

being interested in her? Her heart sped at the thought, and a slow smile crept across her face. The smile lasted until she remembered he was married. Then it disappeared. She slowed her steps but snuck a bit closer to the door. An eerie silence followed.

Logan's voice broke it. "You need to leave her be. She isnae yours." She envisioned Logan towering over Quade on the edge of the pallet as he spoke.

"Why, so you can have her?" Quade whispered.

"How could I stand a chance after you have made your intentions so clear?"

She froze at Logan's words. They were fighting over her? Logan wanted her? Saints above! Truly? Logan wanted her. Nay! She was not interested in Logan. Though he was nice looking, he wasn't as appealing to her eyes as Quade. Holy hedgehogs! She had led a life with only a stable lad interested in her, and now both men wanted her?

"You cannae have her. I am chieftain and my wish holds. Or have you forgotten that? No one else is to touch the Grant lass. I havenae decided yet if I do want her." Quade's voice trembled through the door. She could tell his strength had not yet returned.

"Mayhap I will make it easy on you. You have a few days left to heal. I will return her to her clan while I leave you here. She filled our most pressing need by saving your sorry arse. Taking her to our clan could be a huge mistake. We still kidnapped her and we need to set this right."

"Where are the rest of my guards?" Quade coughed and moaned.

Brenna wanted to run through the door and wrap her arms around him. *Fool! Stop thinking about him. He is married!* Still, she couldn't stop her traitorous thoughts. She paced outside the small cottage.

Logan's voice dropped a bit. "I sent most of them on ahead. There's enough to protect us. We havenae far to go. Mayhap I will take you home before returning her to her clan."

"She stays with me. My original plan still holds. She must come home with us."

Brenna's mind raced. What did she want to happen? Home. She needed to go home—to Jennie, Maddie, her brothers. Still, for some reason her heart wasn't in it, and her gut wanted her to stay with Quade. It was probably because she was a healer. Her mother always had said the same.

She could hear Logan crossing the room. "You are still daft from the fever. Taking her home would be a big mistake and you ken it. I need to return her to her keep."

"My order stands, she returns with us." Quade's voice was losing volume, but he sounded no less stubborn.

"You're my brother and you ken I have always been here for you, but I cannae support this decision, Quade."

"I dinnae ask for your support. If you cannae follow my wishes, then take your leave, Logan. I will escort her safely home with us. She goes with me. If you cannae handle it, then get the hell out." Quade's voice was barely above a whisper, but she heard every word.

Dead silence hung in the air for a few moments before Logan spoke.

"Fine. I'll be on my way."

Brenna was riveted to the spot, uncertain of her next step. Only a few minutes passed before the door flew open and Logan stood directly in front of her. She stared at him, hardly able to believe that he and his brother had been fighting over her. What could she say?

Logan strode around her to his horse, threw his satchel on the back and mounted.

He was gone before she could turn around or utter a word.

Apparently, she was staying.

CHAPTER FOUR

Brenna's eyes followed Logan's furious path away from the cottage. He never turned back so after a while she strode to the door and opened it, feeling somehow guilty for having overheard the brother's crass words to each other. She closed the door behind her and allowed her eyes to adjust from the sunlight. Quade was staring at the ceiling, his eyes not wavering. He was clearly still upset from the conversation, so she gave him time by gathering some of the things that the brothers had thrown onto the floor. A cooked rabbit sat on the table untouched.

"Lass?" Quade's gaze found hers in the dim light of the cottage.

"Aye?" She didn't know what to expect. Would he start bellowing like her brother? Alex often shouted at the air just to relieve his tension. His wife had learned to walk away from him when he needed space. Would Quade be the same?

"I fear you have some patching to do. My wound is leaking." His hands had pulled the blanket back and he was staring at the pink liquid staining the linen strips.

Brenna ran to his side. "Och, you must have pulled a stitch." She gingerly pulled back the soaked cloth, grabbing a clean strip nearby to dab at the drainage. "Aye." She sighed at the thought of causing him more pain. "Quade, I am sorry, but I need to fix it." She grabbed his hand and placed it over the strip. "Hold this and apply pressure while I gather my things."

Moving to the side table, she located her necessary instruments along with a basin of clear water. She moved the chair next to his pallet and set her items down on the blanket beside him.

"Be quick about it, lass. I ken you have to do it, so just do it." He stroked her cheek with his free hand. Brenna jumped as if burned. Married was the only thing that popped into her head. Then why did it feel so good, so tender? Her eyes probably betrayed her confusion, but she refused to ask about his wife. It was up to him to be honest with her. She vowed not to tell him what Logan had said.

She nodded her head and pulled his hand back from the wound.

"Quade, I think it may need a couple of stitches. Would you like something to help with the pain?" She paused in her assessment, unsure of his response.

"Nay, do it, lass. 'Twill no' be the first time I have been stitched. I was lucky I dinnae feel the first you put in me." He grinned and raised an eyebrow at her.

Brenna gathered her thoughts and said a quick prayer as she oft did before stitching. Her feelings betrayed her at the moment. Normally, she would make a quick job of setting the first stitch, but she hesitated. She stopped to glance at Quade. For some reason, she was timid about inserting the needle. Was this what happened when you had feelings for the patient? Her brow creased in doubt.

"Lass? You are making me a bit nervous. Get on with it, aye?"

Brenna gave a quick nod and pierced his skin, hoping she wasn't being any more rough than usual. She was almost finished when Quade's hand reached up to her brow.

"You are sweating, lass. I don't want it to affect your vision." He mopped the sweat from her forehead, but not without adding a soft caress with his thumb.

His teeth were clenched in response to the pain she was inflicting, but there was something else in his gaze, something unfamiliar to her. She tied off the last stitch and breathed a sigh of relief. "Done. You are all right?" She searched his face for any sign of distress, but he appeared in complete control.

His fingers brushed the length of her jaw, his gaze locked on hers. His hand cupped her cheek before reaching behind her neck and pulling her toward him. It was a tentative kiss of warmth, softness, and everything she wanted from him. She heard a soft sound in her throat right before she leaned into him and parted her lips, allowing his tongue to search her mouth. This was nothing she had ever experienced before. The needle clattered to the floor, but she ignored it.

His hand caressed her neck, then threaded through her hair. He pulled back enough to whisper, "Do you have any idea how beautiful you are, Lady Brenna? I think no' and I cannae get enough of your sweet lips." He raised his lips to hers again, angling himself to deepen the kiss. A low groan came from him as he ran his tongue inside her mouth.

She broke the kiss instantly. "You are hurting? You are in pain?"

He smiled. "Aye, lass, I am in pain. But no' from your stitching. From your beauty, from everything about you."

Brenna blushed and pulled away, staring into his green eyes. No one had ever called her beautiful before. What was this chief about? Why did he look at her the way he did, almost as if he wanted to devour her? And he was married, she reminded herself. Married.

She licked her lips and his hand caressed her hip. Dropping her gaze, she bent down to pick up the things she had dropped, but gasped when she noticed the bulge under the blanket beneath his waist.

"Och, you see what you do to me, lovely one?" Quade grinned shamelessly.

Her cheeks flushed so fast, she held her hand in front of her face in an attempt to hide her color from him. He chuckled, the sound sending shockwaves through her body. Collecting her things, she turned away in embarrassment. She puttered with her tools, attempting to clean them. She had heard the servants talk about a man's arousal, but she had never observed it herself. It was shocking that she, Brenna Grant, could actually cause that to happen to a lad. And the sounds she'd uttered from her when he kissed her? He must think her a fool or a wanton.

What would her brothers think of her? She was dallying with a married man. She found a cup and filled it with water, dropping a couple of drops of draught in it before bringing it to Quade. She held the cup to his lips, but her hand trembled and the liquid dribbled down his chin.

"Och, lass, do no' be embarrassed." His hand covered hers to steady it. "'Tis a wonderful thing between us. Enjoy it and celebrate it."

He never let go of her hand, but leaned back and pulled her fingers to his lips. "You are a fine treasure, Brenna Grant." His eyes fluttered shut and he fell asleep.

Thank goodness. She needed to think.

Brenna heard a commotion outside. She ran to the door and listened—horse's hooves without a doubt and from more than one beast. The few guards who were left stood in front of the cottage. Why didn't they pull their swords? How many were on horseback? What if they were raiders?

"Do no' worry, lass. 'Tis probably more of my guardsmen. My guess is Logan sent a few more back to aid our trip home. I am quite useless as a protector right now." He placed his one hand on the pallet and attempted to push himself upright.

Brenna tried to plead with her patient to stay still. "Quade, nay. I just restitched your wound. 'Tis too fresh. Please stay in bed for another day."

Sitting up slowly, he slid to the edge of the bed as he ran his hand through his hair. "You gave me another potion again. Lass, please do no' give me those. I asked before."

A loud banging interrupted their conversation.

"Chief, are ye in there?"

"Aye, enter, Seamus." Quade guarded his belly as he stared at the door.

The door burst open and four new burly guardsmen stepped inside. Brenna stood off to the side.

"Chief, Logan said the boar got you, but ye will live. The Grant lass fixed you fine, aye?"

Brenna couldn't help but smile at the old man. He had a couple of teeth missing, but his smile reached all the way to his eyes when he looked at Quade. He scratched his full beard with one hand and reached for his bum with the other.

"Och, Seamus, 'tis a lady present. Stop, will you?" Quade nodded in Brenna's direction.

The guardsmen all froze at the sight of her.

"Saints above!"

"Och, aye, aye."

"Lucky lad."

Quade barked at the four of them. "Quiet, will you? Lady Brenna. These are four of my best guards, Seamus, Donald, Malcolm, and Mungo. They are at your service. If you need anything, just ask."

Brenna stared at the four men in front of her, blushing at their attention. She realized with regret how this looked to them. Their chief was in a cottage alone with an unmarried woman. She turned her head away, embarrassed to be caught in such a situation.

The other guards had ignored her, but these guards couldn't take their eyes from her. What was the difference?

They were correct in their assessment. She had been kidnapped and left alone in a small hut with a married man who just happened to be their chief. They probably expected her to become his mistress now. While she had attended many married men before as a healer, she had always had a guard as an escort.

She needed to get home and quick. Forget how wonderful this man's kisses were. The further away she was from Quade, the safer she would be. What was taking Alex so long to rescue her?

Logan must have sent the guards back on his way home. Occasionally, his stubborn brother did the right thing. He didn't understand why, but he and Logan oft banged heads. Rarely had it been over the same lass. Logan had completely surprised him with his interest in Brenna.

Quade would not have survived without Brenna's skills as a healer, so he probably owed his life to his brother, who, after all, had been the one to go after Lady Brenna. Even so, that didn't give him rights to the lady. Under no circumstances would he give Logan free rein with Brenna Grant.

Waking up to the vision of her by his pallet was one of the best things to happen to him in a very long time. He would not give her up. Besides, Logan didn't know how to appreciate a woman. He spent most of his time wenching. Brenna did not deserve that. In fact, the thought of her being carelessly used by his brother brought on a surge of anger. The lass's pull was far more potent than even he understood.

The guards roasted meat for their dinner at the cottage. Brenna had been adamant that he not be allowed to sit a horse yet, and he had relented. They would wait one more night, and then leave in the morning. He needed to get back..

"Mungo, get everything together. We leave when the sun rises."

"Aye, Chief. You be sitting a horse yourself?"

"Aye, I can handle a horse."

Brenna stood with her hands folded in front of her. Her chin lifted before she spoke. "I would like to request to be returned to my home."

Seamus and Donald stopped what they were doing to turn and stare at the lass. Quade knew their thoughts. He hadn't told his guards about her kidnapping, so he didn't want any witnesses to their conversation. He nodded to his guards and they left the cottage.

"I'm sorry, lass, but I cannae honor your request. You will be going with me to my keep."

"Why?"

The lass was bold, he had to give her that. She didn't accept a man's statement without question. He gave her a slow perusal before speaking. "I have need of you at my keep. I will return you when your work is done."

"So I am still your prisoner?"

He caught the fire in her deep brown eyes and quashed his urge to smile at her. He had always thought feistiness was a great quality in a lass, though many did not agree with him. "I prefer to think that you are volunteering your skills to assist my clan."

"And who requires healing?"

"You will soon find out. We are no' far from my castle near Lothian. 'Tis all you need to ken."

Quade had sent a couple of his guards back to the Grant keep. He had given them instructions to advise the Grant laird that Brenna had been taken to heal their chieftain and that she would be returned safely when she was no longer needed. He hoped to buy some time with this admission, knowing he could not win against the largest clan in the Highlands, especially under the current conditions. His guards had not yet returned.

Time was his enemy. He had to get her to his keep for his daughter's sake. His heart had been heavy for so long. Mayhap Brenna held the key to Lily's illness.

They left the next morning. Brenna hadn't repeated her request to go home or asked any other questions, and he knew his guards would not offer her information. Everything in his keep was sensitive and Brenna did not need to know what went on there yet. And it would be a long time before he allowed her to go home.

If it were up to him, she would never go back to her clan. He needed her for more reasons than she could begin to guess.

The road was tough going as he was still tender, but not more so than he could handle. He was unable to eat anything more than broth at this point, which was fine with him. But he didn't like the looks of his captive. He worried about her.

Brenna hadn't really spoken much since Logan left, her eyes were lined with dark circles, and she appeared to be losing weight. He shouldn't have argued with Logan. His brother was the best hunter among them. The few rabbits his guards had managed to catch hadn't been enough to feed all of them. He was sure that Laird Grant wouldn't appreciate his treatment of his sister. And he needed Brenna to stay strong for Lily.

He hated to admit it, but Logan was right. He was in no position to start a relationship with this woman, even though she bewitched him. Her beauty took his breath away, even more so because she did not seem to realize her effect on men. One of his guards, Mungo, had given her two oatcakes before they left the cottage. She had devoured them both, oblivious to the way the lads stared at her plump lips as she ate.

He had to get home. His life was in such a turmoil; he didn't know what he would find when he returned. Desperate for help, he had searched all of Scotland for the best healer he could find. They had come and gone, but whatever plagued Lily baffled the very best. Still, he loved her very much and was determined never to give up. When he had heard about the Grant healer, hope had blossomed again. Mayhap she would be the answer to his problems.

They spent much of the trip in silence. Since his side still pained him something fierce, the quiet suited him just fine. Brenna fussed over his wound much like an old hen, but he was grateful for all she had done. Lily needed him. He did his best to rein in his desires for the healer in front of his men. He also did not want to complicate things at his keep.

As they sat around a small fire that night nibbling on rabbit bones, she asked him exactly the same question he had been mulling over in his own mind.

"Where do you think Logan has gone off to?"

"I do no' really know, lass. Logan has done many days of wandering, and oft times, I ken not where. My guess is he will go to our home first to advise our mother that I am on my way home. Then he will be off to some new destination. We have many friends in the Lowlands. He will return when he is ready, though I could use his help now. I shouldnae have let him go; 'twas nae fair to you."

"Why?"

"Because you are hungry, and I am useless when it comes to hunting. My guards have no' provided enough food. I am sorry to push so, but I press on because I want to be home in a hurry. I have worries."

Brenna glanced at him. "About what? Your wife?"

How did she know about his wife? He would kill Logan when he saw him next. "My wife? What do you ken about my wife?" he murmured.

"Your fever. When you had the fever, you kept

asking for Lily. Logan said that Lily is your wife's name."

"Logan needs to stay out of my affairs." He stood up too quickly and clutched his side. "Hellfire, enough!" He glanced at her once more before stalking off into the woods. He would not discuss his dead wife with her.

Brenna watched him go, but couldn't stay quiet. His guardsmen all walked away from her, leaving her alone in the clearing. "Why do you no' answer my question?" Even though she shouted loud enough for all of them to hear her, Quade kept walking.

It had been difficult to get Logan to talk at first. Apparently, that trait ran in the family. Quade would rather run off than answer her questions. Shaking her head, she vowed to never allow another man to turn her head, no matter how he kissed.

Brenna reached for her satchel and searched for her mother's book. Mayhap her mother had written a bit about stubborn Scots and why they never talked. She couldn't find the treasured pages. Frustrated, she dumped the contents of the bag on the ground.

Frustration quickly turned to panic when she realized it was nowhere to be found.

"Nay, nay, this cannae be! Where is it?" Brenna frantically searched the ground, her healer's sack, everything. "It's gone, this cannae be! Where could I have lost it? "

Quade rushed into the clearing as fast as his injury allowed. "What's wrong, lass? What have you lost? No' your healer's salves and poultices? I saw them, they are here."

"Nay, my mother's book. The diary she kept of her healing experiences, her special notes to me. The pages were tied together with rope. They were worn, but I could still read them." Brenna's eyes watered, a very rare occurrence. "I have looked everywhere. I cannae find it. I need it desperately."

"I saw Logan grab something from your satchel before he left. I am afraid I was too angry to notice what he took. I am sorry." Quade stared at her, confused. "Though I do no' know why it would be of any use to my brother."

Brenna stumbled over to the log and sat, holding her head in her hands. What would she do without her mother's book? When she had a bad day, the only cure was to hide in her chamber and read every page, gathering strength from her mother's words. The book was the only possession she valued.

"Lass?" Quade stood in front of her, uncertainty etched into his face.

She brushed her tears away, and forced her gaze to meet his. He made an awkward attempt to sit next to her, but needed to reach for her hand at the last minute.

"Saints above, that still hurts! Sorry for my rudeness, Lady Brenna." He brushed a lone tear from her cheek. "I know you are upset and I apologize for my brother, but I believe you are a fine healer with or without your mother's words. Did you use it much to care for me?"

"Nay," she sniffled. "I have read it so many times, I ken every word in my heart, but it means so much more to me."

"You lost both your parents?"

She nodded, turning toward him a bit. "Aye, they died within a year of each other. It was very difficult for all of us. I have three brothers and a sister. I do no' understand why Logan would take my book."

"I cannae answer for my brother. He always has a reason for his actions, but I cannae imagine what it would be for this. Thievery is no' something he normally does."

"What about your parents?"

"I lost my father five years ago. I really wasnae ready to become chieftain at the time, but I did no' have much choice. Now I feel as if I have been chief forever."

He reached for her hand and cradled it between both of his hands. She sighed, wondering why such a small gesture warmed her heart so. She stared at his large hands, unable to see her own cocooned within them. Wife or not, she did not want to move her hand away; she couldn't help it.

"Your mother is still alive?" She gazed into his eyes, noting how much greener they looked outside.

"Aye, alive and lively." Chuckling, he stared up at the stars. "She never hesitates to give me her opinion on every matter possible."

"Is Logan your only brother?"

"No, I have two brothers and a sister. You will love them all."

One of his guards made his way back toward them. Brenna coughed before pulling her hand away, reminding herself she was traveling against her will and he had a wife. The healer portion of her heart would never allow her to leave him though, and she had complete confidence in Alex's ability to rescue her.

An awful thought crossed her mind.

What if the person he needed her to heal was his wife? Would she be able to do it?

She had to admit that she wasn't sure of the answer.

CHAPTER FIVE

Quade sighed with relief when he spotted his castle in the distance. The purple heather strewn across the meadow always calmed his soul. He loved this section where they were riding, with hills on either side of them, rich greens and browns dotting the landscape, soon to turn to the luscious reds and yellows of late autumn. Even though he had taken the same path many times, this seemed like the longest ride ever. The Ramsay keep was much smaller than the renowned Grant keep, but he was proud of his family and the people of his clan—hardworking folk who supported his family completely and had been with them for decades. He hoped they would support his decision to bring Lady Brenna home with him.

He had worried about whether he should tell Brenna about Lily, and if so, how much. Ultimately, he had decided to wait. Brenna needed to see her and make her own assessment without his input. At least, that was how her many predecessors had handled their visits. How many healers had he brought to see his Lily? Truly there had been so many over the past few years, he had lost count. He had given up all hope until Logan brought him word of the Grant healer.

Quade would give her anything she needed if it would help Lily. He prayed her condition hadn't worsened during the delay caused by his injury. After the last couple of years, the poor lass hadn't changed much. She didn't move far from her bed or her chamber. The stench was too strong for most, so she had few visitors.

Quade let out a war whoop when he caught sight of his brother, Micheil. His brother's arm waved in greeting as he joined them.

"You are alive, brother?" Micheil shouted.

Quade chuckled. "Alive, but not so well."

"Aye, you look a bit green. What did the lass do to you?" Micheil nodded toward Brenna as he came up beside his brother.

He and Brenna slowed their pace as his brother and several outriders joined them on both sides.

"The lass saved my sorry arse, so be kind to her." Quade smiled at Brenna.

The guards followed as they passed through the quaint thatched roof cottages. Many clan members came outside to wave to their chief, which was a normal show of respect for a returning leader. What wasn't normal was that some of the women knelt and nodded their heads as if a holy person was passing.

Quade raised his brow at his brother, Micheil, in question.

"Logan was here for a short time, and he told us of her extraordinary healing powers. He informed us of how close to death you were. They are expressing their appreciation for her hard work and for your continued life." Micheil nodded at the clan's many well-wishers as they passed.

"And how is my Lily?" Quade glanced at Brenna after he posed his question to Micheil. He could tell she was completely focused on their conversation. He didn't have time to worry about her feelings though. Lily's health came first. Mayhap Lady Brenna would come to trust him someday.

"The same. Aggie is with her."

On his left, Brenna rode as if she'd been born on her horse. They had slowed their pace when they neared the village, and she carried herself with regal bearing, her back straight and tall. Tendrils of her hair had tumbled from her plait and blew around her face in the breeze. Her eyes turned to him for a moment, but she blushed as soon as she caught his gaze and glanced away. His early assessment of her had been correct. She definitely was an innocent.

And she was breathtaking.

Micheil's voice cut in from his right. "Brother? Something you wish to tell me?" Micheil's grin told him he hadn't been able to hide his feelings for the lady. Quade gave him a silencing look and Micheil chuckled.

"Have you noted any strangers in the area?" Quade could not help but worry about the Grants. They had to be seeking Brenna by now.

"Nay, Logan asked the same before he left."

"Did he say where he was headed?"

"Nay, he was evasive as ever. Mother attempted to get more information from him, but he denied her, saying something about needing to confuse some Highland laird. Do you ken what he meant by that?" Micheil caught his eye before moving behind him as they approached the bridge.

Quade hid his smile. He could always count on Logan, though he would never admit it. His brother was one of the best trackers in the land, and was more than equipped to throw someone off a trail, even the talented trackers the Grants no doubt had at their disposal. Logan's actions would definitely aid him if the Grant laird didn't trust his explanation for his actions.

The horses carried them over the bridge and past their gate. The stable lads rushed to his side, but he waved them away as he continued toward the keep, motioning for Brenna to follow. She still had dark circles under her eyes, but they did nothing to mar her beauty. He could tell she had not slept well with five

Highland guards surrounding her last night. Though she was no doubt tired and hungry, he was in a rush for her to meet Lily.

He brought Lady Brenna as close to the steps of the keep as he dared to prevent her from tiring further, heedless to the extra work it would cause the stable hands. After dismounting, he reached to help her down from her horse.

Brenna's strong voice echoed across the common area. "Do no' touch me, you will ruin my stitches."

His mother approached as Micheil helped Brenna down and handed her satchel to her.

His mother threw her arms around Brenna. He could tell the gesture startled the healer, but his mother must have been wild with worry ever since Logan told her about the incident with the boar.

Lady Ramsay stepped back and held Brenna's hands. "Thank you for saving my eldest son. I will be forever indebted to you." Tears glistened in her eyes when Quade introduced them, and she swiped at the wetness of her cheeks. "Lady Brenna, your talent as a healer is said to be legendary. I hope it is true. We need your skills desperately."

Quade allowed Brenna a brief chance to return his mother's greeting before he tugged on her hand and pulled her up the steps to the keep.

"Sorry, Mother. She needs to see Lily."

"Quade, where are your manners?" his mother shouted after him as he opened the door for Brenna. "Allow the lass something to eat and the chance to freshen up. How many days have you been traveling?"

"That can wait. Lady Brenna is a strong woman; she needs to see Lily first. After all, 'tis why she is here."

They stepped inside the great hall. He noticed how quickly Brenna's smile left her face, replaced by confusion. Well, soon she would see Lily, and the situation would explain itself.

Rushing her over to the inner stairway, he ushered

her up the stairs and down the corridor to the third door. Grabbing the handle of one of the doors, he turned to her before entering.

"Please help my Lily."

* * *

Brenna prayed for strength as she walked into the room. Was she about to meet his wife? For the first time in her adult life, she was uncertain as to whether she could handle this situation with the neutrality a healer should have. Much as she tried, she could not fight her feelings for Quade. What condition could his wife be in that was so urgent?

The dark chamber carried a strong and distinctive stench, but she couldn't identify it. Furs covered the windows in the small chamber. An array of bowls and urns were stacked in various spots. She wasn't sure what to make of the containers placed in what appeared to be purposeful locations. An older woman sat near the bed wringing her hands, obviously caring for the woman who was swathed under the blankets.

Could she do this? Quade's hand at her back propelled her closer to the small mound of blankets. She turned back to stare at the dark handsome laird behind her. What was he about? She wanted to tell him how much he confused her, but she just couldn't. How she wished that he was unattached and they had met under different circumstances. Turning to face the bed again, she stepped forward.

The old woman stepped into the light, revealing a face stained with tears. "Bless you, my lady."

Brenna steeled herself and turned to the bed as Quade reached for the coverlet and pulled it back.

"Lady Brenna," he said. "Meet my daughter, Lily."

His daughter? Lily was his daughter?

Why did her heart soar at that declaration? The fact that he had a daughter didn't mean he was unmarried. He must still have a wife somewhere. She just hadn't met her yet.

Two small arms reached out from the bed. "Da, you are home? Who did you bring? A new mama for us?"

"Hush, sweet one." Quade reached down and scooped his daughter into his arms, planting a kiss on her cheek. "This is not your mama. Mind your manners and greet her properly. Her name is Lady Brenna Grant and she has verra special skills as a healer."

Brenna's anxiety soared in a second. "Put her down, Quade; mind your stitches, please."

"Och, she weighs less than a feather, Lady Brenna. She is no' hurting my stitches. But I will set her down for you to examine her."

"What stitches, Da?" Lily's angelic face grew wide-eyed as her father lowered her to her pallet.

"Papa ran into a mean old boar, but Uncle Logan took care of him for me. I'm fine. How is my Lily flower?" He beamed at his daughter with pride, causing Brenna's heart to jump when he turned that same smile to her. A man who loved his bairn this much was definitely a good man.

She turned back to her new patient. Lily was a beautiful golden-haired child, probably between three and four summers. Instead of running outside in the fields like a normal wean, she clearly could not move outside her chamber unless carried. She was too thin and there were dark circles under her eyes. Quade's assessment was correct; she was likely too light to upset his stitches. What would cause such a beautiful child to be so frail? Brenna would guess she barely had the strength to walk.

The lass's smile was brilliant for her father, but her skin was dull and dry, and the odor of sickness in the room was still unrecognizable to Brenna. It had been an effort for the poor child to reach up to wrap her hands around Quade's neck. This was no short illness, but something that had sapped Lily's strength over time.

Turning to her caretaker, two wee arms reached out. "Aggie, my bowl."

Brenna's heart broke as the caretaker reached behind her, grabbed the small basin and held it in front of the child just in time to catch the contents of her stomach as it spewed from her tiny mouth. Almost pure liquid, but her frail body continued to heave until not even that came up.

Quade sighed and glanced at the caretaker with his eyebrow raised. "Aggie? What was it this time?"

"Aye, Chief. She had a bit of bread since she was feeling better. I thought mayhap she could handle it. She is getting worse, she cannae hold anything down." Aggie wiped at the child's mouth with a linen cloth.

Tears ran down the wee lass's eyes as her mouth turned into a frown. "Forgive me, my lady, but I couldnae stop," she said to Brenna, her voice weak. Her eyes crinkled, her upper lip trembled as Brenna observed the fight in the little soul. Her weeping continued as she held her belly with one hand.

"Papa, my tummy hurts so. Can she fix me?"

"She will try, little one. You must do as she asks." Quade stroked her forehead.

"Papa, does she have to bleed me?" Her small head turned again toward Lady Brenna. "Please do no' bleed me. It hurts me so and makes me feel terrible." A flood of tears washed over Lily's face once more. Her sobbing broke Brenna's heart, so she sat on the bed and lifted the lass onto her lap.

"'Tis all right, wee one. 'Tis nae your fault." She tucked Lily's head under her chin and rubbed soft circles on her back, hoping to calm her. Brenna turned her head in time to catch the tears in Quade's eyes, but he spun around and left the chamber. "I willnae bleed you, wee one. I ken some healers believe in bleeding their patients, but my mama taught me it is for naught most of the time. We will try something else."

After she managed to calm the child a wee bit, Brenna introduced herself to Aggie, the sickroom helper.

"How long has she been like this, Aggie?"

"Oh, my lady, she has been like this since she began walking. She seems to worsen every moon." Aggie deftly emptied the small basin into a larger one by the chamber door and then stepped outside with the larger one.

When she returned, Brenna continued her questioning. "She has always been sick like this? Always vomiting?" Brenna's brow furrowed at the thought of the stress it must be putting on the child's constitution.

"Aye, sometimes she throws it up, and sometimes she throws it down, if you ken what I mean." Aggie shook her head emphatically. "What comes out of her bum is no' normal. 'Tis foul smelling for such a sweet young thing."

"Does anything seem to make it worse?"

"Naught that I can tell. She has seen so many healers and no one kens what to do. We are all praying that you can help her, my lady. To have our laird's daughter so sick is no' right."

The hopeful expression in Aggie's eyes gave her insight into how much the child was loved within the keep. Brenna continued to rock little Lily until the girl's sobs stopped altogether. She was so unlike a normal child, so unlike her two nephews, Jake and Jamie. The child's frailty was quite shocking. A wee voice broke through her thoughts.

"Please help me, Lady Brenna. I do no' like feeling like this. And it upsets my da."

She placed a kiss on her forehead. "I will try, wee Lily. I will try."

Brenna continued to rub the lass's back until she fell asleep. She glanced at Aggie's sad face as she laid the sleeping child down on the bed. Curiosity got the best of her, and she asked the question that had been on her lips for the better part of an hour "Aggie, why does she want a new mama?" She whispered the words.

Aggie drew herself up tall. "Because she never kenned her mama. Quade named her after her mama because he dinnae think she would be with us for long. She wasnae a strong lass.

"Lilias, that was her mama's name, died less than a month after she was born."

CHAPTER SIX

Quade sat in a chair in front of his hearth. Now Brenna knew he wasn't cheating on his wife. It had been almost four long years since he had buried his young wife, and not once had he been tempted by another until now. He had slaked his lust with a couple of the local lasses, but he had never been tempted to make another woman his own. Even now, he had a difficult time believing he had kissed her. Aye, she was breathtaking, but he could not risk her being affected by his curse. He needed to be stronger.

He shook his head wishing he could rid himself of his past mistakes so easily. He decided it must have been the sickness in his belly, or mayhap something she had put in his broth. Vowing not to fall prey to her beauty again, he convinced himself he was through with his foolishness. He had been so in love with his wife, Lilias, that he'd sworn never to love another. The pull Lady Brenna had on him was mighty strong. Mayhap it was her innocence or her backbone. His marriage had been a long time ago, so much so he could hardly remember Lilias's face lately.

Footsteps on the stone warned him of someone's impending arrival. He pushed up on the arms of the chair to see if it was Lady Brenna. As she came down the steps, she shouted down to him, "Do no' get out of that chair for me. Mind your stitches for a day so I do no' have to redo them, please. The ride was rough."

Quade followed the sway of her hips as she came closer, powerless to move. His vow wouldn't last long. She was a beacon in the dark to him.

She pulled up a chair and tugged his hand away from his midsection. "Good. No fresh blood."

"Lass, do you think of naught else but healing?" He smirked at her. He couldn't help it—whenever she was near, his whole being brightened.

"Aye, I do. Which forces me to pose this question to you: Why did you no' tell me Lily was your daughter and no' your wife?"

"Och, lass. We were within hearing range of my guardsmen. Naught of my personal life is for their ears." He stood, instinctively grabbing his right side.

She sat back and settled her hands on her hips. "Why did Logan want me to believe your wife was still alive?"

"I cannae answer for my brother. Logan and I are competitive and sometimes we are much like oil and water. We battle unless we need to unite, and then we are a mighty force to be reckoned with. Logan has some different beliefs. He wanders because he does no' ken who he is yet. At least, 'tis my feeling."

His mother entered from the kitchens, carrying a basket of bread. "Here, lass, you must be starving. Have a bite to eat."

Lady Ramsay settled her bounty on a nearby table. Glancing at her son, she asked, "Do you no' do as the healer instructed, Quade? Why is it paining you so much?"

"Mother, please, I am fine. I would like to formally introduce you to Lady Brenna Grant, the lass who saved my life. My apologies for being so short upon our arrival."

Brenna stood and curtsied to his mother. "He has good reason to be sore, my lady. I had to cut a poison out of his belly as well."

Quade and Brenna both sat.

"My heavens!" His mother paused, as though she needed to absorb what she had just heard. "Why was there poison in his belly? How did it get there? Why did it no' kill him? How could you cut it out?" His mother's eyes continued to grow as the questions rolled out, one after another.

"Calm down, Mother. As you can see, I am just fine. My belly started to bother me as soon as we left. I feel much better now that she has removed the poison. The pain in my belly was excruciating and I couldnae stop heaving."

Quade's mother brought her hands to her face as a thought occurred to her. He could oft tell what his mother was thinking. "Could that be Lily's problem? Do you need to remove part of her belly to fix her?"

"Nay, Mother. Of course no'!" Quade turned to Brenna after he spoke. "Am I correct, Lady Brenna? We do no' have the same problem?"

"You are correct, you couldnae have the same problem. What you had would have killed you in a couple of days. This has been something slow to develop if what Aggie tells me is true."

"Forgive me, Lady Brenna," his mother said. "I am so hopeful for something, anything, to help my granddaughter." Her hands twisted her gown.

Quade spoke up first. "Is this something you have seen before, Lady Brenna?" He found himself holding his breath. He had watched his daughter's sickness progress since she was just under a summer. How it pained him to watch the wee one's natural energy burn up on a pallet. He knew how much it hurt his mother to watch the lass decline each day. Could Brenna be the one? Was there even a slim chance she could help?

"May we all take a moment so I can ask you about her past? I need to know as many details as you can recall about Lily's illness; how it started, when it stops, what makes it better or worse, anything you can remember."

Lady Ramsay took charge, calling for the servants to bring ale from the kitchens.

"Lady Brenna, we will be happy to tell you everything we ken."

Quade ran his hand across his brow as he got up and started to pace. Why didn't she just get on with her healing? There must be something she could do for his daughter. "Brenna, should you no' be with Lily? Is there naught you can give her from your sack? Some miracle medicine? She is verra ill."

"As you know, my mother trained me. Her advice was to gather information before acting. Has anyone thought to keep a diary of Lily's illness? Have you recorded what she eats, how often she empties her stomach?"

"What good is that, Brenna? We do no' have the time. Nay, we do no' have any records. No one has kept a diary. This is hogswill. Just go and fix her."

"Quade Ramsay! Laird or not, mind your manners!" his mother shouted at him. "Can you no' see this kind lass needs a moment to collect her thoughts? Leave her to do her work and stop telling her how to do it."

Quade stared at his mother first, then at Brenna.

"Fine. Your pardon, Lady Brenna." He pointed toward the dais. "Why do we no' move over here to be more comfortable?"

As he spoke, the servants placed trenchers and ale on the main table in the hall. He ushered Brenna over, then sat at the head of the table while his mother brought the bread over from their place at the hearth.

How could he expect her to understand? He'd had such high hopes for a happy marriage, with four or five healthy bairns at his feet. He had been foolish enough to imagine his brothers married as well. He had dreamed about bairns running in the hall at the holidays, laughter reaching the rafters as his nieces and nephews played with his own children. After his failure, it was no wonder his brothers had chosen to stay single.

He had watched his wife disintegrate and die in his arms. Now his Lilykins, who had been healthy and beautiful for almost a year, was dying before him, day by day. While he was recuperating in the cottage, he had experienced a recurrence of a dream in which his daughter was healed, smiling and giggling at him, chasing around the great hall as any normal wean would do. He had hoped it was a premonition. But nay, she had spewed within less than five minutes of their arrival. Was there any hope at all?

Once they sat, Brenna turned to Quade's mother. "Would there mayhap be parchment and something with which I can write? I would like to get as many details from you both as possible, if you do no' mind."

"Of course, I will fetch them for you. Quade? Mind your tongue in my absence. Remember how to treat ladies, please. We are not your guardsmen." With a raised brow and a swish of her skirts, Lady Ramsay left the hall.

Brenna turned to him. "Quade, I ken you are anxious, but this isnae something that will be fixed in a couple of hours. This will take time. Something is ravaging your daughter's body, and I have to discover what it is before I can decide how to treat it. This may be a long process."

Quade nibbled on a small piece of bread. "Aye, I ken this is difficult for you. I have watched my daughter deteriorate in front of my verra own eyes. 'Tis most distressing and I apologize for my rudeness."

Then he locked gazes with her. "But I hope she does no' die while you are thinking about it."

Brenna stopped in to see Lily again. She had taken copious notes from her conversations with both Aggie and Lady Ramsay. Quade offered some insight, but in a very limited manner. He was clearly agitated by every moment she spent out of Lily's room.

She opened the door and the sun shone down on Lily's golden locks. Her tiny ribs were visible through her well-washed gown, her body finally at rest.

Aggie's hands tugged at the folds of the girl's skirt. "She sleeps too much for a bairn, my lady."

"Aye, for a normal bairn, but no' for one so frail. If she cannae keep any solid food down, she has naught to draw energy from. She cannae grow without solid regular feedings. Her body retains naught long enough for her to use it well. I wish to review my notes before I make any recommendations. Please do no' give her anything but warmed water, and here are some herbs you may drop in the water if her belly continues to bother her when she awakens. Since she is still asleep, her belly must now be at rest."

Brenna gazed at the small bairn in slumber. Lily would be a true beauty when she was healthy again. Her golden hair had lost its normal sheen, and her young skin was dry and waxy. At this tender age, she should be growing long bones and new teeth. Would this sickness affect her growth permanently? Only time would tell. She needed to find out what ailed the child and soon.

She thought of the daily activities of her two nephews, just walking a few months. Alex's guardsmen called them little terrors. Jamie loved to try and pick up a sword twice his size. In fact, Alex had finally fashioned two dull wooden swords for the twins to play with to keep Maddie from losing her head. She couldn't help but chuckle as she recalled the sight of her brother and sister-in-law when the two lads had come into the great hall dragging their uncle's smallest swords. Alex had roared like never before, but the two laddies had just stared at their father and started to giggle.

Sad to her, but the pride in her brother's eyes when

he stared at his wife and bairns was not the same look in Quade's eyes when he looked upon his daughter.

Haunted is the only word that appropriately described his face. Determined to change that expression, she sighed as she stepped outside the door and into the corridor.

Lady Ramsay awaited her. "Lady Brenna, allow me to show you to your chamber."

"My thanks, my lady." Brenna followed her down the long passageway and around the corner.

As she opened the doorway, Lady Ramsay smiled. "I am sure you are anxious to get out of the clothes you traveled in." She pointed to Brenna's satchel on a small chest. "I hope you do no' mind but I had a maid remove some of your gowns to be cleaned. There is a tub awaiting you and a clean gown over the chair near the window."

Brenna glanced around the bright chamber. Lady Ramsay had arranged a vase of flowers on the larger chest. Several beautiful tapestries hung on the wall. An inviting bed sat in the middle of the chamber decorated with a white embroidered coverlet and two plump pillows. She noticed a partition on the other side of the bed. As she walked over to peek behind it, she couldn't help but sigh when she noticed the steaming tub of water behind it.

She nodded to Lady Ramsay. "I thank you, my lady. 'Tis heavenly."

When Brenna was alone, she stripped quickly and sank into the warm water, letting her thoughts overtake her. She had to make a plan first and then share it with the family tonight. There might not be much time to help little Lily, since Alex would undoubtedly come to her rescue soon.

And come what may, Brenna had her heart set on saving the wee lass's life.

The next morning, Brenna asked for everyone involved in Lily's care to meet her in the solar. The Ramsay solar was a large rectangular room with Quade's desk facing the door. A table with several chairs sat in the middle of the chamber with several stools around the perimeter. Various weaponry graced the walls. Since it was on the third floor, a large window with fur coverings allowed the light in. As the day was warm, Brenna had asked Quade to throw the furs back to brighten the room.

Lady Ramsay had arrived early and sat waiting with Lily on her lap wrapped in a soft blanket. The lass's frailty required the extra covering for the cool temperature, but Brenna wanted her to enjoy the fresh air. Lily's precious smile told her she was enjoying the solar, as her own chamber was dark and dreary.

Lily had not vomited again, but she had not eaten anything either. Heated water was all she could tolerate. Brenna's mother had always thought it best for a stressed belly, particularly when mixed with mint.

"How is your belly today, Lily?" Brenna thought the dark circles under the child's eyes had improved slightly since yesterday. Mayhap she had slept soundly.

The lass grinned and held up her arms when her father entered the room. How sad that a child of her size and age could not walk unaided. As upset as Quade was about the whole situation, she noticed that he didn't allow his daughter to see it. He was all smiles and happiness when his wee one was near.

"My belly does no' hurt today. Papa, are you no' happy for me?"

Quade planted a loud kiss on her cheek before lifting her into his arms. "That makes Papa verra happy, my Lilykins."

Lily giggled and clapped her hands together as she peered around at the gathering. She leaned over to whisper in her father's ear. "Papa, I am hungry. Can you find me something to eat, please?"

"No' yet, flower, we need to listen to Lady Brenna."

Quade sat down and settled Lily on his lap. She clasped her hands in the folds of her nightgown. "Aye, all right then. But I am still hungry."

Quade's brother, Micheil, arrived, along with his younger sister, Avelina. Aggie and Cook followed with the kitchen help, trailed by a few of the maids. Seamus and Mungo entered as well.

Avelina was a beautiful young lady with the same green eyes as her brother. She appeared to be a bit older than Jennie, though they had to be close in age.

Quade introduced her to everyone as they entered. They all welcomed her with a bit of hope and apprehension in their eyes. She couldn't take her eyes off the tall chieftain, obviously a born leader, but so taken with his daughter. Her heart melted a wee bit whenever he held Lily, his love evident in everything he did. She caught herself staring at his lips, remembering how warm they had been on hers.

Forcing herself to return to the present moment, she cleared her throat and surveyed the gathering before her. "Is this everyone, Lady Ramsay?" she asked.

"Aye, everyone is here. Please begin, Lady Brenna." Lady Ramsay sat down a couple of seats away from Quade and Lily.

Brenna steeled herself for the reaction she would probably receive while she kept her eyes on Lily.

"This is going to be a slow process, difficult at times, but I have formulated a plan to try and determine what is causing Lily's illness. Since it focuses on her belly and her biles, I believe this might be food related. For most of us, eating any food is all right, but no' for Lily. You probably ken some people that do no' like certain foods because it makes their bellies rumble. For little Lily, she has many things that make her belly rumble and we need to discover what they are.

"The most important concept I need you all to understand is that you cannae feed her whatever she wants." She moved across the room and squatted in front of Lily. "This will be hard for you, Lily, but I hope we will make your belly stop aching forever."

Lily's eyes danced at this and she clapped her hands. "Promise, Lady Brenna? I want to be strong for my da." She patted his big arm with her tiny hand.

"I promise to try my best to help you heal, Lily." She kissed the girl's forehead before standing and turning her attention to the others.

"I have devised a schedule for her diet. Here is what I need you all to ken. It is verra important we only give her food from the prescribed list. If you do no', it will ruin everything we have worked for. This may take us a fortnight or more, but I believe we can discover her trigger foods through a process of elimination. So I will say again, please do no' give her anything to eat without checking with either me, Quade, or Lady Ramsay. We will ken her allowed foods for the day. Even a small morsel of the wrong food could cause problems for her. If we arenae aware of what foods you are giving her, we will never be able to find the problem."

Lily scuttled down from her father's lap and scooted over to her grandmother. Those seated nearby helped her move as she made her tentative steps. Brenna applauded. "Verra good, Lily! 'Tis wonderful for you to walk on your own. Someday you will be running."

As she maneuvered her way onto her grandmother's lap, she said. "Aye, I want to run, so I can be the fastest of all."

Brenna brushed the hair back on the lass's head as she scanned the audience. "Do you have any questions for me?"

Aggie stood up. "How do you ken this will work?"

"I do no' ken for sure. I ken of one person who couldnae eat anything with milk. Once we eliminated cheese and milk from her diet, she had nae problems. I am hopeful we will find the same thing with Lily."

Aggie looked perplexed. "You mean cheese is causing this? I cannae believe it. She loves cheese."

Brenna reminded herself to be patient. "It may be cheese and it may be something else. Remember that liking a food does no' mean it willnae make her sick. The only way we can learn that is by introducing one food at a time to see if she tolerates it. Does this make sense?"

Aggie nodded, still appearing confused, but agreeable. "All right, my lady, we will do as you say."

Quade stood. "I want everyone here to do as Lady Brenna asks. If you have any issues with anyone, you send them to me, Lady Brenna. Understand?"

Brenna answered a few more inquiries, and then a dull voice from the back overtook the others.

"What if it does no' work, Chief? How do we ken she is right? She isnae from around here."

Brenna's throat clenched at the implication. She had expected such a reaction. Why did it feel like a fist to her gut?

Quade's voice quivered as he stared at the group, looking for the culprit. "You willnae question her commands ever. You are to do as she asks or you will answer to me. Is that clear?"

A sigh of relief escaped her as she glanced at him. She had his support. He believed in her so much that she could hear the trembling in his voice. How she hoped she would be able to meet his expectations. She did not want to let him down.

Her belly churned in confusion. Why was that feeling so strong in her? The man had arranged to have her kidnapped, and yet she yearned for his approval.

Several heads nodded and mumbled agreement. Brenna wasn't sure if she had everyone's support, but it was a start. And she knew she had the confidence of

Quade, which mattered most of all.

A low moan broke through the group's discussion.

"Aggie, my bowl, my bowl."

Brenna turned to see Lily lose everything into the basin Aggie had brought with her.

Her head spun as people pushed their way out the solar door, unable to watch as the poor child vomited. This couldn't be. The girl had taken nothing but water. Was she wrong in her thinking? No, she was sure in her plan. Someone must have given her something.

Quade strode over to her. "Brenna, I thought you were sure. You must be wrong. Look at her, look at my bairn. She is throwing up just water. It cannae be food that is bothering her. This is all for naught."

Brenna's mind raced, as she tried to find an answer for what had happened. "Quade, this cannae be. I am sure of my plan. This will work." She felt the sting of tears burn her lashes. But if the lass had only consumed water, she had to be wrong.

When the child appeared to be done retching, Brenna moved over and peered into the basin.

"Och, lass, how can you look at such?" Quade asked, turning away in revulsion.

Brenna understood it was hard for normal folk to comprehend the things she did as a healer. Well, she did what she had to do. Being the primary healer at her brother's castle had given her plenty of experience. With so many guardsmen, she oft saw large slices made by swords, sometimes spilling out trailing innards. Over time, working with her grandpapa and her mother, she had learned not to react to the blood and gore that was so commonplace in their work. Examining a bit of stomach contents did not bother her, and it would help her verify her theory. She needed to be sure of her thoughts.

Her fury rose as she stared at the clump in the middle of the bowl. "I am no' wrong, Quade. Someone fed her. This is why we needed to have this meeting.

We cannae have people feeding her whenever they want. This could kill her. It has to stop."

Lily's tears ran down her face as she stared at her father. "I am sorry, Papa. I was hungry. Grammy gave me just a little bit of pastry."

Quade turned to look at his mother.

"Mother?"

His mother stood abruptly, handing Lily to him.

"I am sorry, Quade, but I cannae stand by and listen to my granddaughter complain of starving. This willnae work. Leave me out of this cruelty."

Quade stood in his daughter's chamber, staring at the beautiful woman to whom he had entrusted his daughter's care. Was she right? Would her plan work or would it cause Lily more pain?

His daughter dozed while Brenna paced with her in her arms, rocking at times to calm her.

"How is she?" He gazed at her expectantly, hoping for good news.

Brenna smiled as she brushed the golden locks back from the lass's forehead. "She is better. She is hungry, but she kens she cannae chew anything. I have given her plain broth and she kept it down. I like to heat her water a bit, and we also add mint leaves. Mint can be verra calming and she enjoys the flavor."

"How long ago did you give the broth to her?" His stomach clenched as he awaited her answer.

"A couple of hours. She said her belly does no' hurt, but she was tired. It has been a confusing day for her."

"Aye, watching her grammy get yelled at by me did no' help her either." He couldn't really blame his mother. She adored her granddaughter and would do anything for her. He wondered how she would react when she found out that instead of asking Laird Grant for the assistance of his healer, Logan had kidnapped her instead.

"'Tis a long process, Quade, but I believe it will work."

"I ken that and I do trust in you. Och, aye, look what you have done for me. You saved my life twice. I need to apologize for my abruptness earlier. You can see I love my daughter verra much.

"I am just an impatient person. I want everything to happen instantly. I have a hard time standing by and doing naught for my daughter, much like my mother, who seems to have trouble with the concept as well." He moved over to stare out the small window, a sly grin on his face. "'Twill be tough going for you, lass, dealing with the two of us."

Brenna quirked her brow. "You are about to see how stubborn I can be. You gave me permission in front of everyone, Quade. She will get naught from anyone in this keep without my approval. I will be a guard for your daughter."

"Are you so attached already?" Hope bloomed in his heart. His gaze pierced hers from across the room, hoping to catch any reaction from her. He could no longer deny the lass had captured a piece of his heart. If it wasn't for the blasted curse on him, he could seriously consider marriage again. She would be a wonderful mother; he was sure of it.

Brenna stopped pacing and met his eyes. "I am a healer, Quade, and you have a beautiful daughter who needs healing. I also ken when my brother arrives with his guards, I will be going home. I am hoping to accomplish something before I leave, for Lily's sake."

Quade strode over and lightly rubbed the back of his fingers across her cheek. "Aye, for a moment I almost forgot Logan had kidnapped you. Mayhap you belong here. You look perfect with my daughter in your arms." Without intending to, he envisioned her as his wife, lying in his bed with her arms outstretched, welcoming him to her side.

Brenna froze at his touch. He sensed her hesitation,

yet she was aware of his situation now and he hadn't imagined her reaction to him in the cottage. Why did his touch bother her?

"No one has offered for you, lass, as beautiful as you are? You are no' betrothed?" He moved in closer, brushing his thumb across her cheek, then her lower lip.

"Nay, my brother would not betroth me to anyone unless it pleased me."

He wanted her to choose him. He leaned in and brushed his lips over hers, careful to avoid jostling his daughter, who was still resting over her shoulder. He was afraid to hear her answer, but he had to ask. "You havenae found anyone who pleases you?"

Brenna's answer came out in a warm rush of air. "Nay."

He had to taste her again. The memory of their kisses haunted his dreams every night, even though he had hoped to forget them. His lips found hers, settling on their warmth, and she tasted of mint, sweet mint. She held back at first, but then gave in to him in a rush of sweetness. Cupping her cheek, he used his tongue to tease her lips until she opened to him, allowing him into her sweet cavern. He swept his tongue until he found hers, mating briefly. Her soft moan of surrender headed right to his groin, turning him hard in an instant.

When he stepped back, he supported her arm, afraid she would stumble with Lily still asleep in her arms. Aye, her reaction now confirmed it. She was an innocent.

And that made him want her even more.

CHAPTER SEVEN

Two days later, Brenna was in Lily's room when Avelina strode in.

"Good morn to you, Avelina." Brenna enjoyed Quade's younger sister, who was just twelve summers and reminded her of Jennie.

"Good morn, Lady Brenna." The lass's green eyes sparked with delight. "How is Lily today?"

Lily jumped up on her pallet. "Look, Lina, I can stand and jump now. Watch me!" She held her tiny arms out so that Avelina would set her on the floor.

Brenna smiled as Lily jumped a bit. After a quick landing, she stumbled, but she was still proud of her one small leap. She had come far in a short time.

"See how high I jump? Da will be so proud of me."

"What is she eating now?" Avelina turned to Brenna with a smile, holding Lily's hands.

"Lady Brenna gave me some porridge this morning. Last night, Cook put some vegetables in my broth, too. I had turnips and some peas. Look at me. No tummy ache. Lady Brenna is going to make me all better!" Her bright eyes shone at her sister and Brenna.

Brenna had to admit she was surprised at how much better Lily already seemed to be. Wee ones were so resilient. She hoped Quade would be about today so she could observe his reaction to his daughter's improvements.

Avelina gazed up at Brenna. "You are fixing her.

You really are. Look at her skin; it is starting to be pretty again. She had the prettiest skin when she was wee."

"Lady Brenna, may I go outside with Lina? Please, I so wish to go outside again."

Brenna pulled the fur back from the window and saw the glorious fall day blooming outside. The leaves had turned the deepest red and were falling off the trees. She smiled at the beam of sunshine as it streamed in through the window, warming her face.

"Why, yes, I think you have a wonderful idea, Lily. I would like to take her out in a wagon, though. She is still frail and may tire quick."

Lily clapped her hands as Aggie helped her change into warmer clothes.

"Mayhap a warm cape with a hood for her head, too, Aggie. And a small blanket."

When she was ready, Brenna picked Lily up and carried her down the stairs while Avelina ran ahead to locate a wagon. Many bystanders cheered to welcome Lily outdoors when they stepped out of the great hall and loaded the girl into the wagon.

They strolled through the bailey, stopping to greet Lily's clansmen. They were more than kind to Brenna, and she was a bit surprised at their quick acceptance.

As they made their way across the courtyard, Brenna heard a woman yelling from afar. She did not know who she was and couldn't make out her words, so they continued with their walk. Lily wished to see her father in the lists and Brenna decided it would give her a good excuse to make sure he was following her orders and doing naught to risk his stitches. As they passed the herb garden, the same flame-haired woman that had been yelling at them from across the way, ran up to Brenna and stopped in front of her, arms folded across her chest.

Avelina stared up at the woman. "What is it, Iona?"

Iona had full breasts and hips and was in possession

of a certain attractiveness. She was not beautiful, but she was striking in the proper light. She had the arrogance of someone who ran the keep, though Brenna wasn't sure why.

"I am here to see the witch, Avelina. You stay out of my business." She turned and pinned Brenna with a look. "I ken what you are and I ken what you want. You may call yourself a healer, but you are a witch who's out to steal our chief. Confess so all can witness." Her hands waved to a couple of people not far behind her. "You are here to marry the chief and you are doing it through his wee lass."

Her heart raced at the accusation, as she was well aware of the impact such a claim could have. Witchery was a nasty charge and she had no idea whether this woman was someone important in the clan. Either way, she would not back down. Brenna returned her glare and stepped in front of the wagon to guard Lily.

"How dare you speak to me in such a tone, especially in front of a sick bairn? It wasnae my intent to come here, but I came at the request of your laird and his brother. I am here as a healer and naught else. I do no' ken how you can claim that I came with designs on your chief. Naught could be further from the truth. Since you clearly do no' ken of what you speak, please remove yourself from our presence."

"Avelina, make her go away. I dinnae like her." Lily's small voice interrupted.

Iona pointed her finger at the bairn. "Lily, close your mouth and do no' interrupt adults."

A few of the clan gathered around them, and Brenna became territorial. Her ire fueled by Iona's crude behavior, she reached for the woman's hand. "Step away from Lily."

Iona jerked away from Brenna's touch. "You stay away from Quade Ramsay. He is mine and no' yours. He loves me and we are to marry soon. Everyone here kens it but you."

Avelina gasped at the declaration, while Lily let out a small moan that erupted into a cry. Brenna reacted as though she had been slapped. Could this be possible? Was Quade betrothed? She glanced at the crowd to gauge their reaction. The nasty looks were aimed at Iona, not at her.

A voice in the back yelled. "Here now, Iona. Leave the healer be. 'Tis the chief's business, no' yours."

Iona snapped her head around. "Stay out of my affairs, Angus. He will be my husband, not hers."

"No' so sure of that, Iona!" Chuckling followed the comment. Iona stared at the offender and all quieted again.

So, not everyone agreed with Iona. Nay, Brenna refused to believe her. This woman was not his type, and he wouldn't allow her near Lily, would he?

"Lady Brenna, please make her leave. She is mean." Lily said in a small voice as she reached for Brenna from the wagon.

Iona's voice raised a whole octave. "You think you have healed her? You'll see. You havenae. You are using trickery, but she will go back to the way she was as soon as you leave. You are naught but an evil witch." She turned to Lily. "And you—I have heard enough of your whining, pretending to be ill when you are no' sick at all, just so your papa will stay near." The woman swung back her arm as if to strike the wee bairn.

Lily screamed, but Brenna caught the arm in mid-air and held tight. "I wouldnae do that if I were you." She twisted the woman's wrist while glaring into her wild eyes, ignoring the obscenities that started to spill from Iona's mouth.

A deep growl caught everyone's attention as Quade descended on the melee.

"I wouldnae do it either, Iona." He stepped between her and Brenna. "I'll take care of this, Lady Brenna. Please return Lily to the hall."

"Papa," Lily wailed. "I do no' like that lady, she is mean."

Avelina peeked at her brother. "Quade, please tell us you aren't marrying her. 'Tis what she said."

Brenna was glad to see Quade's shock at Avelina's question. Nay, Iona was lying.

"Go with Lady Brenna, Avelina. Do as I say. Now." He spoke through gritted teeth, clearly not pleased with the situation.

Brenna turned the wagon around, but not before she picked Lily up in her arms in an attempt to console her. She made her way back to the hall as fast as she could, Avelina trailing behind her.

She didn't believe Iona's claims. That was clear in Quade's reaction. But every man had their needs; at least, that's the gossip she had heard at her keep. Quade's wife had passed away long ago. Had he built a relationship with another woman?

Strange reckoning for her, but she found the idea upsetting. Each time he kissed her, she liked it more. And while his attentions had startled her at first, she welcomed them now. She chided herself for being soft hearted, since she knew she was destined to leave this place, this man, but she couldn't help herself.

Was it just curiosity? After everything she had heard at her own keep, she admitted she wanted to learn more about what went on between men and women. Did it matter who she kissed? Couldn't she kiss Quade as easily as any other lad?

But it *did* matter. There was something about Quade Ramsay that drew her in and got past all her defenses. When he kissed her, nothing else mattered. All she thought of was him. She thought of how furious he had looked when that woman had threatened his daughter. Her brother would have reacted the same way. She liked that kind of loyalty in a lad.

She hoped Iona had been lying about their betrothal. The thought of the two of them together made her want to spit fire.

Nay, there was no use denying it. Quade Ramsay was a verra handsome lad who made her heart race just by being near. She was falling for a chieftain. Actually, it was probably too late, her heart was lost to him now.

And she had no idea what would happen when her brother finally arrived.

Two days later, Brenna reached Lily's chamber and opened the door. Greeted by the smiling wean, she knew today would be even better than yesterday. Lily's eyes shone with brilliance. It had been a few days now since she had retched or experienced any intestinal discomfort. Even the air in the room smelled fresh.

"Lady Brenna!" Lily shouted, her arms reaching up to her. "What may I have to eat today? I am verra hungry. May I have cheese for breakfast?"

Brenna kissed her cheek, enjoying the renewed softness and the sweet aroma of the lass's skin. Her hair had a soft sheen to it now and was curling at the ends.

"Nay, no cheese yet, my sweet. I have something new for you this morn. I think you are strong enough to go downstairs for breakfast. How does that sound?"

Lily squealed with delight. "Is Papa breaking his fast, too? May I eat with my him?"

"I am no' sure if he is still there, my wee one. He may be out in the lists already. Let's go find out." Brenna laughed as she watched the lass jump about. How delightful it was to see her acting like a normal wean.

Aggie chuckled and held Lily still. "Wheest, hold, wean, so I can wash and dress you."

The young one could not keep her excitement contained.

"Careful, or you will use up all your energy before

we eat," Brenna said with a laugh.

Aggie cleaned Lily up quickly. "My lady, she is so much better. You have been a wonder for her."

"We must stay diligent, Aggie. Do no' bend from her diet."

When Lily finished dressing, Brenna held out a hand to her. "Come, let us see what Cook has created for you today."

"What is it, Lady Brenna? 'Tis something special, I ken it. Will I like it? Can you tell me now?" Her chattering persisted all the way down the corridor and the stairwell. When they entered the great hall, the few people who remained turned to stare at them.

Brenna overheard one of the kitchen maids. "Oh my word, 'tis a miracle. Look at the wee one. Where is the chief? He should be here."

She hoped he would stop in to see his daughter, but it seemed unlikely. Quade had avoided them after the mishap with Iona. She was learning the patterns to Quade Ramsay's behavior. He clearly did not like conflict, though she had a difficult time understanding how he managed to be chieftain of his clan without dealing with conflict. Perhaps his tendency for avoidance only pertained to women. He apparently didn't have any problem fighting when necessary.

Or was his issue just with her? Or worse yet, had the scene in the courtyard with Iona turned into a night of hot passion? That thought ripped at her heart, so she shut it down as quickly as it had started. A laird had many obligations. She was sure he had other things he needed to tend to besides his daughter's health.

Lily and Brenna arrived at the kitchens and proceeded through the doorway in search of Cook. They found her over by the hearth, but she stopped short when she turned to greet them.

"Saints preserve us, look at this bairn." Cook stopped and blessed herself with the sign of the cross.

"My lady, see what you have done for her. For all of us. She is the image of her mother, and how we loved her so. The chief has been so tormented since his wife's death and the illnesses."

"Illnesses? Have I missed something, Cook? What other illnesses have there been besides Lily's?" She set the lass down beside her, but held fast to her hand.

Cook changed the subject with a hasty wave of her hand. "Miss Lily, wait until you see what I have for you this morning."

"Tell me, Cook. What is it? Please, I am so hungry! A pastry? Do you have a sweet pastry for me again?" Lily's exuberance spread to all the helpers in the kitchens as one by one they snuck over to look at the chief's bairn and whisper.

"Nay, lass." Cook bent over and picked the child up into her arms. "No pastry yet. Lady Brenna said I could bake you an apple today to eat with your porridge." She carried Lily over to see her bowl. "And here it is. Do you want your apples mixed in or by themselves? I skinned the fruit, just as you requested, Lady Brenna." She pointed to the steaming bowl of cooked oats and the skinned chopped apple next to it.

"Both!" Lily squealed. "I like both. May I have both, Lady Brenna? May I have an apple mixed in and another one by itself?"

Brenna had to admit that the aroma was tantalizing. "Aye, mix one in, Cook. We will see how that settles before we have the other apple."

The maid carried the food out and helped them to settle at the table in the great hall.

Avelina joined them. "Och, you have apples in your porridge, my favorite!"

"Aye, Lady Brenna said I could try them today. Where is Papa, Lina? I want him to see." Lily giggled right before she shoveled a spoonful of food into her mouth, her blonde curls bouncing with exuberance.

Brenna's eye caught movement from the corner of

the room, and she cast a glance in that direction.

Lady Ramsay moved as if in a trance, her eyes never leaving her granddaughter, her cheeks wet with tears."Oh, my Lilykins! Look at you. What have you done with her, Lady Brenna?" She sat across from Brenna and reached over the table to grab her hands. "May God bless you, Brenna Grant. How can we ever repay you? Look at her. She is almost normal again. What have you given her? I cannae believe my eyes."

Lily finished her porridge in a flurry before making her way to the other side of the table to her grandmother. "Grammy, don't cry. I am fixed. See, I can eat apples in my porridge without a belly ache. Lady Brenna, may I have more apples? Please? They are so sweet; they are my favorite."

The door to the hall burst open, and the outline of a large man filled the doorway.

"Papa!" Lily walked across the room, hanging on to Avelina's hand, only stumbling once before launching herself at her father. He picked her up and swung her in a circle, before hoisting her up so he could kiss her cheek.

"Papa, guess what? I had apples in my porridge today. Lady Brenna said I could." She promptly lifted her gown and pointed to her belly. "Look, no tummy ache after breakfast. Papa, can I have another apple? Cook has another waiting for me." Quade kissed her belly, sending her into a shrieking fit of giggles, then strolled over to the table and greeted his mother before stopping next to Brenna. He set Lily down, and aimed her toward the kitchens. "Go, Lilykins. Ask Cook for another apple." His gaze caught Brenna's and stayed there. "Och, cease, Lily. Did you no' check with Lady Brenna?"

"May I have another apple, Lady Brenna?" Lily said with polite solemnity, holding onto the bench.

Brenna couldn't help but smile. "Aye, lass. See if Avelina will help you to make your way to the kitchens."

"I see I have much to thank you for, Lady Brenna," Quade said with a brief bow as he watched his daughter disappear through the doorway. "My daughter hasnae been able to walk the length of the great hall in a verra long time. What a greeting for me when I opened the door. I thank you for helping my daughter."

Lady Ramsay continued to stare at Brenna. "What a blessing you are," she said.

Moments later, Lily burst through the door holding Avelina's hand, followed by a maid who was carrying her apple and a bowl of porridge for the chief.

Quade sat down, still staring at Brenna. "What have you given her to create this miracle?"

"I havenae given her anything other than good cooked foods," Brenna said.

Lady Ramsay glanced at her. "Perhaps we are nae longer in need of your services. We can prepare an escort for you to return you to your home."

"Nay!" Quade barked at his mother. "She cannae be finished yet. Am I correct, Brenna? You arenae done helping her?"

A fist slammed into her gut. Return now? Impossible. She could not leave Lily. Why, her work with the lass had just started . She had to settle this in a hurry. "Aye, you are correct, Quade. I still havenae isolated the food that has caused her illness. Fruits, vegetables, broth, and oat porridge are all I have tried. I did not suspect vegetables to be the cause since there isn't any particular vegetable she would have eaten enough of to cause the problem. She is doing fine with the porridge, so I think we can try another new food, something more common. Bread tomorrow, then cheese."

"Whatever you say, Lady Brenna. Clearly you ken how to handle this." Quade finished his porridge and leaned over to kiss his daughter before striding to the door.

Brenna rubbed her forehead at the thoughts racing through her mind. She had to admit that Lily was not the only one who held her here. The mysterious chief was always on her mind. She followed him with her eyes as he strode out the door without another word.

Lady Ramsay smiled at her granddaughter. "Sit with me, Lilykins?" Lily plopped onto her grandmother's lap with a smile.

"He has probably gone to ride and shoot, Lady Brenna," Avelina said, giving her an unreadable look.

She tried to stop the flame that brightened her cheeks. She was being so obvious that the chief's sister could read her thoughts.

Lady Ramsay spoke in a soft whisper, a wistful look on her face. "Oh, I do hope you are right, Lina. He has not done that in a long time. Perhaps he is finally healing."

"Ride and shoot?" Brenna said, shaking her head in confusion. "What does he shoot?"

Avelina smiled with pride. "He used to ride his horse while standing on her back and then shoot with his arrow. He is the best hunter in the Lowlands, mayhap the Highlands as well. He loves to practice just outside the gate in the heather field near the loch. His horse, Star, is so in touch with him. 'Tis amazing to watch them move together."

"Ride standing on the horse?" Brenna said, alarm shooting through her. "He cannae. He could fall. It hasnae been that long since I stitched up his insides. He could ruin everything. One fall and I could have to cut him open again. You have to stop him."

Lady Ramsay and Avelina both smirked at her.

Quade's mother spoke first. "You willnae be able to stop him. This is how he releases his energy, and he must practice to maintain his skill with the bow and arrow. Frankly, I am thrilled if Avelina is right. I have been worried because he does no' do anything for enjoyment anymore. All he does is torture himself about all the things he should have done differently."

"What do you mean?"

"Quade thinks he is responsible for his daughter's illness and his wife's death." Avelina added.

Brenna couldn't stop her reaction. "That is ridiculous. Where did he come up with that idea?"

Dead silence followed her declaration, but she was grateful for it. She had something more important to do.

There was no way in hell she would allow that man to ruin her stitchery.

CHAPTER EIGHT

Brenna charged across the courtyard to the stables, her hair whipping around her head. She grabbed her skirts and lifted them to allow her to move faster, not the least bit concerned if her ankles showed. Seeing her in advance of her arrival, the stable lad anticipated her need and brought a horse out for her.

Another helped him saddle the horse. She hopped from one foot to the other, imagining his wound popping open under his leine. "Where did the chief go?"

The lad pointed. "He likes the heather field, my lady."

Her heart threatened to pound out of her breast as she turned the horse and shot out through the gates, heading in the direction the lads had sent her. Her brothers had all made sure she rode, and rode well. She flew over the ground.

Foolish, foolish Quade. Her mother had told her men were driven more by emotion than reason.. Always thrill seeking, her father and brothers had risked their lives many times without regret. A man needed a woman to use reason and logic for him, her mother had said, because men were not capable. Now she understood what her mother had meant.

As she galloped outside the castle walls, she couldn't help but admire the beauty of the Ramsay land. Rich green hills surrounded her, the trees resplendent with fall colors. She breathed of the autumn air as she kneed her horse to speed up. When the shades of lavender and purple in the meadow across from her came into view, she was tempted to stop to drink in the beauty. Instead, she plowed ahead, intent on saving Quade from himself. Didn't the man have any sense? He had just had part of his insides cut out about a sennight ago. How could he think his body was sound enough to ride standing and risk a fall?

When she drew near, she slowed to a trot, a warmth spreading through her belly at the sight of him. Quade stood on the back of his horse, his arms stretched to the heavens. He hollered as he rode, but she couldn't make out any of his words. Much of it sounded similar to her brothers' whooping when they competed. Mayhap he was just shouting in joy. He was so in tune with the movements of his horse that horse and rider seemed as one. She stopped not far away, just to enjoy the sheer pleasure of observing him without his knowledge.

Star had a beautiful brown coat with a white face. Quade had removed his shirt and his muscular torso had a fine sheen of sweat. The beauty of his body caught her breath. His scars did not bother her. How could they, since she had put them there? A week ago he could barely walk, yet now he rode like he'd been born on the back of his horse. Amazing. He held his bow, aimed, and let an arrow loose into the distance before releasing a whoop of excitement.

He then tumbled off his horse with a shout, landing on the ground with a hard thump.

Her heart lunged in her chest. Fear crept up her spine as she imagined that he might be seriously hurt or even dead. The fool! She spurred her horse closer. She would kill him if she had to cut him open again. The place her thoughts traveled next she refused to acknowledge. Nay! He was alive. He had to be alive.

She bounded from her horse as she pulled near to where he lay on his side in the deep grass.

"Quade! Quade, are you all right?" She fell to her knees at his side, afraid to turn him in case she caused him greater injury, or worse...

He rolled over in a flash, and tugged her down on top of him, kissing the breath out of her. His warm mouth caressed hers, and his tongue slid between her lips, teasing hers. He tasted of apples, of autumn, and she yielded completely, lost in the moment and dizzied by his touch. He caressed her cheek and she groaned as his tongue mated with hers, clutching his arms to bring him closer. She was confused by the longing and insatiable need he brought out in her. What did it mean?

He rolled her onto her back and continued his assault, kissing her neck, his lips trailing a path of fire down to her breast. Boldly, he stroked his hand over her breast, and she started at her own reaction. She had no idea such a caress could feel as it did. She was filled with the mad desire to rip off her dress and feel her skin against his. He reached inside her shift and cupped her breast in his hand. Pulling back, his green eyes locked with hers as he teased her nipple with his thumb. "Do you like that, my sweet?"

Brenna wrapped her hands around his neck, wanting him closer. He leaned toward her for another kiss, but instead his mouth found her nipple, and he ravished her breast until she moaned in sheer ecstasy. His hand gripped her bottom and tugged her closer to him. At the sudden contact with his hardness, her sanity returned.

She hit him square in the chest and pushed away.

"You jest? Did you fall from your horse on purpose? How could you frighten me like that? I was terrified that you were hurt, really hurt!" Brenna shouted loud enough for half the valley to hear her.

Quade chuckled, a smug look on his face. "Och, I fell honestly, but I also saw you and decided to wait in the grass for you. You have feelings for me, my fiery lass?"

She shoved his shoulder. "Nay, just feelings of a healer, foolish lad!" She slugged him again for good measure.

Quade stopped and stared into her eyes. His smoldering gaze caused her breath to catch. No one had ever looked at her like that. Her belly fluttered as she returned his stare. His sweet breath warmed her cheek as he brought his lips down over hers again, gentle at first, until she conceded. She should have pushed him away, but she had no strength of will. She wanted his lips on hers again. Angling his mouth over hers, he used gentle pressure to deepen the kiss. She finally opened for him, a slight moan erupting from her as his tongue swept inside her mouth. She could taste the apples and porridge and something else—Quade. What she tasted was him. He pulled back and gazed into her eyes.

"Brenna, you make me want to live again. I havenae felt like this in a verra long time."

He kissed her again, deeper still, possessing her. His tongue mated with hers as his hand swept up the side of her body. His hand cupped her breast, rubbing her nipple through the thin fabric. She arched her back to get closer to him. What was she doing? His hand was on her breast again and she liked it?

She didn't just like it; her body was on fire, and she burned for his touch everywhere. His mouth devoured hers as if she were the only woman in the world. He kissed a trail down her throat before daring to slide his hand under her skirts. She was briefly aware of his touch, but her senses were on overload. Shocked at what they were doing, she was more surprised that she didn't want him to stop.

He caressed her thigh, boldly touching her where no other man had before. His fingers found her core and grazed her entrance. Her breath caught as she gazed into his eyes, trusting him, but wanting him to explain what was happening to her. He continued to fondle her core, sliding his thumb against her nub. The sensations overwhelmed her, the thrum in her body urging her into the unknown. Nibbling her lips, she groaned into his mouth, embarrassed by the power of her reaction.

Did she want him to stop? His fingers slid into her wetness and she opened for him. Her mind was rife with confusion, yet the cravings inside her were undeniable. Clutching his strong arms, his bunching muscles, she wanted more of him, every wonderful inch. The tension in his body matched her own, and his breathing became raspy the more he touched her.

His horse made a loud neighing noise, and just like that he stopped. "Blast it!" he mumbled. Giving her lips a final peck, he straightened her skirts. Before she knew what was happening, he was standing above her.

She was momentarily stunned, unable to comprehend what had just happened—what he had done to her, why he had stopped. She rolled on her side in the meadow, trying to catch her breath before sitting up. Vaguely aware of his movements, she followed him with her eyes.

Confusion clouded Brenna's mind as Quade moved to his horse and turned Star back in the direction of his keep. The sound of approaching horses reached Brenna's ears and she finally understood. Thankfully, the way he held Star prevented the oncoming riders from seeing Brenna fumbling in the grass. The harsh reality of visitors forced her to get control of her senses. Once she righted her clothing, Quade reached down to help her to her feet. He brushed the grass from her skirt and her hair in an attempt to repair her appearance. He still kept his back to the oncoming horsemen, blocking their view of her.

"Forgive me, I was out of line." His voice, husky, was barely audible.

She blushed at the implication of his comment. What was he asking her to forgive him for? Kissing her? Brenna gazed at him, but he ignored her. He shouldn't be apologizing for that, she had enjoyed every minute of it. Didn't he realize that?

She didn't know what to think. The grim line of his mouth made her question what their encounter had meant to him. Had he regretted everything or just the interruption? She doubted she would ever know. She had no experience with men. What had gone wrong? He shut down on her completely, barely even looking at her. He cupped his hands and held them next to her horse to help her mount, still refusing to look at her. His coldness had her more confused than ever, particularly when he slapped the horse's flank, sending her back toward the keep without another word.

It was time to return. Quade had stayed away from the keep ever since his interlude with Brenna. The lass made him daft. She brought out feelings in him that he hadn't experienced since the early days of his marriage. He had loved his wife, but stress had pulled them apart during their last few years together. But this? This reminded him of new, butterflies-in-the-belly love.

He couldn't do it. From what had happened in the meadow, he could tell she'd never been touched that way before... yet she was so passionate once she gave in. He loved to hear the little sound she made in the back of her throat when he kissed her. Had his horse not warned him of the oncoming riders, he would have shamed her and his guilt tore at him for that. He just couldn't stop himself with her. And that meant one thing: He couldn't allow this relationship to go on any longer.

He would not get involved with another woman and kill her the way he had killed his wife.

The men on horseback had told him there were

signs of poachers or reivers on his land. His trackers were the best, so he didn't doubt their accuracy. He just knew what it meant, and he didn't want to accept it.

Laird Alexander Grant had sent someone out scouting for his sister. He would have to let her go soon, though every ounce of his being screamed against it. For some reason, he felt as though she belonged here with him. She belonged with Lily, his Lilykins, to watch over her, to keep her healthy.

How wonderful it had been when Lilykins ran toward him this morning in the great hall, throwing herself into his arms. He loved her so much, and he was so excited to see her happy again, acting as any normal lass should.

Brenna couldn't leave him yet. He wouldn't allow it. But what was he to do?

Trudging up the steps to the great hall, he sighed and ran a hand through his hair. How could he keep her here? The only possible way would be to marry her, but that was out of the question. He wouldn't allow her to risk her life by becoming his wife. He had killed his first wife. Not intentionally, but he had certainly been the cause of her death. If not for Lily, he may have ended his life long ago.

He could not marry Brenna. But if he didn't, would she stay just to help him with Lily? He doubted it. He had to come up with another reason. Time was running out.

When he reached the keep, he headed for the great hall, taking a chair in front of the hearth. Soon after he sat, a maid came out with ale for him. He sat and stared at the flames, willing an idea to come into his mind. When his mother entered the room a few moments later, he still hadn't thought of anything useful.

"I did no' ken if you would return tonight." Lady Ramsay stared at her son with her arms crossed.

"Something must have happened outside the gates today."

He glanced up at his mother with a sigh. "Why do you say that, Mother?"

"Because Lady Brenna was so flushed when she returned." She moved over to sit in the chair next to his.

He took a sip of his ale. "Mayhap she ran back to the hall." He turned away and stared into the hearth.

"I do no' think so. My guess is she followed you because she was worried about your stitches. I am thinking things got out of hand."

"Do not concern yourself. It will never happen again." He continued to stare into the flames, no inflection to his voice.

"Quade, you have to stop punishing yourself for what happened."

He turned to stare at his mother.

She continued. "It wasnae your fault. You have to let it go and start to live again. I can tell that you have feelings for Lady Brenna. I couldnae be happier. You need to get involved with people again and stop looking at life from the outside. Truthfully, I hope you rolled in the meadow with the lady. And I hope she helped bring you back to life. She has brought your daughter back to life, now it's your turn." Tears welled in her eyes as she spoke.

"She did for a moment, Mother. For a moment, I felt alive again." He took another swig of ale. "But I cannae let it happen again. You ken I am cursed. Look at my life thus far. I wouldnae do anything to hurt her."

"Quade, let it go. 'Tis time." She waited for his answer, but he didn't offer one. "Has it occurred to you how unfair this is if she has developed feelings for you? Are you no' hurting her more by pushing her away and always keeping her an arm's length from you?"

"There is something else you do no' understand,

Mother. She will never stay here." His chin rose as he glanced at her.

"Why? She has feelings for you. I believe it with all my heart. And she is wonderful with Lily. Rejoice that you have found a woman who is perfect for you."

He hated to hurt his mother, but he had no choice. The truth must come out. "Cannae be." His guilt over the way he had treated her—and her innocence—in the meadow still ripped his heart out. She must hate him. How could he have allowed it to go so far? The lass drove him over the edge.

"Why? What do I no' understand?" She leaned forward awaiting his answer.

He plunged ahead, knowing how she would receive this news. "Because Lady Brenna was kidnapped. She was stolen out of her bed in the middle of the night and Laird Grant is probably on his way here as we speak."

His mother jumped out of her chair, one hand pressed to her throat. Her reaction was just what he'd expected it would be. He hated letting her down.

"Dear lord, Quade. Why would you do such a thing?" she gasped. "What have you done?"

Micheil came in just as Quade stood to address her. "Mother, I had no choice. You saw Lily! She was near death. The lass could nae longer walk on her own. I willnae stand by and watch my daughter die."

"I agree with him, Mother. He had to take action." Micheil stood next to Quade. "I did no' go along, but I kenned what they were doing and why. We had no way of kenning Quade would take ill on the way."

"But 'tis wrong! Your father and I did no' raise you to act so rash." Tears clung to her lashes.

"Mother, I watched my wife die, I wasnae going to stand by and watch my bairn die, too. What else was I to do? All the other healers did naught but bleed the poor lass."

"Quade, you kidnapped the sister of the laird who

has cut down the best swordsman in all of Scotland! The Comming was dead in less than an hour. He will kill you. Or worse, hang you where I can watch. Aye, praise the saints! What are we to do?"

Tears ran down her cheeks in a torrent. He couldn't bear to see his mother cry. She had been through too much.

"Logan and I left to find out more information about the Grant healer. We would have talked to her brother, but I was struck down by the boar. Logan did what he thought was right. And according to Brenna, I wouldnae have lived another day without her intervention. Father taught us to do what we had to do for our clan. 'Tis exactly what we did."

He enveloped his mother in his arms. "Had we waited to talk to the Grant, I wouldnae be here now. I willnae hold what Logan did against him. I am still here, aye?" He forced his mother's chin up to look at him.

"Aye, I am so thankful for Lady Brenna. She has saved you and my granddaughter both. But to what end? What will her brother do to you? I am so frightened."

"Aye, I ken you are and I am sorry for that. 'Tis why I did no' tell you the truth before now. We also heard from more than one source that Laird Alexander Grant is a fair man, and Niles Comming deserved what he got. I am hoping that Laird Grant will at least be willing to talk."

"I hope you are right. How soon before he arrives, do you think?"

"Unfortunately, it could be on the morrow."

❧ ❧ ❧

Her eyes flew open. It was the middle of the night, but she knew something was wrong. She heard the crying even through the thick stone walls, she had left her door open just a touch so she could hear Lily if she needed her.

Brenna stood up, reached for a goblet of water to rinse her mouth and then grabbed her plaid and her slippers to protect her feet against the cold stone floor. She ran her fingers through her hair to help make herself presentable. Aggie slept in the room with Lily. She would be with her this night.

She padded down the corridor after washing her face and hands, dreading what she was to find in wee Lily's chamber. She reviewed what the child had eaten that day in her mind. Lily had done so well with the porridge and apples. The middle meal had been broth with carrots and turnips with some chopped greens thrown in. All had settled fine. She was full of energy all day, tearing around the great hall and the outdoors as never before.

It must have been dinner. Cook had thickened her broth a bit and Brenna had allowed Lily to have a small piece of dark rye bread with it. She should have known better than to allow so many new foods in one day.

She stepped into the chamber quietly. Aggie sat on the bed with Lily on her lap, doubled over in pain. The lass's sobs reached her ears, instantly breaking her heart. The bairn was clutching her belly, her screams alternating with sobs as waves of pain tormented her insides.

"How long has it been, Aggie?" Brenna rubbed the sleep from her eyes as she spoke.

"My lady, she has been having belly pains for some time, but they have just now worsened. What can I do for her?"

"Here, let us give her some mint in warm water and see if that helps."

Brenna called for a maid and sent her to the kitchens for the hot water.

"Lady Brenna, my tummy hurts, please make it

stop. Oh, it hurts so bad. Fix me. I want my papa. Where is he?" Lily's arms reached out to Brenna, who lifted her into her warm embrace.

Brenna could feel the tension in the wean's body, alternating with shivers from the stress of dealing with so much pain. Children should not have to feel this way, they were too innocent. Her eyes watered as she shushed wee Lily on her shoulder, rocking her from side to side in the hopes of giving her comfort.

"My bowl!" Her little hand reached out. "Aggie, my bowl. I need my bowl."

Aggie held the small basin under the girl's chin just in time to catch the fluid spewing from the tiny mouth.

When Lily came up for air, Brenna could barely understand what she said, but she knew she had to act fast.

"The pot. I need the pot, Aggie. Oh, I need them both." The poor girl didn't know what to do first.

Yanking Lily's gown up with one hand, Brenna moved her over the pot in the corner in time to catch the foul smelling, bulky stool that ejected from her tiny quivering body. How could something so awful come from something so sweet? Brenna's nose wrinkled at the strong assault. She turned her head in time to see Quade step in the door before turning around as soon as he saw the pot.

She read his lips before he left. "I cannae."

Fortunately, Lily had not seen her father before he left. The poor lass spewed from both ends for several more minutes before finally sighing and closing her eyes.

"My lady, what do you think did this to her?" Aggie whispered as they both struggled to clean her up without awakening her.

"The bread. Without a doubt, Aggie. Everything else settled fine today. She cannae have anything at all with any rye in it. I thought it would prove to be cheese, as I kenned another that couldnae tolerate cheese. It has to be the rye, the grain, that is assaulting her insides. We will go back to the broth and baked apples."

"But she had porridge, my lady. Why didn't that cause her harm? I don't understand. I thought oats and rye were both grains."

"Aye, they are, but one is from oats and the other from wheat. While this was awful for the poor dear, this is good news. Now we ken what her problem is. Wheat! She cannot eat wheat. That is easy to avoid. She can eat oatcakes and porridge, she just cannot tolerate any wheat bread."

Brenna kissed Lily's forehead. "Poor lass is exhausted. She may still have a bit more to lose, Aggie, can you stay with her? I will talk to Cook in the morrow. Let me mix the mint water for her in case she awakens. I don't want her to have anything else until morning. Then we will see how she feels."

Aggie finished placing clean sheets on the little one's bed. She ran her hands across them to smooth the wrinkles. "Aye, my lady. I will stay with her. Let me rid the room of the pots, and then I will return to hold her."

Brenna settled Lily on the soft sheets and covered her with a warm blanket, tucking her in tight. She still did not have much fat to warm her thin body, but she had made great strides in a few days. Brenna smiled as she leaned down to kiss her cheek again.

"Finally, we have an answer, lass."

CHAPTER NINE

Brenna flew down the stairs, hoping to find Quade. She was so excited that the mystery had finally been solved. She never would have guessed that the problem was wheat. This would be simple to fix for the poor little lass.

She had wanted to scream at Quade when he turned around and walked away from his sick daughter. But her mother had told her it was the way of men.

A man could run another man through with a sword, but if his baby girl had a cut on her hand, he couldn't handle it. Why, she had seen lads almost swoon at the sight of blood on someone they loved, yet the very same lads could fight their way through twenty men to protect the clan. Grown men would heave at the sound of a child vomiting, but could walk ten fields with their belly sliced open.

She vowed not to chide him for leaving his daughter. She searched for him at the bottom of the staircase, but didn't see him until she passed the hearth.

She headed toward his chair to check on him. "Quade? Are you all right?"

He jumped at the sound of her voice.

"Sorry, Lady Brenna, I dozed for a moment." He rubbed his face in an attempt to wake up. "How is Lily? Is she still spewing? I am so sorry, I couldnae stay. I ken she wants me there, when she's sick, but I just cannae do it."

She stifled her grin at his tousled hair and tired eyes. How could a chieftain look so handsome? "I understand. I ken men have a difficult time around illness. Nay, I have come to give you good news. I think I have determined what food gives her trouble."

He stared at her. "You do? But you said it would take a long time." He sat up straight, his eyes wide. "Tell me, lass, what is it? What ails her? She did no' sound well to me a few moments ago."

"Wheat, 'tis wheat that sickens her. She had a piece of rye bread at the dinner meal. Cook also thickened her broth a bit and I want to check to see what she used for that."

"Wheat? So what does that mean, she cannae eat any wheat or rye bread? No grains at all? I do no' understand. How will she grow strong without bread to fill her belly? Bairns need bread, we all need bread." His full attention was on Brenna as he awaited her answer.

"She can eat oats, she has had porridge. I have not tried barley yet, so I am not sure, but it could just be wheat. We will keep her on oats for now and see how she does. Oats will help her grow."

"Could it be that if she does no' eat any wheat, she will ne'er be sick again? How could it be so simple? What about vegetables and fruit? Pottage? Can she have pottage?"

"We need to talk to Cook to see what she uses as a thickener in her pottage. If she uses rye or wheat, we will just have to make Lily's separate and use oats as a thickener. I think she will like it." Brenna smiled at Quade, her excitement overflowing. "I think 'tis it! She will grow strong again."

Without thinking, she embraced him, pulling him close in her excitement.

At first she thought he would push her away, but then his arms wrapped around her and held her tight.

"Lass, I do no' know how to thank you. I am forever in your debt if you are right about my Lily." His whispered words were warm in her ear.

He stepped back while still holding her arms. "Do you ken how long and hard my family has searched for an answer to her ailment? I cannot believe 'tis so simple. Are you sure, lass? Did she eat wheat that much? I do no' think she ate bread at every meal."

"Mayhap she only ate bread at dinner, but your cook may use wheat as a thickener in many things. Sometimes cooks throw a bit of it into pottage, into pudding. Wheat is in all the pastries." He hadn't let go of her yet. Why did her heart skip a beat just because he held her hands and didn't let go?

"Och, aye, Lilykins was always sneaking pastry."

"And if your cook likes to bake, wheat is always in baked goods. 'Twill be in cakes and pies and tarts."

"What will Lily be able to eat if 'tis in everything? Just vegetables and oats?"

"Nay. Any good cook can make sweets with oats. She just has to leave out the wheat flour for anything intended for Lily. She can have sugar and fruit, so 'twill just be a bit different. Pears and oat crisp or strawberries and oats. She may still have the cheese she loves so and goat's milk. Trust me, she will be fine."

Quade's smile improved the more he thought about it. "Och, aye. Then this is something we can handle. Lily will be so excited. I cannae wait to see her in the morning and tell her."

Brenna's smile left her fast as the realization hit her. If this was the key to the bairn's problems, he didn't need her anymore. She could go home, if only to avoid causing trouble for the Ramsay clan. His mind appeared to follow the same path as hers.

"You are probably ready to go home, lass? Aye?" Quade said with a frown. He stepped back, releasing her.

"Nay, I would like to see this finished. I want to make sure I am right. I need to test a couple of my ideas. I am still no' sure about barley or cheese. But, aye, I am close to being ready to go home." She cleared her throat, unsure of what else to say.

"Lass, I have not had the chance to speak to you about a couple of things." He ran his fingers through his hair before continuing. "I ne'er made any promises to Iona. I made the mistake of spending a night with her a little over a year ago, and she clearly misunderstood my intentions. I ne'er made any mention of marriage to her. Iona sees things a little differently than the rest of us."

"Quade, you do no' owe me an explanation."

"Aye, I do. She attacked you, and had you no' intervened, she would have attacked my bairn. I have no' had the chance to thank you for that. I had a conversation with Iona to clarify the situation. She was no' happy, but she willnae bother you again."

He cleared his throat before continuing.

"I must also apologize for my actions in the meadow. I promise it will ne'er happen again."

Brenna did not know what to say. She could not stop herself from blushing. So, he was sorry? Did that mean he wished it had never happened? At first she was embarrassed, but then anger blossomed inside her. How dare he insult her! He tells her that he didn't enjoy their interlude and it would never be repeated. How heartless was this man?

"Brenna? Are you all right?"

"Aye, I am fine." Her chin lifted. She would not allow him the satisfaction of seeing her disappointment. "Was there aught else you wished to speak to me about?"

"Aye, I probably should tell you I expect to see your brother soon."

"And why is that?"

He paused for a moment before answering. "He has

had scouts in the area. My lads have seen them, but they have no' intervened. They left after questioning a few of my people. My guess is he wants to move a large number of guards here, so he sent scouts ahead to make sure you are here and no' harmed. I made sure the scouts understood that."

"You spoke to my brother's guards?" Her hands fisted at her sides. How could he have kept this from her?

"Nay, I have not. I have my ways of making sure that his men receive the correct information. I do no' want him to think you are in danger."

"Nay, of course not, just kidnapped against my will."

She spun on her heel and headed to the kitchens. She had wasted quite enough time on Quade Ramsay.

Quade paced in his solar, stress emanating from his pores. He had been pacing since dawn.

His brother, Micheil, leaned against the table, watching him. "Quade, did you think this moment would no' come?"

Quade stopped for a moment to glare at his brother. "Aye, I ken. But I still am no' sure how to handle it."

"Seems quite clear to me. Tell the laird you want to wed his sister." Micheil smiled and crossed his arms.

Quade could not lose her now, but he still questioned the wisdom of marrying her. Without responding to his brother's statement, he barked out, "How far away are they? How much time do you think I have?"

Micheil chuckled. "A couple of hours."

"And how many guardsmen are you guessing he brought?" He began pacing again.

"My lads tell me over a hundred guards, could be closer to two hundred. But what does it matter? All you need worry about is facing Laird Alexander Grant in one-on-one combat. You heard what he did to the

Comming laird who was a great swordsman in his own right. I imagine Grant's youngest brother, who is traveling with him, is quite a swordsman as well."

He stopped again to glare at Micheil. "Aye. You are no' helping me at all, brother."

"Nay, facts are facts. Logan kidnapped the man's sister. I do no' think he will feel kindly toward you."

Quade stopped his pacing to yell at him. "Do you think they will just attack? Or will Grant want to spear me at once? You are head of my guard for a reason—to offer me advice. My head has been wrapped up in other things lately."

"Aye, I heard you were in the meadow with the lass. Your head, your arms, and your lips have been wrapped around Laird Grant's sister. How did Logan manage to ignore what was going on in front of him? He had to have seen it."

"Forget Logan! He left us. I do no' care about him right now. What should I do?"

"As I said, tell Grant you wish to marry his sister. That will put a stop to everything. Do no' be a jolthead. Tell the truth."

Quade sat in a chair and crossed his arms as he stared at his brother. "Aye, what a mess I am in now. After all the battles I have seen and all the times we fought next to Da, the thing that frightens me most is a beautiful lass. I am no' indecisive. This lass has brought me to my knees." He rubbed his hand across the stubble on his chin. "You ken I can no' marry her. You ken of the curse on my family. I cannae do that to her."

Micheil move to an inch away from his brother's face. "By my sword, shove the curse! Marry her and have some happiness in your life, Quade. Lily loves her and needs a mother. She's a perfect solution to all your problems."

He couldn't recall the last time he had seen his brother this way. Was he right? Should he marry her? It would be wonderful for his daughter. He had to admit he would be quite happy to have her as his wife. She was bright, beautiful, and compassionate. What more could he ask for?

Quade stood up and strode out the door, his decision made. "Nay, I cannae marry her, but I will meet her brother on my own." He turned in the doorway. "Tell your guards to ready themselves. Then you alone will go with me. We will meet the Grants head on."

Micheil grabbed his brother by the arm. "Och, aye. According to everyone I have asked, Laird Grant is a fair man. I am sure he will be willing to listen to you. Just be sure you do no' insult him by being nonchalant about kidnapping Lady Brenna or letting him think you treated her with anything less than the respect the lass deserves."

Quade tore out the door, heading for the stable. His mind was filled with sheer panic at the thought of losing Brenna, but he knew he had to let her go. Lily was healed. Of course, it was time for her to go back to her clan. Yet he still needed her for one more task.

He knew she wanted him as much as he wanted her, but he couldn't marry her and she was an innocent. She was also a strong, beautiful lass with a healer's gift and a brother who almost ruled the Highlands. The Grant would never allow her to stay here without a marriage contract. Even with a contract, he might not allow her to stay so near the Lowlands. She would be a long distance away from her clan here. Alexander Grant wouldn't be losing just his sister, but his healer as well.

The stable lad led Star out to him. He mounted in a hurry and galloped out the gate. He stood on his horse for a moment to see how far away Grant was. Not far.

He then fell back in his saddle and headed out to meet Laird Grant.

He had no idea what he would say. Mayhap it did not matter.

He could be a dead man.

CHAPTER TEN

Brenna heard the pounding of the hooves in the distance the moment she left the chapel. She turned to see a flurry of lads running to the stables, rushing to mount their horses. Chaos reigned in every direction.

"'Tis the Grants. They've come for us." The lad's shout carried back to her.

She had known her brother would come for her.

Brenna rushed to the keep, hoping to catch Quade before he headed out. A figure stood at the base of the stairs inside the doorway to the great hall. Lady Ramsay.

"I hope your brother is a kind man, Lady Brenna." Her hands twisted in her skirts as she turned to look at Brenna. "He willnae kill him on sight, will he?"

"What? Nay! My brother does not kill or maim without good reason. Where is Quade?"

Her eyes roamed the hall as she searched for him.

"He has gone to meet your brother. My hopes are he wasnae foolish enough to go to your brother alone." Lady Ramsay's voice dropped to a whisper. "Lady Brenna, please do no' leave us yet. My family needs you."

The woman's expression tugged at Brenna's heart. Had it been so long since this family had possessed any hope?

"Trust me when I tell you that you do no' understand everything yet," Lady Ramsay said, reaching for her hand. "'Tis amazing to me that one slight young lass has given me more hope than any of the old wizened healers who have passed through these gates. Please, lass, *do no' leave us yet.* I havenae seen Lily or my son this happy in years." She brought her hands to her face in an attempt to mask her sobs.

Brenna wrapped her arms around the woman. How could she deny such a request? The woman only wanted her family back. "Aye, I will stay for as long as I am able. However, my brother can be verra stubborn when he wants to be. This willnae be easy."

"Foolish old woman, I am," Lady Ramsay said through her tears. "My hope was that my son would fall in love with you. He so deserves some happiness in his life. This clan has lived under stormy clouds for too long. I saw you as our much needed and deserved blessing, child."

Brenna stepped back, rubbing the woman's arms. "I will see what I can do. But I must go after Quade. I wish to speak to my brother before he makes any quick decisions. He is sometimes too hasty."

Lady Ramsay nodded. "Then go, lass. Do what you must."

Brenna was heading up the steps to the door, when the other woman said her name. "Aye?" She turned around, her hand still on the door handle.

"I am so sorry my son felt the need to kidnap you. I had no idea. You just do no' understand everything yet, though, and desperate men do desperate things. Trust in him. He is a good lad and a good father."

After nodding her understanding, Brenna bolted out the door and headed for the stables. She could feel the pins coming out of her hair, but she didn't have time to fix it, so she let it go its own way. She had to get to Alex before he did or said something he would later regret. She yelled to the stable lad and rounded the corner in time to almost collide with the slight lad leading a horse to her.

She mounted with his help and headed toward the gate, her head roiling with so many thoughts she didn't know which one to give her attention to first.

What did Lady Ramsay mean by telling her she didn't know everything yet? Quade had lost his wife and his daughter had been on death's door. Did she fault Logan for kidnapping her? Nay, she had to admit with a grudge that she might have done the same thing in his place. His brother's life was at stake and his niece's. Had Logan not gotten her there sooner, Quade would not have survived. Chieftains had done far worse for their family.

Lady Ramsay's admission that she wanted Quade and Brenna to marry had also thrown her. He was adamant that he could never marry. Convinced he had killed his wife, he must have made a commitment never to marry again, regardless of the circumstances. Why did he think he had killed his wife? His mother didn't appear to agree with him. Would she ever be able to understand the inner workings of Quade's mind? She had to admit that if he persisted in kissing her the way he had been in that meadow, she might not care.

The wind in her hair, she urged her horse onward, reveling in the feel of freedom as the beast cantered across the Highland meadows. Peering out at the landscape, she saw her brother's guards in all their glory. What an impressive sight they were. Her two brothers led with their flag carriers off to the side, and a sea of horses covered the horizon in majestic splendor. It did not surprise her that they evoked such fear in many clans in the Highlands. She nudged her horse from a canter into a gallop. She could see Quade up ahead—he had almost reached her brother, and Micheil was just behind him.

She hoped her brother would not act until she arrived.

Her brother's battle cry reached her ears seconds later and she screamed.

CHAPTER ELEVEN

Quade heard the Grant's battle cry and cringed.

"Grant! By my arrow, give me a moment before you finish me. Every man should be granted a last request. Aye? By your Scottish honor?"

Alex's arm reached across the sea of warriors. Instant silence followed.

Grant nudged his magnificent stallion forward, bringing it within inches of his horse. "You kidnapped my sister, Ramsay. There is no honor in you as a Scotsman."

The Grant was massive and every bit as impressive as he was rumored to be. "Aye, I acted in haste. God's truth, my brother acted in haste because I was on death's door. Your sister has come to no harm. I ask you to come to my hall and speak to her before you pass judgment on my clan. The actions I took were for my own benefit and not for my clan's."

Quade's eyes met the laird's. He thought he saw a glimmer of softening there, enough to give him hope he was not about to have his head cleaved from his body in one swoop from the man's giant claymore. Grant's brother flanked him. He had eyes like Brenna, more soulful than the laird's. Quade reminded himself he spoke to the family of the lass he loved, and he would give them as much respect as he gave her.

Grant's powerful warhorse whinnied and pawed the ground, anxious about something, but he couldn't tell what. Then Quade caught the subtle shift of Grant's eyes back toward the keep. What had he seen? He turned his head to look in that direction and drew back.

Brenna.

Brenna flew across the meadow on her horse in all her glory.

He tried to return his gaze to the Grant, but couldn't. Powerless against the siren flying toward them, his chest swelled with a strange kind of pride as she galloped toward them. Her hair was unbound, chestnut locks waving in the sun, but she didn't let that stop her. He knew Brenna by now. She never cared about her appearance, whether due to her innocent misunderstanding of how it affected people or because it wasn't important to her, he wasn't sure. Her hair had been back earlier, but it was always in a bit of disarray, so it hadn't taken much for the wind to pull it from its confines.

She was magnificent—glorious in her beauty, steadfast in her strength. Everything about her called to him without speaking. He couldn't let her go, he realized as he watched her, he would never let her go. Beyond her beauty, she was the most intelligent lass he had ever met. She knew things most men could not begin to understand, things *he* couldn't begin to understand. They belonged together. He knew he couldn't marry her, but mayhap he could settle with having her stay in his keep as the healer. He would force himself to use restraint and stay away from her just to keep her near. His people needed her, his children needed her.

He needed her.

He loved her and admired her more than he had ever loved before. That thought frightened him, but he knew he would do whatever it took to make her stay. What Laird Grant wanted did not matter. This called for extreme measures.

She approached their group and nodded to her brothers, situating herself almost between the two chieftains. "Alex, Brodie." She greeted both with a stiff countenance that puzzled him.

"Lady Brenna," Alex greeted her. "How do you fare?"

Her mouth curved a touch. "I am well."

Quade still could not take his eyes from her. She sat her horse as a queen would, regal in her bearing, her brown eyes taking in everything at once. Grant's entire army of warriors stood as still as can be, awaiting any word from her.

"Brenna, move your horse behind mine." Alex barked his order without flinching.

She didn't budge.

"Brenna? Your laird gave you an order." Brodie glared at her.

"Aye, Alex. I heard your order. Excuse me, my laird. I would like permission to speak first." Her eyes bored into her brother's.

Stubborn woman! What was she thinking to deny her laird? Quade wanted to shake her before she made any more poor decisions. He glanced back at Laird Grant and decided he didn't like the menacing look he was giving his sister.

Quade moved his horse over in front of Brenna. "Lass, go behind me."

Brenna paused for a long moment, clearly thinking about her decision and its implications, before slowly moving her horse behind him.

Quade's heart soared. Mayhap there was hope.

A muscle in Alex's face twitched. "You give your life for my sister, Ramsay?"

"Aye, I do."

"You've made your choice." Alex pulled his claymore out, wielding it high enough for all to see.

"Alex, stop! Please listen to me. If you have any regard for me at all, you will stop this nonsense and enter the hall. I have need to speak to you and no' in front of your guardsmen. Quade, you will allow my brothers into the keep for purposes of negotiation?"

Quade's eyes never left the laird's. "Aye, your family is always welcome. As long as I have your brother's word that he will not harm you or force you to do anything against your will."

Alex's eyebrow rose. "I would never harm my sister, but she may not like the decision I make. I agree, for her sake only, to discuss the situation."

Quade looked to Brenna for confirmation. "Lady Brenna? Is this agreeable to you?"

"Am I allowed to be part of the discussion?" she asked, her eyes pinned on her brother. "Alex, I will not have important decisions made about my life without my input. You know how our mother felt about such things."

Alex's mouth quirked before he nodded in agreement. "Stubborn lass. You have my word."

"I welcome you at my table, Laird Grant. You and your brother. We will send food and ale out for your guardsmen."

"Agreed. Brodie, get the men settled and I will see you in the hall."

※ ※ ※

The two lairds squared off in the hall. Alex was the taller of the two, but Quade was still impressive. Brenna's brother was dark, bulky and tended to appear brooding to others. She knew how soft his heart was, but he kept that side of him well hidden, part of the mystery about Laird Grant of the Highlands.

Quade Ramsay was every bit as impressive. He was handsome, of course, and muscular and bronzed from the sun, but his beautiful green eyes were what made him special. They held a knowledge of life that many did not possess. Brenna could see the strength and wisdom in his aura, but she was a healer, and as her mother oft said, healers saw things in a different light.

And it was true, she did see Quade Ramsay in a different light. How does a leader of his clan continue to function when he is forced to watch the ones he loves crumble in front of him? She knew he had a heart of gold and more patience and strength than most, so she enjoyed watching him with her brothers, acting as the laird he was and not just as a father.

Quade explained why they had made the decision to travel as far as the Grant lands in the hopes of convincing Brenna to come and help Lily. He talked of traveling to neighboring lands and of all the healers who had come and bled Lily without making her better. He explained how Brenna's reputation had just reached them since they were near the Lowlands. Her reputation of having an uncanny ability to work with bairns had struck a note with him, as well as the stories of how she had successfully tended many of her brother's guards.

Quade explained that he had been gored and near death when his brother, Logan, had made the decision to kidnap Brenna instead of talking to her laird first— a decision that had saved his life. Of course, he had no explanation as to why his brother was no longer at his side.

Brodie had joined them eventually, listening quietly to both sides. After several long passes of explanations, Brenna could tell Alex wasn't swayed yet.

She had to call on her reserves. She had hoped it wouldn't come to this, that her brother would listen to reason and do what was best for the Ramsays, but she would have to do what was necessary.

Ever since he had married Madeline MacDonald, her brother's heart had softened. Once she had given him twin boys, his heart had softened even more. His exterior was still a laird's hardened countenance, but he had one weakness and she intended to use it.

When the twins were born, he had hoped for a lass.

Alex so loved his wife that he had wanted a lassie with blonde curls, just like Madeline's. He loved his lads with all his heart, but he still longed for a wee lass to settle on his lap, and hoped for one with Maddie's present carry.

He wanted a lass just like Lily. Wee Lily with her long yellow curls and infectious giggle would bring Alex Grant to his knees.

Or so Brenna hoped.

"Alex, I must leave to check on wee Lily. I will return promptly, I promise." She glanced at her brother before heading to the stairs. His forehead furrowed, but he nodded, indicating that she would have time to retrieve Lily before he acted.

A few moments later, she descended the steps with Lily in her arms, the wee lass bubbling with excitement to be allowed back in the great hall, especially to meet someone new.

"Lady Brenna, who is the really big lad? I think he is bigger than my da, and I thought my da was the biggest ever. What is his name? Is he one of your brothers? What are their names? Do you love both your brothers? Who is the biggest? Can I talk to them?" She waved to the group below stairs.

When Brenna set her down in at the bottom of the stairs, she charged over to her father as fast as her wee legs could carry her. Brenna was so proud to see her nearly running—not quite a full run yet, but she was so much improved.

"Papa! I am so happy to be here. See how fast I am now!"

Quade stood up and caught his daughter before lifting her in the air and planting a big kiss on her cheek. "Lily, use your proper manners." He set her back down. "You must curtsy to Laird Grant and greet him."

The plan had worked. Brenna watched as her big brother stood, clearly charmed by the wee lass. Her heart swelled because her instinct had been correct. A smile had broken out across Alex's face counter to his will.

Lily stood in front of him, attempted a curtsy but stumbled. "Good day to you, Laird Grant." Her father helped her straighten and her mop of curls tipped back as she stared up at Alex.

"My, he is big. Why is he bigger than you, Da?" Her innocent grin seemed to hit Alex right between the eyes.

Quade sat and picked Lily up, lifting her into his lap. "Sit, Laird Grant. My daughter is a bit talkative now that she has more energy. I have never seen her this way. I must confess that I owe her good health to your sister. She is the only healer who had been able to determine Lily's problem."

"And I am all better, Laird Grant. Watch me."

Lily jumped off her father's lap and turned to look at him. "Watch how fast I am. Papa, I will run to the other end of the hall and back."

She took off, only stopping once before she came to the other end. "Papa, see? Am I no' the fastest ever? Watch me, Laird Grant! I am the fastest."

They all followed Lily as her little legs churned back toward them, her arms swirling furiously.

"See, Laird Grant?" She stopped in front of Alex. He stared at her wide-eyed and nodded his head.

"Watch me again. Lady Brenna," she tapped her knee, "watch how fast I am." As soon as she was sure she had everyone's attention, she sailed off in the opposite direction once more.

Brenna and Quade both started to laugh, trying to keep quiet about it.

Alex looked at them both in turn. "Brenna?"

"Aye, Alex?"

Four pairs of eyes followed Lily's journey back and forth in the hall, all of the watchers smiling except for Alex.

"Why does the wean run so slow? The lads are much faster than she is and they are quite a bit younger...And why are you two laughing?"

Brenna and Quade glanced at each other and broke into louder laughter. When she was able, Brenna finally answered her brother. "Because she does no' ken she is slow."

Brodie whispered, "I was going to say the same thing, Alex, but I did no' want to hurt anyone's feelings. Why does the lass think she is fast when she is so slow, Brenna?"

"Because this is the fastest she has ever run." Quade's shoulders shrugged as he offered his explanation. "She is the fastest ever in her terms."

Alex stared at him with wide eyes.

"Aye, she could barely walk before your sister arrived. She had been frail for almost three summers. She rarely made it off her pallet, much less out of her chamber. She was too weak. " Quade's face stretched into an indulgent smile as his daughter ran back toward them. Brenna couldn't take her eyes off of him. He was so taken with his daughter.

"Here I come again, Papa! Look, I am even faster now!" Her arms swung over her head in her excitement.

They all watched her tear back across the hall toward them, and Brenna and Quade laughed hard enough to make Lily giggle. She stopped in front of Alex and stared up into his eyes, her face beaming with pride. "Do you want to see how high I can jump, too, Laird Grant?"

"Aye, aye, Lily!" Brenna said through her laughter. "We are so proud of you! Keep running and jumping."

Alex continued to stare at the three of them. He finally bent down and patted the wee one's back. "Aye, lass. You are the fastest."

Leaning over, Lily gave him a kiss on his cheek. "Thank you, Laird Grant. I hope you do no' take Lady

Brenna away from me. She fixed me. See how much better I am now?"

The big laird was conquered.

Brenna covered Lily with her blanket after their evening meal. She still smiled at the thought of how easily the girl had changed her brother's attitude. She leaned down and gave Lily a kiss, taking in her sweet scent, marveling at how much she had improved in such a short time.

Alex had been unable to argue after seeing Lily. He agreed she could stay another fortnight and then Quade would escort her back to Dulnain Valley with his guards.

"Sweet dreams, wean."

Lily reached up and patted Brenna's cheek with a tenderness she had never experienced before. "I love you, Lady Brenna. Thanks for helping me. I am glad you are staying." She rolled on her side and fell fast asleep, just like that.

The wee lass had just squeezed her heart as surely as if she had reached inside her. Why did she suddenly want to cry? Brenna made it to the door before turning around to stare at Lily. Aggie, who sat in the corner, smiled at her and nodded her head. She opened the door and stepped into the hallway. Quade strolled toward her.

"She is already asleep, Quade. I think it was an exhausting day for her."

Quade strode over to her in the dark stone hallway and cupped her cheeks in his hands. "I have wanted to do this all day since I saw you riding your horse toward us." His lips took hers in a possessive kiss.

Brenna fell back against the wall for support. Quade's arm reached behind her to keep her from falling. He pulled back and gazed into her eyes. "Am I doing something I shouldnae?"

Losing herself in his green eyes and his scent, Brenna wrapped both arms around his neck. "Nay, more." She decided not to hide her desire from him and pulled his head toward hers until their lips met. He chuckled under his breath and tugged her tight to him.

His mouth covered hers, his tongue plunging into the warm cavern of her mouth. She opened for him, allowed him in, and tasted the mint on his tongue. Her hands moved to his forearms, then ran up to his solid biceps, tracing the rippling muscle as he pulled her to him. Her body was helpless to fight him. She savored the rush of warmth spreading through her body until she clung to him. His mouth ravished hers, penetrated deeper until she was almost breathless.

He pulled back, panting. "You make me lose all control. I wanted you so much when I watched you on your horse. I wanted to throw you down in the meadow and make you mine and I did no' care who watched. It took all my control no' to pull you onto my horse and run off into the forest with you, to leave everything behind and just be you and me, alone."

His lips crushed hers again in a searing kiss, teasing her with his tongue, making her forget where she was. She grabbed at him, confused by the sensations coiling in her body, forcing her to rub against him for something, anything, but what? Her body was on fire and she knew not what to do about it. Following his lead, she touched her tongue with his and he growled, lifting her against him and pinning her to the wall. She yearned for more but what?

He balanced her on one arm and ran a trail of kisses down her neck until she wanted to explode. Her skin burned with an unknown desire. His hand cupped her breast and a hum sparked through her core that felt heavenly.

"You are so beautiful, I cannae imagine how glorious you would be with naught on. Your breasts are perfect, and I want to taste you everywhere."

Beautiful? No one had ever called her beautiful before. His lips covered hers again. His fingers brushed her nipple and she jolted, arching toward him as if it was the most natural thing in the world. Her body swirled with a fever she had never known before meeting Quade.

"Aye, you are a passionate one, Brenna. You have no idea how much I want you."

He lowered her feet to the floor and pulled back, his forehead touching hers. Several seconds passed as they both attempted to calm their breathing.

"Aye, this is the wrong place, my love."

Had she heard him correctly? Had he just used the word love?

He kissed her again, though this time it was less hungry. Instead, it was a tender, deep kiss that scorched her heart. His hands were braced against the wall on either side of her head. When the sound of footsteps echoed down the corridor, his hands moved to her and pushed her behind him. She peeked over his shoulder to see her brothers.

"Och, what a surprise. Looks to me like there will be a wedding before we leave, Brodie."

Alex stood at the end of the corridor, his arms crossed, a grim expression on his face.

"Either that or I will kill him with my bare hands right now."

CHAPTER TWELVE

Five of them now stood in Quade's solar. Alex's arms were crossed in his laird stance—as Brenna oft called it—and Brodie looked equally serious next to him. Quade and Micheil stood against the opposite wall with Brenna somewhere in between.

Alex spoke first. "Ramsay, since you had your tongue halfway down my sister's throat, I expect you will be agreeable to marrying her as soon as possible."

"Alex!" Brenna could not believe he had said such a thing. Even if it was true, it didn't need to be said in front of everyone. She blushed a dark shade of red. She had blushed as soon as she had seen the look in her brother's eye after he caught her in such a compromising position, but it had been dark in the passageway, even with the torches. Plus, after the way Quade had been kissing her, it was hard to think clearly.

All right, she shouldn't have been kissing Quade, but she wouldn't change it. She had liked it too much. Her whole body would still be tingling if not for her brother's angry countenance. Brodie wasn't any better, except she could see his smirk trying to break out. She knew he didn't dare smile in front of Alex.

Hellfire, what was she to do now? She supposed she could marry Quade. Her feelings toward the lad had grown, especially when he kissed her like that. Whew! How long had they been standing in the hallway devouring each other anyway?

Either way, her brother was just being a big bully. He had promised their mother she would have a say in who she married, and he had promised her the same thing. Alex would never force her against her will. Would he?

"The marriage will take place in two days time. Find a priest, Ramsay. I need to get home to my wife." Alex's eyes were pinned on Quade, daring him to argue again.

"Alex, stop!" It was time for her to get involved. She would not allow Alex to run her life. "This was clearly a mistake and it willnae happen again. I promise."

"'Tis too late, Brenna. The damage is done. I did no' notice you pushing him away, so you should be agreeable."

"But I am no' agreeable," she shouted.

"You were agreeable enough to let him run his hands all over you."

"I am no' agreeable to marrying him. I willnae force anyone to marry me."

"I do no' care if you are agreeable or no'. This man, chief or no', willnae shame my sister and get away with it. You will marry him, Brenna."

"Nay! You promised our mother that I would have my say in who I married. And I say nay!"

"Sorry, but it appeared to me you were saying aye when you had your arms wrapped around his neck and you were pushing yourself against him. You will marry him!" Alex's bellow shook the rafters.

Quade stepped forward. "I do no' care if she agrees. I willnae marry her."

Alex strode forward until he was but an inch away from Quade's face. "What do you mean you willnae marry her? You had your hands all over her. Or is that how you treat every lass, like a common wench?"

Quade did not back down. "Nay, I do no' treat every lass as such. Brenna kens how much respect I have for her. But one kiss does no' force a marriage. I repeat; I will no' marry her."

"You have an odd way of showing your respect, Ramsay. You will marry her at the end of my claymore, if you wish."

"Nay, I will no' do it, no' for you or for anyone."

Brenna suddenly realized what Quade had said. Her brow furrowed. It was one thing for her to deny a forced marriage, quite another for him to react this way, as if marrying her would be the worst fate in the world.

She marched over and stood in front of Quade, her hands on her hips. "What do you mean you willnae marry me? Was everything you said to me a lie?"

Quade gaped at her. "Nay, Brenna. I have never lied to you."

"Lady Brenna to you, Ramsay," Alex barked.

"Aye, Lady Brenna. But nay. I wasnae lying to you. I meant every word I said. Could we nae discuss this somewhere else, Lady Brenna?"

"Nay, now you are insulting me. What is so wrong with me that you willnae marry me?" Brenna's throat constricted on her, but she couldn't stop. "You were going to kiss and run? I have heard of men like you. I thought you had feelings for me." She swung out in frustration and slapped his arm. "How could you?" Tears threatened to fall, but she would not give him the satisfaction. She should have stayed away from him. Never again would she fall prey to a lad's kisses, no matter how they made her feel.

"Stop, will you no'? You know I cannae marry you. We have discussed this." He reached for her hand, but she pulled away.

"You also said it was a mistake when you kissed me before before and it wouldnae happen again. But now it has happened again. What is that supposed to mean? You do no' want me at all? Or do you?" She dared him to deny her again to her face.

Hellfire, she was in a room full of men, each of them trying to run her life. Quade said he wanted her with his actions, but then he insulted her by denying her brother's direct order. What in blazes did he mean? Was he using her? Had he no feelings? When she was in his arms, he acted as if he couldn't get enough of her, but now he could hardly look at her. This lad was making her absolutely daft.

And Alex? Alex just wanted to order everyone about. Wait until she informed Madeline how miserable he was when he was away from her. There was no reasoning with any of the men in this chamber. She wasn't daft, they were. She glanced at her brothers again and narrowed her eyes when she saw that Brodie had finally broken out into a grin. She promptly walked over and slapped his arm. "And that's for laughing. How dare you laugh at me when they are all trying to tell me what to do! You were there when Mama said I was to have a say when it came to marriage."

She squared off with Alex. "And I am going to have my say. He does no' want me and I do no' want him. This was a big mistake and I can promise you, without a doubt, that it will never happen again. You will never see me kiss Quade Ramsay again."

Brenna marched in a circle with her hands on her hips. She had to get out, that was the only solution. She had to leave while she still had an ounce of her mind left. Finally stopping in the middle of the room, she glared at all of them before whispering, "I will no' marry Quade Ramsay and you cannae force me, Alex. And neither can you, Quade Ramsay. I want you out of my life."

"I want to go home. Now."

Quade panicked. Now what had he done? She was leaving him. She couldn't leave him. He would have to convince her. One way or another, she needed to stay. As she flew out of the solar, he followed her without hesitation.

He would have to tell her the rest of his story, reveal what he had tried so long to hide.

Should he involve the Grant, too? Or just Brenna?

"Ramsay, we arenae done with this conversation," Alex said, trailing behind him. "I do no' care what my sister says. We need to finish this."

Quade couldn't respond. He didn't know what to do. How had his life gotten to this point? He should have given up long ago. There was no way out of this misery. What had he been thinking when he kissed Brenna in the first place? He wasn't entitled to any joy in his life anymore. There had been little to smile about in his life until Lily's arrival. Then he had killed his wife. Shortly after, his Lilykins had gotten sick. Just like before. It would never stop.

But he had to try. Brenna Grant had saved his daughter, and maybe she was his chance out of this cyclone of curses. Wasn't it worth a try?

He turned and reached his hand out to her. He could hear Grant yelling from behind them, but he ignored him. "Will you trust me one more time before you leave, Brenna?"

He stared at her. *Please, Brenna. I need you. You have no idea how much I need you, but do no' leave me now. Please come with me one more time.*

"Please, Brenna. I am asking you to trust me one last time." He gazed into her beautiful eyes and prayed she would listen. He waited, his hand outstretched.

She nodded her head slowly.

"Then come with me, please." Quade's eyes bored into hers.

"Why? What more is there to say? You have said it all." Brenna took a step back, clearly wary of him now. It broke his heart to see the change in her.

"Please, Brenna. I need to show you something. I

need you to understand why I have been acting so strangely. I have held the truth back, but I cannae any longer."

⁂

Brenna stared into his green eyes and was lost again. Totally powerless against him, she felt her head nod. He held out his hand and she reached for his warmth.

"Hold. Do not move, Ramsay." Alex's powerful voice broke through her haze. "You dare to consider bringing my sister somewhere without an escort after all your trespasses? That willnae happen."

Alex strode over to stand in front of them. Of course, her brother would interfere.

"Alex, please."

"Where are you taking her?" Alex glared at Quade, ignoring her completely.

"I need to take her to a cottage just outside the village."

"Again, I do no' think so, Ramsay. Not without me or my brother."

Feet braced, hand on his claymore, this was her brother in all his glory. The laird who could send Highlanders running in the opposite direction with a single look stood in front of her. The last thing she wanted to see was a power struggle between Quade and her brother.

"Alex! Stop. Would you listen to me?" Brenna grabbed the arm that was braced on his sword.

"Brenna, you have naught to say in this. You willnae go anywhere with him without an escort. He has made his lack of intentions clear." Alex spoke forcefully, his eyes never leaving Quade's.

Quade didn't back down. "Then you are welcome to follow us, Grant." Holding her hand in his, he turned toward the door without waiting for her brother's answer.

Clearly ruled by powerful emotions, Quade's steps were fast and furious as he continued through the bailey and out toward the gate. Brenna glanced over her shoulder to see that Alex was behind them. He would never stop acting as her protector. How could she get him to trust her? And the man in front of her? When would she ever understand Quade? She was allowing him to drag her off to some unknown location, with no idea of where or why. Yet she trusted him.

Soon both men were in front of her, and she was racing to keep up with their long strides. Brodie, who must have followed Alex out of the keep, strode behind her. They had to be a strange sight together. Everyone in their path cleared out of their way, standing back in an attempt to see their destination.

It wasn't until they reached the end of the village that Quade's steps finally slowed.

Standing outside a small cottage hidden behind the main path, he turned to speak to her. "I have wanted to bring you here before, but I had my reasons for waiting. I just could not risk everything at once. I wanted to see your methods as a healer before I fully confided in you. I bring you here now because of my absolute trust in you and your abilities. I want you to know that. Do as you see fit. You have my complete faith."

He turned to Alex. "Laird Grant, you may not wish to step inside. There could be bad air inside the cottage. I also must caution all of you that none of my clan except for my family is aware of what goes on inside this cottage. I am asking you to keep my confidence."

Brenna couldn't believe her ears. More sickness? And no one else knew? Who would she find inside?

Alex didn't hesitate. "Agreed. But I will follow my sister in and stand beside the door. Brodie will wait outside. She goes nowhere with you alone, Ramsay."

"As you wish. This is why I cannae marry your

sister, Grant. My whole family is cursed and I would never want to do anything that could hurt her."

His statement hit her like a fist to her gut. What was he talking about? Lady Ramsay had alluded to some other problem, but she had no idea what she was about to see.

"Brenna, please agree to stay a fortnight, I beg of you." He turned and pushed against the door.

Brenna held her breath, unsure of what she would find inside. He held the door for her to enter before him. As soon as she did, the odor assaulted the hairs of her nose. It was vile, disgusting, and foul—not an odor she would ever forget. But it *was* something she had already encountered once in her life.

When she had first arrived at the keep, a similar stench had hung in the air in Lily's room. But who was the patient in this cottage?

Quade stopped at the end of the pallet and held his arm out as an introduction.

"My son, Lady Brenna. Meet Torrian."

CHAPTER THIRTEEN

His son? He had a son with the same disease?

Brenna sank into healer mode immediately and approached the bed from the side.

Kneeling down on the side of the pallet, she searched the lad for clues. His eyes were open, but his breathing was shallow. When he glanced up at her, he lacked the ability to lift his head from the soft pillow. His bed consisted of mounds of materials, and was probably the thickest she had ever seen.

She reached for his head, but stopped when Quade spoke.

"Do no' touch him, Brenna. Sometimes, even touch pains him." He sat on the other side of the pallet, the pain in his face clearly visible. "How do you fare today, my son?"

Brenna's heart broke in two. How could Quade have dealt with so much anguish on his own? Tears threatened to spill down her cheeks, but she fought them, intent to do what must be done as a healer.

"Da? 'Tis you?" A brief smile touched the boy's thin lips. His voice was weak and raspy, barely discernible in the quiet of the cottage.

"How many summers, Quade? And how long has he been like this?" She glanced up at him, noticing how his eyes filled with love as he stared at his first born.

"He is seven summers, and he has been ill ever since his second summer. It broke his mother's heart when he became sick. Does your head hurt today, lad?"

"Aye, a bit. Not too bad, Papa. Who is with you?"

"Torrian, this is Lady Brenna. She is a healer, and I've brought her here to see if she can help you."

"Have you seen Lily yet, Lady Brenna?"

"Aye, I have met your beautiful sister, Torrian." Brenna watched him closely as they talked. She noticed the paleness of his skin, the wasting in his muscles. The disease had ravaged his body far more than it had Lily's. She pulled the blanket down a touch so she could see more of him. Thin, spindly arms and legs poked out of soft night clothes.

"May I look at your skin, Torrian?"

When she reached for his arm, Quade grabbed her hand. "Nay, Brenna. We do no' ken what he has. He has always had a terrible rash. 'Tis verra painful for him. Take care to avoid touching his blisters."

Brenna removed Quade's hand from her own, and she wrapped both her hands around his. "I am no' afraid of your son. 'Tis all right if I touch him. I promise no' to hurt him." She searched over Quade's shoulder for her brother. "Alex, the lad is fine. 'Tis no' something in the air. You may come closer if you wish."

Quade stood, his face etched with concern. "Lass, how can you ken that for sure? Every healer who has seen him has cautioned against allowing others to come inside the room and breathe the same air."

"I believe this is the same illness Lily has. It isnae in the air. I can help your son, too, by adjusting what he eats."

"Brenna, every other healer who has been here has said that what ails Torrian is nae the same as what ails Lily. Are you certain?"

"Nay, not certain. But I believe there are enough similarities between the two that it is the same disease. Torrian has had it longer, aye? His symptoms are worse." She grabbed his hand. "I believe I can help him. You need to trust me."

Alex moved over to the bed. "Greetings, laddie. 'Tis my pleasure to make your acquaintance."

"Da, who is this big lad? You have brought two people to see me? How exciting." His voice crinkled with what little exuberance he could muster.

"This is Laird Grant, Torrian. You must address him proper."

"Aye, Laird Grant. I thank you for visiting me. You must be a warrior because you are so big, even bigger than my papa." Torrian's head turned to the side so he could take in the full sight of his visitors.

While he talked with his father and her brother, Brenna did a quick examination of the wee lad. At seven summers, he had the size of someone who was just four or five summers. She lifted the sleeve of his top and noticed the blisters and rash on his elbows and how he winced when she moved the fabric. He never cried out, which saddened her. Opening the ties on his shirt, she noticed the same rash across his belly and, rolling him a bit, also on his back.

"The bumps are in my hair and on my bum, too, Lady Brenna."

How curious. The lad knew why she searched. He knew his symptoms better than anyone, probably. Her gaze took in the sallow color of his cheeks and the dull whites of his eyes, though she could swear they almost glittered as he conversed with Alex and his papa. She also noticed how the rash on his elbows had been scratched and how he wriggled in bed in an attempt to relieve the itching on his backside.

What struck her most was how the young lad tolerated his discomfort. While anyone else would be writhing in pain from the blisters that were so evident across his skin, he bore the burden as if it didn't exist. Occasionally, there was a slight twitch in his countenance that told Brenna how much he suffered, but that was it. She had seen this in one of her mother's patients. After dealing with pain for so long, she had no longer reacted to it, accepting it instead with great dignity. However, that woman had been a lass of many years. How could one so young handle pain with such grace?

Noticing the presence of his caretaker in the corner of the room, Brenna walked over to introduce herself to the young lass, Margaret. She asked a few questions before returning to the boy's pallet. The lad's lids were already closing, even thought they had been there for a short time. She found it sad that one so young would be so quickly fatigued.

She put her hand on Quade's shoulder. "Mayhap we should let Torrian rest."

"I am a wee bit tired, Lady Brenna. Will you come visit me again?"

She placed a kiss on Torrian's cheek. "How would it be if I returned on the morrow? Mayhap I could help bathe you. I have some herbs I could add to your water to help soothe the blisters and your itching. And we can start talking about finding a way to help you heal."

"Do you think you can help me, Lady Brenna? Will you promise no' to bleed me? It hurts too much and I do no' like it." His eyes misted, but they retained their focus on her.

"I think I can, Torrian. I do no' believe in bleeding for this illness. I promise I will give it my best. You rest up. I will probably tire you over the next few days."

The three of them left, but Brenna couldn't help but stop and stare at the poor lad again before walking out of the cottage.

Quade fetched Micheil and the five settled in Quade's solar: Quade, Brenna, Alex, Brodie, and Micheil. A few moments passed before anyone spoke.

Quade turned to Brenna. "Lady Brenna, my

apologies for my rudeness before. I am asking you to forget that for now and ask—nay, beg—you to stay a fortnight to help my son."

Brenna's eyes misted as she stared back at him. "Why have you no' told me this before? Why have you kept Torrian hidden all these years? I do no' understand."

Alex interrupted. "'Tis the laird's son, Brenna," he said gently. "Many would try to harm him if they kenned he was ill. 'Twould be easy to take him out."

Brenna gasped at her brother's declaration.

"I am sure you ken how some people feel about sickness they do no' understand," Quade said. "They fear for their own children. I had many healers here to see him when the sickness first started, and they only had one consensus. It was the type that spread through the air. The healers did no' want anyone near him. Lilias and I loved him too much to stay away from him. But others were afraid. We were fortunate to have Margaret and her husband Ennis to stay with him. They had a young lad at the time so Torrian had a playmate.

"Most healers did no' think my son would live long. They bled him often, but to no avail. Some thought to let him die, but Lilias wouldnae allow it. The clan was upset after Margaret's son died, thinking Torrian was to blame, so we spread word that our lad died of the same red throat a few days later. It was easier for my clan to accept. No one but my close family kens he still lives. We could not risk his life. Aye, he is weak, but Lilias and I couldnae have loved him more. We had to protect him."

Brenna rubbed her hands together in thought. What could she do? She had no choice. She knew she could not walk away from this bairn. "Quade, I would like to speak to my brothers alone for a bit."

Quade nodded and stood from his desk. "As you wish. I would like to say to you and your brothers that my reasons for no' marrying you are no' because I do no' care. In your heart, Brenna, I believe you ken this to be true, but some say I am cursed. First my son, then my wife, and then Lily became ill. 'Tis in your best interest to stay away from me." He directed his next comment to Brenna alone. "Lass, I refuse to marry you because I am trying to protect you from my curse."

After Quade left, Brenna watched Alex to gauge his demeanor. "Alex, you ken I have to stay."

"Aye, I would expect nothing less of you, lass. Healing is in your soul, much like it was for our mother. I cannae comprehend it, but I think both our parents would prefer if I support you in your healing work." Alex paused before continuing. "I ken you do no' wish this, but in view of what has happened, including in the corridor before we met Torrian, I still believe you and Quade should marry."

"Why did you try to force us to marry, Alex? Help me understand. You ken we agreed that I would have a say in such an important matter." Brenna stood and started to pace. "Aye, you are correct, there is something between us, but a forced wedding? Why would you do such a thing to me?"

Brodie spoke up. "Aye, Alex. I agree with her. I was surprised by your reaction." He turned to his sister. "I thought Alex would change his mind after he calmed down. You ken how his temper is."

They both turned to their laird with expectant gazes.

Alex did not speak for a few minutes. "Part of it was my temper. You ken how it looked to Brodie and I, do you no'?" Alex asked his sister. He continued without waiting for her answer. "I tried to force the match because I thought it would be the right step for you. Ramsay is a good man and he needs a mother for his wee ones. You are a perfect match for him."

Brenna crossed her arms before stopping in front of

him. "You ken 'tis no' a good reason for a marriage. We all hope for a love match like Mama and Papa and like you and Maddie."

"But I believe 'tis a love match. By the way you two had your arms wrapped around each other, it did no' appear you were against it. And Brodie can vouch for how the lad couldnae take his eyes off you from the moment we arrived. Perhaps your feelings for each other are stronger than you realize."

"Aye, he's right, Brenna. When Ramsay saw that you were on your way out across the field on your horse, he turned and awaited your arrival. He had the look of a love struck lad, and he was powerless to tear his gaze from you."

"You are jesting, Brodie. He believes that anything that's happened between us is a mistake." Brenna shook her head before sitting again. "He confuses me."

"He loves you. He either doesnae realize it yet or he's fighting it. But now you understand why, lass? He intends to protect you. That statement speaks volumes to his feelings for you."

"Aye, at last I am starting to make some sense from the man's mind. How terrible to have lived with so many tragedies in such a short time."

"I agree, "Alex said. "This is against my better judgment, but I will give you a fortnight to see if you can help the lad. After, Ramsay is to return you to our clan with a good amount of his guardsmen as escorts. We cannae risk losing you, lass. You are invaluable to our clan and our family. Jennie and my wife are verra worried about you, and they will be pleased to hear tidings of your safety. Are you agreeable to this?"

"Aye, I should ken within a fortnight if my plan will help the lad at all. He has had this ailment for a long time. I hope we arenae too late."

"Shall I leave Brodie or a guard to protect your honor?"

"Nay, Alex!"

Alex smiled before he stood. "Use your good judgment, lass. Then come home to us. You know Maddie wants you at her birthing. She will rest better when you are home, even though her time is no' near yet."

Brenna embraced both her brothers. "Please tell Quade I will remain. Right now, I would like to clean up and make a plan for the lad. Then I will check on Lily."

"You have the power to heal the lad, which is why I allow you to stay. Mama and Grandpapa both believed that your healing skills were more powerful than theirs. Believe in yourself." Alex smiled, kissed her cheek, and left, Brodie following behind.

Brenna didn't know what to make of what her brother had said.

But she hoped he was right, for Torrian's sake.

CHAPTER FOURTEEN

Alex left with Brodie and his guards early the next morning, anxious to return to his pregnant wife. It was difficult for Brenna to bid farewell to her brothers, but she couldn't do anything else. She had to help Torrian. If she couldn't heal him completely, perhaps she could find a way to control his symptoms so he did not have so much pain.

Brenna headed down the hill with her healer's satchel and extra towels. She stopped to chat with a few villagers on the way but was careful not to discuss her destination. Quade had sent word ahead for Torrian's helper to fill the tub for him.

Still shocked by the revelation that Quade had a son, she was even more surprised that the child had been kept hidden all these years. Having discussed the situation with Quade's mother at breakfast, all she'd learned was that the family felt it was risky to let anyone know the chieftain's son was alive and ill. That was why he was kept in a separate building, along with the possibility that his illness was in the air.

Brenna had tried to reason with Quade that the boy's condition was clearly not catching since he had been with the child many times without developing it, but he did not seem convinced. Too many other healers had persuaded him otherwise.

When she entered the cottage, Margaret greeted her along with her husband, Ennis, who had just filled the tub with steaming water from the hearth. Brenna had asked Quade for some time alone with Torrian, and so Margaret and Ennis left the cottage once the tub was full.

Brenna glanced around at the homey cottage. It didn't look like a cottage for a laird's son on the outside, but inside, she could see nothing was spared for Quade's son. A wooden box held a few toys, but they didn't appear to be used much. Margaret had everything she needed to cook and care for Torrian, including a beautiful tub. A couple of illustrated books sat near the bed. Soft blankets and pillows were everywhere along with tapestries of horses and dogs.

Before assisting Torrian into the warm water, she added lavender oil and oatmeal to help with the itching. She had also brought special gloves for him to wear while he slept to prevent scratching.

After he settled in the tub, the lad anxiously chattered away.

"Lady Brenna, I am so glad you came back today. Do you think you can help me?"

"I think so. I believe you have some variation of the sickness your sister has."

"How is my sister? I havenae seen her in a long time." He peered anxiously at her, anxious for news from outside his small prison.

"She is doing much better."

"How? Have you healed her? What did you do to help her?" The look of hope on his face tore at her heart.

"Well, she is eating only certain foods, Torrian. I think some of the foods you eat might be making you sick." She carefully washed his hair as she talked, meticulously allowing the lavender oil to settle on the blisters on his scalp.

"But how can that be? Lily has never had the blisters or the rash like I have. It must be different."

"Sometimes the same illness will show different

signs in different people. I think 'tis the case with you and your sister. There are problems you and Lily share that are very much the same. Later I will talk to you about what you eat. Since you are older than Lily, you can take a larger role in your own care. I want you to know which foods are safe so you can be sure you are eating the right things."

"May I see Lily?"

"When was the last time you saw her?" Brenna drenched her cloth again and soaked the lad's torso in the warm water.

"I do no' remember. She wasnae talking much yet. Papa was afraid I would make her sicker."

Brenna blinked back tears at the thought of this poor lad's life. She needed to be strong, though, and couldn't let him see her sadness. Thinking of sweet Lily, she smiled. "How would you like to see your sister in the next couple of days? I will bring her here if you like."

"Would you? May I play with her?"

The wistfulness in Torrian's weak voice wrenched her gut. "Aye, I will bring her to see you. How long has it been since you have seen the great hall?"

"I have never seen the great hall, Lady Brenna. I have been here since I can remember. I have never stepped outside. My da willnae allow it. Even when Todd was alive, we had to play inside."

Brenna had to force her hands to continue their healing ministrations. How could this have happened? How could Quade not see what he had done to his son? No friends or family time at all? How was it possible that the lad was so good-natured and intelligent with such an upbringing?

"Lady Brenna, he does no' do it to make me feel bad. He has to keep me here. That is what he always tells me. Please do no' be angry with Papa. He loves me, I ken it. He even taught me how to read." He hung onto the sides of the tub as she washed.

Brenna wasn't sure if she was doing the right thing, but she plunged ahead. "Why, Torrian? Why does your papa think you have to stay here? Why does he no' tell anyone else you are here so they can visit?" Somehow, she thought there must be another reason behind the boy's isolation.

"Papa says I have to stay here or I could die." His wee head stared down at the glassy surface of water.

"Why, laddie?"

"Because he says that if people saw my rash, they would think I had evil spirits in me and would put me out in the forest and leave me to die."

Brenna dropped the cloth in the water.

"Lady Brenna?"

She collected herself enough to pick the cloth up again before speaking. "Aye?"

"You willnae do it, will you?"

"What, lad?"

"You willnae put me in the forest and leave me to die, will you?"

Brenna couldn't help herself. She grabbed a linen towel, wrapped it around the lad and picked him up in her warm embrace. Looking him directly in the eye, she said, "Nay, Torrian, I willnae."

"Papa doesnae allow any hugging either," Torrian warned. She noticed a slight cringe in the lad.

"Aye, I do. Hugging willnae hurt you, aye? Am I hurting you, lad? Am I too rough on your blisters?" She sat in a chair and settled him on her lap wrapped in the soft towel.

"Nay, it does still hurt a wee bit, but I do no' mind. I would like to be hugged sometimes even though my da does no' allow it. He is too afraid someone will hurt me. I ken it." He whispered as if his father was near.

After a few minutes, she dressed him in a soft gown and sat back down with him still on her lap. He took up hardly any space and was light as a feather. This lad needed to gain some weight.

"May I ask you a question, Lady Brenna?"

"Of course, Torrian. You may ask me anything." She wrapped her arms around and helped him settle against her chest. "Are you comfortable, like this?"

"Aye, I like sitting on your lap."

Of course, he would love any human contact, no matter how much pain it caused him. His blisters did seem better, but it would be awhile before they were completely healed. "Is the itching better?"

"Aye, the bath helped it. It is nae so bad as before." His face beamed.

Poor lad. Silence filled the air for a few moments. She decided he would ask his question when he was ready.

"Papa was really angry with me a short time ago."

"Aye, that happens sometimes. It does no' mean he does no' love you. He wasnae angry with you yesterday." Brenna rubbed his legs as they talked. It was the only place he didn't have a rash.

"I asked him if he would please take me to the forest and let me die."

Brenna steeled herself not to react. She remained silent, hoping it would encourage him to continue. He needed to share this with her.

"You see, my rash hurts me really bad some days. Sometimes, I just want to cry all day, but I ken it upsets my da if I do. He wants me to be strong so I can be laird some day, and he gets upset and leaves when I cry. Not because he is mad but becauses he feels bad. He says he is sad when he can't help me feel better. So I try no' to, but 'tis verra hard no' to when it hurts really bad. I tried to tell him that 'twould be easier for me if I was in heaven, but he wouldnae let me finish. Do you believe in heaven, Lady Brenna?"

"Aye, I do. I am glad you do, too."

"Aye, I thought if I was in heaven and I did no' have to hurt or itch all the time, I might like that better. Sometimes, I scratch so much I sob. But never in front of Papa. Margaret wants to hold me when I cry so hard, but then it hurts to sit on her lap." He paused to turn and smile at her. "The bath helped my blisters, though, and it does no' pain me to sit on your lap."

Brenna kissed the top of his head and settled him back against her.

"I just tried to tell Papa I would rather be in heaven and no' itch all the time than to be here like this. My mama died when Lily was a wee bairn, so she would be in heaven to greet me. I told Papa he could stay with Lily and I could go with Mama, but he was verra upset. He did no' understand. Do you? Do you understand why I would rather be in heaven?"

"Aye, lad. I understand. Do you still wish to be in heaven?"

"Nay, I do no' anymore because I saw Mama in my dream one night. She told me I couldnae leave Papa yet."

"You saw her in your dream?" Brenna tried to encourage Torrian to finish his story. She thought he would feel better if he shared it with her.

"Aye. 'Twas after Papa was so mad at me. After he told me I couldnae die, he left and did no' come back for three days. I was afraid he would never come again. That's why Mama came to see me in my dream, I think. Because Da would no' come and I was so afraid."

Brenna marveled at the strength of the young lad in her arms. How was it right for a young lad and lassie to go through all that he and Lily had suffered? And poor Quade. She was beginning to see that the man she had fallen in love with had a reason to be a tortured soul.

In love? Had she really just thought that?

Aye, seeing Quade with his ill son had caused her to lose her heart to him completely.

CHAPTER FIFTEEN

"Tell me more about your dream, Torrian." Brenna wrapped the blanket around him a bit tighter as she spoke.

"Aye, I fell asleep, but then I woke up right away. I only kenned I was dreaming because I was *different.*"

"How were you different?" Brenna didn't know how much more heartbreak she could handle, but listening was the best thing she could do for Torrian right now.

"I did no' hurt anymore. I did no' itch and there was nae pain. I looked at my arms and the rash was all gone. I did no' ken where it went. I was looking at my belly when I heard Mama's voice."

"What did she say?"

Torrian tipped his head to stare into her eyes. "Do you believe me, Lady Brenna? Cause Papa thought I made it up when I tried to tell him. He wouldnae even let me finish."

"Go ahead, laddie. I believe you. Tell me what your mama said." The important thing was that Torrian believed it, so she wanted him to finish.

"There was this long tunnel with a white light at the end of it." He rested back against her chest before continuing. "I kept looking down there, but I did no' see anything. Then I heard Mama's voice. It sounded like she was at the end of the tunnel. I kept staring and then I saw her walking down the tunnel toward me. Lady Brenna, my mama was so beautiful, she looked just like an angel. She hugged me when she reached me. And I told her I did no' hurt anymore. She said she kenned it. She told me she couldnae bear to see me in pain anymore, so she had brought me home just for a few moments to help me understand."

The wee lad turned to look at her, as if to make sure she was taking him seriously. Brenna nodded. "Go on, lad."

He settled back against her. "She told me I would never hurt when I was in heaven. But she said it was too soon for me to stay there because I had some important things to do yet. Then she asked me no' to say that I wished to die to Papa anymore. But I told her I wanted to. I told her that it was true, that I did want to die. Does that make me a bad person? It was so nice there, I really wanted to stay. I could walk by myself. I wasnae scart and I did no' itch or anything, and I miss my mama. She said too many bad things had happened to Papa and he couldnae handle losing me yet. But I told her I wanted to stay with her, and that I did no' want to come back where I hurt all the time."

She could feel the hot tears on her lashes and was thankful he had his back to her.

Torrian continued. "I told her how tired the itching makes me, how it keeps me from sleeping or playing. That I used to play with Margaret's son, but after he died, I did no' have anyone to keep me company. Papa wouldnae let me play with Lily. He's always been afraid I will make her sicker and Lily wouldnae be able to keep the secret. And then every time I eat, I throw up and have an achy stomach and I do no' want to anymore. Still, she said I couldnae stay. And I said then I will stop eating when I get back to my bed, or I will go out and show someone my rash so they will take me to the forest so I can die."

The tears flowed freely down Brenna's cheeks now.

"What's a forest, Lady Brenna? I do no' know what

it is."

She cleared her throat before speaking. "A forest is a group of trees."

"'Tis really dark? Could I walk to one? Is there one near here?"

"Nay, you would have to walk a bit, Torrian. I do no' think you could walk that far."

"Aye, Mama said I couldnae go to the forest to die. Then I cried. But she promised me something before she sent me back."

"What did she promise you?"

"I did no' believe her then." He sat up in her lap and turned to look her straight in the eye. "But now I think I do."

"Why is that?"

"Because she promised to send me someone who could fix me. She said she kenned someone who could fix both Lily and me so we wouldnae be sick all the time. I thought she would send a priest."

He continued to stare, his wan face glowing with hope.

"'Tis you, Lady Brenna? Did Mama send you to fix us?"

Brenna didn't know what to say. How did one answer such a question? "Lad, I do no' ken your mama. I have never met her. But I can promise you that I will try to help you."

"And will you fix Papa, too?" His gaze never faltered.

"I do no' know what is wrong with your papa. I do no' know if I can fix him."

The lad stared at his hands in thought. "Then if you cannae heal him, will you tell him something for me?"

"All right, but why do you no' tell him, Torrian? He might like to hear it from you."

"You see, Mama promised to send someone to fix us, but then I had to make a promise to her, also."

Quade walked into the doorway as the boy spoke.

He came to a complete stop when he saw Torrian in her lap and stood transfixed as he listened to his son. Since the boy had his back to the door, he was totally unaware of his father's presence.

"And what did you promise her?" Brenna asked.

"I promised I would tell Papa that he did no' kill Mama. Mama said Papa thinks he killed her, but he did no'. She said to tell him that she was already dying and she kenned it."

"You havenae told him that yet, lad?"

"Nay, I am afraid. Papa doesnae believe I saw Mama in my dream, and he always gets angry when I talk about it. But I promised her. Will you? Will you tell him that Mama said she wants him to ken that he did no' kill her?"

Brenna glanced over Torrian's shoulder at Quade's retreating body.

"Aye, I will tell him, lad."

Brenna covered Torrian with a soft blanket after settling him back on his pallet. Now she understood the thick layers of soft padding under him. The poor lad was exhausted from all his confessions, and he fell asleep instantly.

Margaret had returned to the cottage with Ennis, and Brenna hoped to get some information from her. They sat at the beautiful oak table, staring at Brenna expectantly. Ennis brought more wood in for the large hearth not far from Torrian's bed.

"Margaret, you have been with Torrian a long time?" she asked, sitting at the table across from the other woman.

"Aye, my lady. I have been with him ever since he started throwing up and couldnae eat anything. Quade asked me to take care of him. He was afraid someone would hear and try to attack him because he was the chieftain's son. Since I had a son about Torrian's age, he hoped the two would be friends."

"Were you no' afraid for your son?"

"Och, nay, my lady. Ennis and I were honored to take care of the chieftain's son. Then, when he kept getting sicker and developed the rash, Quade told everyone but his family that Torrian had passed on. I have kept him here for all that time. I love him like he is my own."

"I can see that you do, Margaret. I believe Torrian and Quade are blessed to have you in their lives. But what about your son? Did he have the same sickness?"

"Nay. Torrian and Todd loved to play together. Then he caught the red throat and died when he was five summers. I tried so to save him, but I couldnae." She paused to regain her composure before continuing. "Torrian never caught the red throat so he survived. I am honored to care for him still." A slight smile tipped up her face, but the pain in her eyes was evident.

Brenna reached across the table and wrapped her hands around Margaret's. "I am so sorry for your loss, Margaret. Losing a son must be very difficult." The woman nodded her head without speaking. Brenna couldn't imagine Maddie or Alex losing either one of their laddies. Her brother would be totally distraught. She marveled at the strength of the young woman in front of her.

"Margaret, I would like to ask you another question, if I may." Brenna patiently awaited her response.

"Aye, I will help in any way I can, my lady."

"How did Quade's wife die? Was it from birthing Lily?"

"Nay, she had childbed fever. It was quite a while after Lily was born. But the midwife told me Lilias never lost the part attached to the cord. The part that comes after the baby never came out of her. Gunna, the midwife, searched for it, but couldnae get it free. She said sometimes it willnae let go."

"Thank you. You have been very helpful."

So that explained it. Lilias had never expelled the full afterbirth. It must have stayed inside her and rotted. This probably caused her to have childbed fever, as her mother had called it. Her mother had explained that some women would develop a fever after childbirth, sometimes fatal. She had thought there were different causes, and this must be one of them.

Brenna gathered her things and straightened her skirts.

"My lady? May I ask you something before you leave?" Margaret wrung her hands in her skirts.

"Of course. Anything."

"Do you think you will be able to help wee Torrian? I feel so bad for all his itching and pain. Sometimes, I cry with him. I do hope you can help him."

"I think I will be able to improve his symptoms, but I do no' ken if it will be possible to completely heal him. We shall see. I would like Torrian to eat only broth again today. No bread, no milk, just plain broth. Hopefully, he will be able to follow the same plan as Lily. Can you do that, Margaret?"

"Aye, only broth. He wasnae hungry. It was enough for him last eve." Margaret escorted her to the door. "Thank you, my lady. Until the morrow."

Brenna's eyes searched the area around the cottage when she stepped out. She had noticed Quade leave, but she had no idea where he could be. She headed to the keep because she had something very important to do.

She needed to find Quade and explain to him why she knew he hadn't killed his wife.

CHAPTER SIXTEEN

She was almost up the last hill to the keep when she saw Quade fly over the small valley to the north at a pace that could only mean he was in a fury.

Screaming his name, she tore to the stables. He did not stop or show any recognition of anything but his own raging thoughts. As she rounded the corner of the stable, she collided with the stable boy, Ian.

"Och, Ian, forgive me!" she paused for a breath. "I need my horse saddled."

A small grin spread across the lad's face. "Aye, my lady. He is saddled. I left him inside the building."

Brenna stared at him, puzzled. "Lad, how could you ken I wanted my horse?"

His face turned beet red under his carrot-colored hair. He stared at his feet and whispered, "My lady, where my laird goes, you usually follow." He turned to retrieve her horse.

Brenna cocked her head as she thought about his statement. Was she that obvious to all? Ian returned and brought her horse near the mounting block. She waved her hand and muttered, "Och, I do no' have time for that thought." She mounted and flew toward the gate.

Once outside the gate, she allowed her horse to choose his gait and enjoyed the wind in her hair, yet she couldn't stop worrying about this lad she loved. How had it come to this? The brute's brother had kidnapped her, and they both had kept her a virtual prisoner. Quade had kissed her thoughtless, denied his feelings for her yet, in a mere fortnight, she could not imagine her life without him.

She knew how he had suffered, more than anyone should. She couldn't imagine what it must have been like for such a strong man to watch both his bairns fall prey to such a debilitating illness. He had been powerless to do anything for the ones he loved most. Wouldn't anyone in his shoes have resorted to desperate measures?

Now she understood Lady Ramsay's strange comments about his wife. For some reason, Quade blamed himself for her death. But if Lilias had died of childbed fever, why did he think he had caused it? Childbed fever was clearly a result of giving birth. What could have transpired to make him believe her death was his fault? And what was his reaction to Torrian's declaration that his mama had said Quade had not killed her? He had turned and fled after he heard that.

Determined to help him get his life back and his bairns healthy again, she vowed not to stop until he understood he was not the cause of any of his family's problems. Then she could at least go home with a clear conscience. Somehow, she would deal with the fact that he didn't love her enough to risk another relationship. After all that had transpired, it really wasn't that difficult to comprehend why he was not interested in marrying again and, possibly, having more bairns.

When she finally gained on him enough to catch sight of him, she noticed he had dismounted near a cliff and was standing near the edge.

He couldn't be thinking of throwing himself over?

"Quade!" She had to get to him before he did anything reckless. "Quade, do no' do it!"

Frantic to get his attention, she galloped in his

direction as fast as her horse would take her. When she was almost there, she heard him bellow a raging growl over the landscape.

"Quade!"

His head jerked around as if he had only just realized he wasn't alone.

"What? Brenna?" He threw his hands up in the air. "Leave me be, please! Can you no' see I prefer solitude? Take yourself back to the keep."

"Nay, I will not. I am not leaving you on the edge of that cliff." She jumped off her horse and ran toward him. "Do no' do it, please." He had turned back to stare out over the cliff, his back to her, his head tilted up toward the sun.

"Do what, Brenna? What is it you think I am about?"

"Jump, promise me you willnae jump. It wasnae your fault. Naught is your fault." When she reached his side, she was panting from the exertion, her arms holding her quaking sides.

Quade turned and shook his head. "Jump? I am no' going to jump."

"The cliff, you are standing in front of a cliff."

Quade's brow quirked. "Nay, lass, I come here to clear my mind sometimes. I admit I like to hear my voice bounce off the stone. 'Tis beautiful, is it no'?"

Brenna cleared her throat, unsure how to apologize for her folly. "Umm, aye, forgive me for intruding." She turned to walk away.

"Wait, please. Why are you here, Lady Brenna? Last I heard, you did no' want anything to do with me. You wanted to get away from me as fast as possible."

"I came to talk to you about your wife."

Immediately, his barriers went up. His hands fisted at his hips. "I would rather no' discuss my wife with you. Why is my marriage any concern of yours?"

"Not your marriage. Her death. I wish to speak with you about her death."

"Lass, there is nothing to say. 'Twas my doing, and I prefer no' to share it with anyone else. It is verra private to me." He turned to stare over the landscape again. "Go home, Lady Brenna. Do what you can for my son and go home. 'Tis where you belong. No' here with a lad with a curse on his kin."

Brenna stared at Quade's profile. She wished she knew how to help him. This was something she was unprepared to handle. She knew how to fix people physically, but she had little experience in dealing with emotions. She thought of her brother, Alex, and his wife and twin sons. How would he handle losing Madeline and having both lads so ill they spent most of their time in bed? She pictured Alex swinging his sons in a circle, the bairns giggling as they clung to his arm, pealing with laughter as their mama held her breath. That was how life should be for a young father, not the way Quade's life had unfolded.

She moved back to her horse, obliging his request for solitude. Mayhap he was right, and she had infringed too much upon his life. Her steps slowed as she thought of the original mission that caused her to go to the stables. As usual, the man had distracted her from her purpose. She stopped and strode back to stand directly in front of him.

"I am sorry, Quade, but I willnae leave until I have had my say."

"Your say about what, lass? There is naught to say." His gaze caught hers and her heart broke at the pain that was clearly visible in his eyes.

Glancing at the ground before squaring her shoulders, she cleared her throat and began. "Chief Ramsay, I understand this is private for you, but I would like to explain to you why your wife's death wasnae your fault." She paused to gather her thoughts and then plunged on. "From my understanding of your wife's condition, she died from childbed fever. 'Tis nae uncommon for a lass to develop a fever after giving birth. I have seen it happen before. Some are able to fight it and some cannae. Either way, 'tis no' your fault your wife was unable to recover from giving birth. There were certain circumstances that probably caused her death."

Quade's hand went up to stop her. "Lass, I ken about childbed fever. That is no' what killed my wife. She was recovering. I killed her."

Brenna's eyes narrowed as she thought about how difficult it would be to convince him of the truth. This man was a stubborn one. She started again. "I did no' wish to bring up this sensitive subject, but I feel I must. After a woman gives birth, there is another part that needs to be born. I was told that, in your wife's case, that never happened..."

"Stop, Brenna," Quade said, taking her shoulders in his hands. "I ken all I need to ken about birthing bairns. I ken of her fever. 'Twas over, Lilias was recovering."

"She couldnae have recovered..."

"Aye, I am telling you she had recovered."

"Quade, 'tis no' possible to recover..."

"I killed her, Brenna, accept it." His shout echoed off the stone walls of the surrounding area. "I killed my own wife, the mother of my children."

"Nay, there is nae way..."

"She died in my arms." He bellowed louder with each word and stretched his arms toward the sky as he shouted.

Brenna froze. She had died in his arms? How tragic! But still...

"We hadnae stayed in the same bed since Lily's birth. Lilias asked me to stay and hold her that night. I did no' think she was strong enough, but she was insistent."

Suddenly, it all made sense to her. "Because she was dying."

"Nay, she was calm and smiling. She was still weak,

but she was better. I held her in my arms and when I awoke, she was dead. I must have taken the breath from her lungs. Somehow, I ken no' how, I killed her."

She grabbed his forearms, hoping to calm the tremors in his body caused by his memory. "Because she kenned she was dying. I have seen it many times. She had accepted her fate. People ken in their last hours...."

His shout was loud enough to hurt her ears, and he reached for her shoulders again.

"I killed her, Brenna. Accept it. I killed my wife. She died in my arms because I must have rolled on top of her or something." His grip tightened as he spoke, and he shook her in his desperation. "She chattered on and on about the bairns and taking care of them. She was tireless that night, so she couldnae have been near death. I was so exhausted from battling my brother in the lists that day that I must have rolled over on her in the middle of the night and crushed the life from her. 'Tis my fault my bairns lost their mama."

"Nay, Quade, listen to me. A lass will never survive if the after part from the birth is no' delivered. 'Twill stay inside and rot until it takes her last breath. 'Twas no' you. It couldnae have been you."

Quade's gaze changed as he stared at her. A flicker of hope crossed his face.

She continued, hoping to convince him of his innocence. "If no' that night, mayhap the next day. She was near death, and she wanted to die in your arms. Sick ones ken when their time is up. I have seen it many times. They have last thoughts they need to share, which gives them energy near the end. She was telling you in her own way that she was about to die."

Quade turned to stare out over the cliff again. His hands fell to his side.

"You couldnae have killed her," she said again. "She would have died anyway."

Quade didn't move but continued to stare into the

horizon.

"Your son has been trying to tell you such, Quade. Whether a dream or no', somehow your wife wants you to ken 'twas no' your fault." She watched as the man she loved swiped at his eyes. Was he crying for his wife? There was no reason for her to stay. She strode back to her horse, knowing Quade now had all the information he needed to come to the right conclusion. She could not do that for him.

He was on his own.

CHAPTER SEVENTEEN

Quade didn't know how long he stood there, staring out over the Scotland landscape that he loved. Glancing over his shoulder, he realized Brenna had left. The lass he adored, loved more than he would have thought possible, had left and he hadn't noticed. What was wrong with him?

He thought about all she had said. Was she correct? Had Lilias known she was dying? He remembered her face when she had asked him to hold her close that night. In her face, there had been something—a wistfulness, a calmness—he hadn't seen there before. He tried to recall what they had talked about before he had fallen asleep.

Their conversation returned to him in bits and pieces. She had talked about the bairns. Aye, she had made him promise to always take care of Lily and Torrian. He had considered her daft comments part of her fever. She had questioned their decision about keeping Torrian hidden. It had been such a tough choice, but Quade loved the lad and wanted to protect him from everything, even cruel comments. Lilias had begged him to reconsider that night, to bring Torrian out of hiding, saying that Torrian should take his rightful place at his father's side.

As the words returned to him, the truth finally fell into place. She had spoken as if she had known she would not be around forever. Had she been trying to let him know she was dying? Had she been expressing her last wishes? He had dismissed her words as a mother's worries at the time.

Brenna was right. He had been too tired to notice, but Lilias had known she was dying. She had wanted to be held. She had wanted to make sure that she didn't die alone, that her bairns would be cared for forever. How had he missed that?

A great weight lifted from his shoulders. Clarity settled in his mind. He hadn't done anything wrong. His wife had known she was about to die, and she'd wanted him to hold her while it happened. And he had held done exactly that. There was no reason to feel any more guilt. Och, he could regret that he had not been awake for her last breath, but he had not caused her death. Then another memory struck, one that sent a shockwave through his system.

He raised his head to the heavens and said, "I love you, Lilias. I always did and I always will. But I must move on. I recall your last wish now. You made me promise not to grieve forever, to find another."

Quade had one more visit he had to make to set his mind straight. He had gone over everything again and again last night and let it settle in his mind while he slept. Everything told him that Lady Brenna was correct in her assessment, but he needed to see one more person to be convinced.

He knocked lightly at the door of the old cottage over the hill. He had told the old woman many times to move into a hut closer to his keep, but she always refused. She had covered her yard in flowers that returned year after year. Purples, whites, and yellows covered the outside even though it was autumn, and Gunna had said she was too old to replant. He smiled at the colorful landscape as he waited on her doorstep.

The door opened and he stared into the wizened old

face of the woman who had been his clan's healer for years. "Good morn to you, Gunna. How do you fare?"

"Och, my laird. 'Tis been a long time since you have stood at my door. Bend down and come inside."

Her instructions made Quade grin. At this point in his life, he had learned to duck through the old doorways. "Aye, I will. 'Twould no' have to if you moved into a new cottage, as you so deserve."

Gunna chuckled as she ushered him over to a stool at her small table. "How can I assist you today, Laird Ramsay? I am too auld to heal you, but I can always listen."

Quade sat in the stool and rubbed his hands together before he spoke. "Gunna, I need to ask you some questions about my wife's death. Forgive me, as I should have come many moons ago, but I needed to talk to the expert."

Reaching over, the woman wrapped her hands around his. He was startled by this small act, but he gave her his complete attention. "I expected you a long time ago, my son. You have grieved for your young wife for too long. 'Tis time for you to move on and find a lass to be a mama for your bairns. What is it you need to hear from an auld woman?"

Her words, which he had finally accepted as true, were like a punch to the gut, but he needed to complete his task. "My wife, why did she die? I have been told there was a problem with Lily's birth. Things did no' happen the normal way. 'Tis true?"

"Aye. When a lass delivers her bairn, she must also deliver the part that feeds the bairn for nine moons. Lilias never delivered hers. I tried to find it, but 'twas not free for me to take. If 'tis no' free, death can happen immediately if it is pulled out, so I couldnae do that. 'Tis rare but no' unheard of. Others have had the same happen, but no' many."

"Is that why she died? 'Twas no' because I smothered her in the night?"

"Och, nay, lad, 'twas no' you. Just as I told you many moons ago. She couldnae survive with it still inside her. 'Twould have killed her eventually. In such cases, it usually takes less than two moons."

Why did he not remember any of this? "Did Lilias understand her fate?"

"Aye, she kenned it. I believe in being honest with everyone. She fought verra hard to stay for you and her bairns, but it just couldnae happen. It never released from her body."

Still, Quade would not be able to rest easy unless he allayed all of his concerns. "The day she died, she seemed much improved. I held her in my arms that night, and she chattered on and on. I believed she was better. Was I wrong?"

"Aye, lad. She kenned 'twould no' be long. We had discussed it that day. That happens; a burst of energy oft comes before the last breath." She released his hands and sat back.

He stood and paced the cabin. He had a difficult time understanding how he could have been wrong all these years. "Gunna, why did you no' tell me this when Lilias passed?"

"Och, lad, I did tell you. You were so distraught you couldnae hear me. 'Tis why I kenned you would return to me some day. I kenned that when you were ready, you would ask me the right questions."

He turned and stared at the old healer. "I was wrong. All these years, I was wrong. Do you ken I just remembered her telling me to take care of the bairns? Then yesterday, one of the last things she said to me came back. She asked me to promise to find another. I couldnae recall this before yesterday. I do no' understand."

"Aye, lad, I do. Sometimes the mind blocks out what it cannae yet handle. But time was bound to heal you eventually. 'Tis time for you to do what you were born to do."

He smiled at her. "Time to be a good laird?"

"Och, you have always been a good laird. 'Twas these auld hands that brought you into this world." She stared at them as if remembering all the details. "I recall what the stars told me about you when you were born. You were to be a great leader, but also a great father to many and a great husband to two. I am sorry to tell you 'twas in the stars for you to love twice. Now 'tis time to move on. 'Tis time to lead and love."

She paused for a long moment before continuing. "Many have come to tell me of the new healer, whose great mind solved a problem that this auld mind couldnae. Your bairns will both be healthy again. Do me a favor and do no' lose her."

Quade moved over to the table and helped Gunna to stand, then enveloped her in his arms. "I thank you, Gunna. And I thank you for all you have done for our clan. You are a treasure." He stood back and held her at arm's length. "Are there any other words from the stars you wish to impart?"

"Aye," she said with a broad smile. "Get on with your life. You have many more bairns waiting to be born."

Quade strode down the hill toward Torrian's cottage. All his wife's words had returned to him over the last two days. He had kept to himself, working in the lists when necessary, but eating alone. He needed to sort out everything Lilias had said before he moved on. He would never understand why he had blocked out her words for three years, but he was glad to finally have them back.

He had enjoyed his visit with Gunna. Some of her comments still ran through his mind. Was he truly meant to love twice? Were there more bairns in his future, and if so, would they be healthy? Did it even matter if Brenna was right about the cause of the sickness?

He hadn't wanted to ask Gunna if Brenna was meant to be his wife. He had to make that decision on his own. He loved Brenna with his whole heart, without a doubt. But after the cruel way he had rejected her, he didn't know if she would allow him back into her life. Granted, he had only done so because he wanted to protect her. Brenna was an intelligent, compassionate woman. He believed she would accept his apology and he would not give up until she did.

He so hoped he would have two healthy bairns soon. Lily's recovery had amazed him and his mother cried daily as a result. Would his beautiful, skilled, brilliant healer be able to perform the same miracle for his son? He believed she would. In truth, he believed in Brenna Grant with all his heart.

As he made his way to his son's cottage, his heart hammered in his chest. He imagined Torrian strong, walking at his side, working with him in the lists. Would such a dream ever be possible? He promised himself to be content with any small improvement, and not to get his hopes too high lest he be disappointed.

Striding to the door, he took a deep breath, preparing himself for whatever he might encounter inside. He was stopped in mid-step by the wonderful sounds echoing from inside. Giggling voices reached his ears. Had he ever heard such a sound emanate from this cottage before? He knocked on the door and held his breath before entering.

"Papa!" Lily ran to him as he closed the door behind him. His eyes instantly searched for his son. He saw a smile on his Torrian's face that held something new and unbelievably beautiful—hope. Margaret stood in the corner washing kitchenware.

His gaze found Brenna's and held it. Her smile drove right to his heart and he knew, without question, that his love for her was as real as any he had ever experienced. He had made his peace with his first wife, and it was time to move forward.

Brenna was sitting on the bed next to Torrian, carefully patting a towel over his skin after his bath. Instead of wincing in pain, as he usually did when his skin was touched, Torrian smiled. Quade reached down for Lily and swung her up into his arms, kissing her when she giggled.

"Look, Papa! I am playing with my brother, Torrian. I did no' ken I had a brother. Did you? I love my brother already. He is sick like me. I hope he gets better, too. Lady Brenna will make him better. Do you no' think so?" She placed her tiny hand on his face, awaiting his answer.

"Och, aye, wee one. You are still doing well, no throw-ups?"

"Aye." Lily wiggled until she slithered down his leg and ran toward the bed. "I am eating cheese now and I am still no' sick. You ken cheese is my favorite. Look at Torrian. See my brother?"

Brenna blushed under his gaze. "I am sorry, Quade. I wasnae thinking about Lily no' kenning she had a brother. I wanted Torrian to have company, so I brought her with me today."

He leaned over the bed to give Torrian a kiss before turning to her. "No need to apologize, Lady Brenna. How does my son fare today? Is it the same sickness?"

After Brenna put a clean night shirt on him, Torrian stood up on his small pallet. "Aye, Papa! See, my blisters are much better after just two days, and I do no' hurt much anymore. I am only eating broth and vegetables now and my tummy is much better. But Lady Brenna said I can try porridge today. She said I can only have oats and porridge is made from oats. No wheat or rye. But I can do that. And I need new clothes. I do no' have any trews like you or the other lads. The very best is that I am starting to walk again.

Watch me, Papa!"

The wee lad reached out and Quade lifted him and set him on the floor. He released the boy for a second and he actually stood on his own for a moment before teetering to the side. Quade closed his eyes and enveloped Torrian in his arms. Could it be? Would his son heal? Would he finally be able to hold him as he had yearned to do for so long?

"Aye, lad, can I hug you without hurting you?"

"It does no' hurt me if you do no squeeze much. I am almost fixed. And now I have a friend to play with again—Lily." He pushed against his father's chest and pointed his finger at his sister as she ran in circles in the small room, her energy evident in her constant motion. "Papa, do you think I will be able to run again like Lily someday?"

Quade turned to Brenna. "Mayhap, Torrian, but we must ask Lady Brenna. You are to do as she says at all times. Understood?" His gaze locked on hers again, and he was powerless to turn away.

She cleared her throat before she spoke. "Aye, I believe it is the same," she said, answering his earlier question. "He hasnae had any sickness since he started on the broth. His skin is much better, so I would like to start him on porridge today. The true beauty of youth is how fast they can recover. He needs to begin to build his strength back up. He has lost much over the years, but he is young. I think he will fully recover." Brenna folded the sheets. "I spoke to Cook this morn. She is making extra porridge and baking apples for them both. I will retrieve their food as soon as I straighten everything here with Margaret."

Brenna set the damp towels out to dry while Quade swung his son in a circle around him. He had kept Torrian hidden for too long, and it was time for the lad to come out of hiding. It would probably be a shock to his clan members, but he would do it today. It was time for a fresh start.

"Och, aye, 'tis time for my son to return to the keep. We will go eat in the hall."

Quade's smile reached in and grabbed her heart. She stopped to watch his revelry. How he loved his bairns! He was so good with them, too.

He turned to the boy's caretaker. "Margaret, bring your things to the keep. We willnae be hiding my son anymore."

Lily jumped and clapped her hands. "Can we play in the great hall, papa?"

"Aye, you can play wherever you like. We need to introduce Torrian to the clan again."

"Quade, at least allow me to wrap him in a blanket. He is still verra thin and 'tis chilly out." Margaret fussed over her charge.

"Och, then find my plaid. My son will wear it and take up his rightful place. And Margaret? Tell Ennis when he returns from the lists that you both may move into the keep. "

Brenna heard Margaret gasp. She glanced at her and shrugged her shoulders as she wrapped Torrian in the Ramsay plaid which was a beautiful shade of blue and black. Torrian's face beamed with pride.

"Ladies first, Lady Brenna," Quade said. "After you. Margaret, follow us when you and Ennis are ready." He held the door for Brenna. As soon as he stepped outside onto the grass with Torrian in his arms, the boy held his hands over his eyes.

"Papa, the sun is too bright."

"Och, you will get used to it, lad. 'Tis cloudy today. 'Twill no' bother you much." He swung him up on his shoulders and started up the hill. Lily grabbed Brenna's hand and skipped along behind her father.

Micheil joined his brother on the path since he had been not far from the cottage. The shock on his face was evident. "What's this, brother? My favorite nephew is doing better?"

Quade radiated excitement at his son's improvement. "Aye, Lady Brenna is healing my son as well. He will take his rightful place at my side on the dais for meals." He spoke loud enough for everyone in close range to hear his pronouncement.

Micheil shouted a Ramsay whoop and Torrian giggled. Micheil winked at his nephew. "'Tis about time. Torrian needs to spend more time with the lads."

Quade let out a whoop loud enough to bring more clan members out of their cottages. Brenna didn't know quite what to do. Many dropped to their knees as they saw the lad on his father's shoulders.

Whispers abounded as they passed.

"'Tis the chief's son. I thought he had passed."

"Saints above, 'tis a miracle, nothing less."

"Where has the lad been all this time?"

"He is very thin and small. Has he been sick?"

"Look at the lass. She is so much better."

Then the stares turned to her.

"The Grant healer, she did it."

"She is a miracle worker. Look at what she has done."

"Aye, the lass has saved our clan. Look at the two bairns and how wonderful they look."

Quade shouted for all to hear as he continued on his way to the keep. "My son could use some lad's clothes now that he improves. Who would like to bring him some trews to wear? Come up to the great hall and meet my son."

Many of the women who had wandered out onto the path ran back to their cottages in search of clothing.

"My lad's clothes will fit him for sure, Chief."

"We will make new for him. He is your son, Chief. Only the best for him."

Lily waved at the well-wishers, then stopped to stare at something on the ground in front of her. "Lady

Brenna, I have my sack. May I collect some pretty stones to take to the keep?"

"Of course, you may, lass. May I see it?"

Lily held her tiny hand up to display her find. "See how pretty?"

Brenna peered at the small stone. "Lily, 'tis beautiful. What a pretty pink and gray it is."

"I must find more, Lady Brenna." She hopped from side to side on the path. "I can hide them for Torrian and he will have to find them."

They had almost made it to the great hall when Quade turned to address the crowd that had gathered behind them.

He waited until all was quiet, and then he brought the lad down from his shoulders, setting him on the ground in front of him so that Torrian could lean against his strong legs. "My son has been sick for a very long time, but now he heals. I have Lady Brenna Grant to thank for healing both my son and my daughter." He nodded his head toward her. "Please make her feel welcome here. I am forever indebted to her healing skills."

Brenna blushed as she turned to gauge the reaction of Quade's clan. Would they accept her? A strong hush descended over the group, then a slow rippling of shouts of approval began. Some even kneeled. She nodded her head in thanks and ducked her head toward the door to the keep.

Then Iona made her way through the masses and yelled, "She's a witch!"

Brenna fled into the keep without waiting for anyone to say another word.

CHAPTER EIGHTEEN

Lily ran inside after Brenna. "I do no' like that lady," she said, a tremor in her voice. "She does no' have to come in here does she, Lady Brenna?"

"Och, lass, we will see what your da wishes. 'Tis up to him."

"But I do no' like her! And she is mean. She wants you to leave, and I do no' want you to ever leave me." Lily reached over and wrapped her arms around Brenna's leg.

Brenna picked her up and hugged her, then said, "Why do you no' hide the pretty stones you found for your brother? He can try to find them when he comes in with your da." Lily smiled and scrambled away to complete her task after Brenna set her down.

As she stared after the wee angel, Brenna thought about how good it felt to know that Lily wanted her to stay. Had anyone other than her sister ever said that to her? If so, she could not recall. Lily's father had certainly never uttered such a thought in her presence. Why did that not sit well with her? Because no matter how much it ended up hurting her—and she was certain that it would—she had strong feelings for Quade Ramsay.

Her eyes continued to follow Lily, who carefully chose her hiding spots, her tongue between her teeth as she worked. A sly grin passed her face when she lodged a stone into a nook that would be extra difficult for her brother to find. Brenna grinned at the impish pleasure that danced across the girl's face and stepped over to the dais, settling into her usual chair.

Moments later, the door flew open and Quade strode in. He hurried over to the dais and gently settled Torrian into the chair next to Brenna's before marching back out. He glanced at Brenna before departing. "I will return soon, Lady Brenna." He had almost reached the exit when he swirled about and returned to her, planting a soft kiss on her lips before winking and leaving.

What could he mean by that? Brenna peeked around the hall to determine if any others had noticed the kiss, and if so, how they were reacting. A few whispers funneled to her, but none close for her to pick up any words.

Brenna turned to Torrian. "Will you be all right if I leave you alone for a moment, lad? I want to go see Cook about your porridge." He nodded his head, his eyes busy following wee Lily with her stones, so Brenna left for the kitchens. As she walked, her mind churned with questions. Was Quade out there dealing with Iona? How would he handle her rudeness? She couldn't tear her mind away from the screeching voice that had declared her a witch.

Forcing herself to focus on his kiss instead of Iona, she stepped into the kitchens and smiled at Cook, searching the large work area for the children's porridge.

"Is he ready, lass?" Cook stared at her, awaiting her opinion.

"Aye, I believe he can handle the porridge today, Cook." Peering into one of the bowls and swishing it, she declared, "I think you have made it thin enough for him."

Cook kneaded her hands before she spoke. "Lady Brenna, we are so grateful for all you have done for our clan. You have not only returned Lily to us, but the chief's son. We will be forever grateful for your skills and devotion to our wee ones."

Brenna's head dipped, as she was unsure of how to receive such compliments gracefully. "I have done what any healer would have done."

Cook shook her head, her lips pursed. "Nay, we have seen many others come and go. Mayhap another may have eventually helped Lily, but none could have helped our chief as you have. I have no' seen him like this in many, many moons, and I thank you. Whate'er you wish for the weans, you just ask. I will make whatever they need to push away their sickness, my lady."

Brenna blushed as she grabbed the two bowls of porridge and some baked apple, arranged the warm dishes on a platter, and turned to the door. When she entered the hall, she called out to Lily, "Please come eat your porridge with your brother."

Lily popped onto a stool near Torrian. "Aye, my favorite! Lady Brenna, may we have the apples mixed in? Torrian, wait until you taste this. 'Tis my favorite."

Torrian peeked up at Brenna. "Must I, Lady Brenna? I am feeling very good today. I do not want my tummy to start hurting again."

Brenna sat between the lad and Lily. "I think this will be all right. Try a few slow spoonfuls of the porridge to start."

Torrian stared at the bowl, picked up the utensil, and tasted the sweet dish. "'Tis tasty. I will wait a minute, though, to see how my tummy feels. I do no' want to ever be sick again, Lady Brenna. Please? I do no' ever want the rash to come back, either. My sores are so much better."

Brenna brushed a lock of golden hair back from his forehead. "Try it slowly. You will see."

The door burst open and Quade entered, followed by a series of well-wishers. They streamed over to smile at Torrian and offer him words of welcome. Torrian studied his bowl and nodded at each newcomer. How strange this must be for him after being hidden for so many years. Lily was young enough to adjust quickly to her improved health. Torrian's journey would be more difficult as his muscles needed time to heal, but Brenna was determined to make it as easy as possible.

When Quade reached the dais, he brushed Brenna's arm and whispered, "I am sorry. Iona's rudeness will not happen again."

"Good, Papa. I do no' like her." Lily peeked up at her father to gauge his reaction.

"Thank you, Lily. Now, please mind your manners and eat the good meal Cook has prepared for you."

Quade took the seat next to Torrian so that his clan would have a clear view of his son. Brenna sat between Torrian and Lily.

In between visitors, they were alone for a moment. His gaze caught hers. "I meant what I said. Iona will never insult you again. I promise you that, Brenna."

The depth of feeling in his voice sent a shiver down her spine. "Is she the only one who believes I am a witch? Do others of your clan feel the same way?"

"Nay, they do no'. No one has mentioned such a daft thought. Iona, you must understand, is acting out of jealousy. I do no' ken why she expects to marry me, since I havenae encouraged the idea. I have no' been with her in a very long time. I apologize for her crass insult."

"Papa, I am finished. May I go hide more stones for my brother?" Lily awaited her father's permission before bouncing off her stool.

"How is your porridge, lad?"

"Delicious, Da. But I am afraid to keep eating it. I do no' want to be sick ever again. Do you think it will be safe for me to eat more?"

Quade's gaze went over his son's head to find hers. "Aye, I believe Lady Brenna with all my heart. You should, too, Torrian."

Brenna swallowed at the depth of affection in Quade's voice and gaze. What was he about? One never knew what the lad was thinking. He made her daft at times.

Torrian thought before speaking, his hands trembling in his lap. "I am a wee scart, but I will eat it. I want to be big and strong like you, Papa."

Quade ruffled his son's hair, smiling with pride. "You must eat to be big and strong, lad."

"Papa?" Torrian's spoon moved to his mouth as his eyes followed his sister.

"Aye?"

"What do I do when Lily asks me to find her stones? I cannae walk well enough on my own yet. Do you think I will be able to walk soon?"

"Aye, soon. Do no' worry about Lily. She was like you no' long ago. Do you realize she was unable to walk alone less than a moon ago?"

The three followed the wee lass's antics until she charged back to the table. "Come, Torrian, see if you can find all my stones. I hid them so you cannae find them. Hurry."

Lily gazed at her brother, playfulness and hope dancing in her green eyes. Torrian gave his father a desperate glance, unsure how to respond to Lily. Just before he spoke, the lass jumped up and clapped. "Wait! I will find them for you."

Two wee feet glided around the hall as Lily picked up several shiny pebbles, oblivious to those around hr. Each time she located a new stone, she pivoted to show her brother, her face beaming with her new joy. Torrian's puzzled face gave way to his thoughts. "Lady Brenna, why is she finding the stones she hid? 'Tis no' a challenge if she hid them herself, is it?"

Quade's laugh was a low rumble that Brenna and the boy joined, creating a low chorus of laughter. Each time Lily threw her arm into the air with another stone, their laughter increased.

In between her giggles, Brenna finally gave Torrian her answer. "Aye, at her tender age, 'tis a challenge for her. She does no' need anyone else to play with her; she is happy in her own world as long as we are close." She leaned over to give Torrian a light kiss. "She is very happy to have a new brother, lad. That knowledge shines in her eyes."

Much later, Lily launched herself in their direction to show off the bounty she herself had hidden and found. As she handed the last of her treasures to her brother, Lily leaped onto Brenna's lap and clapped her hands with satisfaction.

Brenna wondered how she would ever be able to leave this family. The sense of belonging that had settled into her heart took her totally by surprise.

Quade leaned back and balanced on the back two legs of the chair at his desk in the solar. Rocking carelessly, he observed the faces of his mother and his brother, waiting patiently for their response to his declaration.

His mother's lips pursed before she shared her thoughts. "You are sure of this, Quade Ramsay? You cannae toy with the lass's feelings. You do understand what you are implying?"

Micheil spoke up, his eyes wide. "Aye, you cannae do this again, brother. 'Twas less than a sennight ago when you denied the lass. I fear I ken lasses well enough to know she willnae believe you this time. And who would blame her for denying you? You cannae play with her feelings as you have."

Quade dropped the chair to the floor before standing, his hands held high in front of him as if to stave off an attack. "I ken what you are saying. I need to talk with Brenna again and explain my reasons. I need to apologize for my previous behavior, I ken that."

"Telling her how much you loved your first wife is no' going to help the situation." Micheil glanced at their mother for support.

Quade jumped in. "That is no' what I wish to tell her. Aye, I did love my wife. But now I love another. My feelings for Lady Brenna are very strong."

"You are sure this is love you are experiencing and not just gratitude for all she has done for your bairns?" Lady Ramsay's worry was etched onto her face. "I cannae deny that I hoped you and Lady Brenna would be wed, but I want to ken you are doing it for the right reasons."

Quade strolled over and kissed his mother's cheek. "Aye, Mama. I understand your concern. But do no' doubt my love for the lass. It has been in my heart ever since I first saw her. But I have been thick-skulled. The only reason I denied Laird Grant's directive to marry his sister is because I was afraid of hurting Lady Brenna. You understand I couldnae live with myself if I hurt the lass? I couldnae risk bringing harm to her, as I thought I had done to Lilias. Brenna helped me to see the truth of what had happened."

"What is this you speak of? You are daft sometimes, I swear." Micheil paced the floor, while their mother just stared at Quade with a question in her eyes.

Quade held his arms up in surrender. "Och, aye, I will explain." He moved over to the hearth, gathering his thoughts before speaking. "The night Lilias died, she asked me to lie in her bed with her. I had no' slept in her bed since Lily was born because I kenned she had childbed fever. But that night, she told me she wanted me to hold her, so I did." He paused, a slow smile building on his face as he recalled his first wife. "She chattered on about taking care of the bairns, but I was so tired, I did no' really listen to her. Lady Brenna helped me see that she was sharing her last wishes with me. I must have fallen asleep while she still spoke."

Moments passed before he was able to continue. "When I awoke, Lilias wasnae breathing. I panicked and called the healer in. I do no' remember what the healer said, but I believed I had smothered my wife in my sleep. I had worked hard in the lists that day and was exhausted. I thought I had rolled over on her and somehow crushed her.

"Lady Brenna suggested Lilias had known she was dying and wanted me there so she wouldnae die alone. After mulling it over, I went to talk to Gunna and she confirmed Brenna's thoughts. In fact, she told me she had advised me of the truth when it happened. For some reason, I never heard her or did no' want to hear her. I believed I had killed Lilias. By accident, aye, but I still felt responsible for my wife's death. I was so horrified by my actions that I could no' discuss it with anyone. And I could no' ever consider marrying again with such on my conscience. Can you no' see why I thought I was cursed? I believed it and couldnae risk harming Lady Brenna."

He lifted his gaze to his mother and his brother. "I do love Lady Brenna, but no' for the reasons you think. She is a caring, loving, beautiful person. I would be honored to have her as my wife. Whether she will accept me or no' is yet to be seen. I willnae allow her to leave without fighting for the lass first."

Lady Ramsay strode over to her son and enveloped him in her arms. "Quade, how awful. Why did you never share this with me? I kenned she had died from childbed fever. We all did."

"Aye, but I believed you all said so for my benefit. In my heart, I thought I had caused her death."

When Quade stepped out of his mother's embrace, Micheil clasped his shoulder. "Brother, you have chosen well, but I think you have some courting to do. You will have to be persistent."

"Aye, I ken that and I will no' give up. She is worth it to me. I will no' ever find a more kind or clever lass."

A single tear rolled down Lady Ramsay's cheek. "Aye, she is special. I cannae believe all she has done for our family. The bairns are beautiful again. Most everyone in the clan is taken with Lady Brenna. She is a strong woman, and I would welcome her into our family. I hope you are successful, son."

Quade winked at his mother. "Och, aye, I will no' take no for an answer."

CHAPTER NINETEEN

Two days later, Brenna headed to the gates of the keep, a large basket with gloves inside swinging on her arm. She stood at the entryway and spoke to the guard. "Mungo, do you know the shortest direction to find wild herbs in a forest? I wish to find as many as possible before the snow buries them all."

Mungo crossed his arms and widened his stance. "Aye, my lady, but the chief said you are not allowed to exit the keep unescorted."

Brenna's face contorted in the sun. What had possessed Quade to restrict her now? It wasn't as if there was a risk that she would start running toward home.

A shout caught her ear and she turned, shielding her eyes from the bright sun with her hand. Quade ran toward them, his expression all pleasure. She was almost afraid to hear what he would say. It was impossible to know what he was about at any given time.

"Mungo! I will go with the lass."

Brenna saw the astonished look pass over Mungo's face before he recovered. "You, Chief? You will take the lass foraging?"

Quade cupped her elbow when he reached her side. "Aye, Mungo. 'Tis my pleasure to take her for a stroll into the forest." He nodded his head to her. "Good morn to you, Lady Brenna. How do you fare?"

She mumbled a quick, "Fine." What was this about? She had to agree with Mungo; this was totally out of character for Quade.

Quade stepped forward and tugged on her elbow. "Come, Lady Brenna. My mother told me your supply of healing plants needs replenishing. I will show you all the great hiding spots. I know the forest well."

Brenna didn't try to hide her surprise. "You ken what I'm seeking?"

He chuckled. "Nay, 'twas just an excuse to walk with you. You do no' mind, do you?"

Brenna sighed. Would he walk away if she said she did? Probably not. "Nay, of course no'." Why not allow him to escort her so he could confuse her all over again. As usual, the butterflies in her stomach had started as soon as he cupped her elbow. How she wished her mother was alive so she could ask her about this strange anomaly. Had it ever happened to her mother? She would have to ask Madeline if the same ever happened to her when she had first met her brother.

She sighed in exasperation as she remembered how Logan had taken her mother's book. She thought her mother had mentioned something about love and how it affected the body, but she just couldn't remember what. Curse the lad for stealing her beloved book.

"Careful, lass. With a frown like that, you may convince me to turn around and run." Quade's sheepish grin caught her right in the gut. She blushed before apologizing. "Sorry, my laird, I was thinking of another. Where do you suppose Logan is?"

Quade's hand covered his heart. "Och, I stroll with you and all you can think of is my brother?"

"Nay! I mean, well, aye...."

His eyebrows rose as he stared at her. Why did he make her so daft? She never stumbled for words unless she was with him.

"I was thinking about my mother's healing book. Do

you recall the one that Logan took?"

Great, now she had to think of why she wanted it. She gazed at him as he stared back at her, a sly grin on his face. "Um, I..." Curse it, Quade Ramsay! "Uh...My mother's book had sketches of plants and information on why each was important."

"And you have forgotten all those plants?" He quirked an eyebrow at her as they strolled to the edge of the forest.

"Nay, but I was wondering if I would ever see my mother's book again."

"Ah, lass. I cannae tell you why Logan took it. He runs for many moons and then returns for a fortnight or two. He is searching for something, but I do no' believe even he knows what. We ne'er know when he will return. He just shows up one day. I do no' think he took it to sell it. I believe he will take care of it and return it one day."

"You do? You do no' think he took it to make me angry and threw it in a stream or something?" She gazed into his eyes, hoping to see the truth in them.

"Nay, he would not take your property lightly. He is a good lad, just confused. He was always fond of his niece and nephew, and he took it very hard when Torrian fell sick. Sometimes, I think he thought it was an insult to our family that my boy wasnae a strong lad. He acted tough, but I could see how upset he was when the blisters sprung up on Torrian's skin and we could no' stop his pain. He runs because it is too difficult for him to see the weans in pain, I believe. He would ne'er admit it."

"I hope you are right. I treasure my mother's words. Perhaps he will return soon if word reaches him that your children are improving." She stared at his profile and shivered, astounded how his gaze could get under her skin so swiftly.

Quade tucked her in close and wrapped his arm around her shoulder. "Are you cold, lass?"

Brenna nodded her head, unable to speak when she was close enough to feel his warmth and the beat of his heart, a pulsing that mesmerized her like no other. How was that possible? Usually, she listened to a heartbeat to judge the soundness of the body, of the strength the person's blood. But Quade's heart called to her and beckoned her closer, threatening to enrapture her like no other. The healer part of her flew away whenever he was near. Her thoughts were illogical, confusing, and dysfunctional at times.

His lips touched her forehead for but a second, leaving a searing heat behind. He stopped and turned her to face him, pulling her in for a quick kiss. All the powers in heaven could not have stopped her from leaning into him, wrapping her hands around his neck, and searching for more. He kissed her again, angling his mouth deeper over hers. He tasted like apple and Quade. He pulled away briefly, but she tugged him back to her and he chuckled deep in his throat.

He coaxed her mouth open and plunged his tongue into it, searching for hers. Groaning with pleasure, he cupped her bottom and pulled her against him until she felt something hard against her belly.

Realization hit her like cold water splashing on her face. She shoved him away.

"Sweetness? I did something you did no' like? I thought you were enjoying my kisses as much as I was enjoying tasting you."

"I do. I did. Curse it. What are you about? I do no' understand you." She didn't know how to explain her thoughts, but she had to try. He rejected her. How could he have rejected her in front of her brother if he wanted her? This was just like before. He had kissed her senseless, then walked away as if he wanted naught to do with her.

He tucked a stray hair behind her ear. She pushed his hand away.

"What is it, Brenna? You do no' want me?"

"Nay, 'tis no' it." She willed her breathing to slow so she could speak reasonably.

"Talk to me, sweetness. What are you thinking?"

Tears welled in her eyes as she recalled how he had denied her in the solar.

His finger touched her chin, forcing her gaze to meet his. "Brenna, talk to me, please."

She brushed a tear from her cheek and gazed into his eyes. "You rejected me. We did the same thing in the passageway, then you embarrassed me and you rejected me. My brothers probably thought I was a loose wench when you said you would never marry me. I ken you make me weak in the knees, but I willnae allow you to play with my feelings. Leave me be, and do no' ever touch me again."

She had to get away. She pushed at his hand, dropped her basket, and ran back toward the keep.

Quade had to admit he probably deserved that. The lass's loveliness took his breath away, even when she was in a fury. She tasted so sweet and he would have loved to toss her on the soft moss to make love to her, just the two of them and the sky and the trees.

He charged after her. She should have done exactly as she did. He had intended to talk to her before allowing the relationship to turn physical again, but, hellfire, how could he resist her? Those rosy pink lips and brown eyes, that sable hair curling about her face, how could he stop picturing her naked in his arms? Saints above, he was only human.

When he caught up to her and grabbed her arm, she swung around and caught his face with her hand.

"Leave me be, please! Get away from me, Quade!"

After rubbing the side of his face where she had caught him—aye, he had deserved that as well—he caught both her hands in his. "Brenna, two minutes, please. Allow me to speak. Listen to me for just a few minutes and if you still want to go, I will escort you back. I promise no' to touch you unless you want me to. Please, Brenna. I will beg if you'd like. Please?"

She hesitated for a moment, then slowly nodded her head. "Two minutes, 'tis all you have."

He took a deep breath, kissed the back of each hand he held, and said, "I love you. 'Tis that simple." He gauged her reaction to be somewhere between shock and anger, but then he caught a flicker of softening in her eyes. That would be the reaction from the woman he loved—strong, warm, thoughtful, and sensual. Heavens above, he adored her, and he needed to convince her of that. He swallowed and plunged ahead. "And I think I have since you popped your mop of curls up by the side of my pallet in that cottage. I cannae explain it, lass. Sometimes I am a wee bit dense and do no' see what is in front of my face and 'tis you. Us. We belong together.

"Aye, I rejected you in front of your brother, but 'twas because I love you so much that I did no' want to force my curse on you. Every time your brother mentioned the word marriage, all I could see was Lilias lying dead in my arms when I awakened. 'Twas the worst day of my life. I couldnae ever risk that happening again. 'Twould no' be fair. You must admit, I have had a challenging life since my marriage. I have watched both my bairns fall ill with a sickness that befuddled all the healers in the nigh area. Except you. You are the one that saved my bairns."

"Then you love me because I saved your bairns? Is that why, Quade? Because if 'tis the reason you say you love me, then I do no' want you. I need someone to love me for who I am, no' because I am a healer. Being a healer is a large part of me, but 'tis just that—a part of me, not all of me. I do have value in other ways."

"Och, and I ken it. You have the patience and compassion that make you a brilliant healer, but you are also the toughest lass I have ever met. Your mind is brilliant, greater than any lad I ken. You will make a wonderful mother to my bairns."

He heard her sigh and knew what she needed to hear. "But most of all, Brenna Grant, I love you because you make me weak in the knees like I have ne'er felt before." He kissed her cheek when she blushed. "And I cannae wait to watch you blush from your head all the way down to your toes with naught around you but your beautiful hair. You excite me like nae other.

"When I am old and gray and cannae lift my claymore anymore, I want to see your face next to me, lass. I want you to be by my side, holding my hand." He tucked her hand in his and turned back to the forest. "I ken you want to learn more of my marriage and I need to tell you, so will you stroll with me?"

"Aye." She leaned into him as they wandered aimlessly.

"Lilias and I married because of a match made by our fathers. I remember the first time I saw her, I thought she was pretty enough. We married quickly, and we were happy. She carried within our first year and when I saw our son, Torrian, for the first time, why, I havenae been that proud since. Lilias and I both adored him. It was such fun to watch the wee lad grow that I did no' want to go out in the lists many days. Sometimes I would send Logan to lead in my stead. He was almost as taken with the lad as I was. Every time he giggled and wandered toward Logan, the man dropped everything.

"Shortly after his first year, Torrian became ill. We tried many things and many healers but for naught. He would have good days and bad days. We lost my da around that same time, and our keep was saddened for a long time. Losing my da and having Torrian so sick was hard on all of us, but it was hardest on my mother.

"We plunged along, finding more and more healers

that bled him or fed him horrid potions, but all was for naught. Lilias became pregnant again and she focused on the new bairn while still trying to heal our son. When she delivered a wee lass safely, we were all so thankful, though we worried she would fall ill like her brother. Lilias doted on her, but 'twas less than a sennight before I realized how ill she herself was. I heard talk of childbed fever, but I couldnae or wouldnae listen to what the healer said. It devastated me.

"I was fond of Lilias in the beginning, but I grew to love her. I so admired how hard she worked to try to save our weans. They say illness tears people apart, but nae for us. Our love grew each year. You cannae go through what we did without building a strong bond. I couldnae handle it when I lost her."

He grabbed Brenna by the waist and drew her in close so he could nuzzle her neck. "Aye, I loved my wife, but I love you even more, Brenna.

"I rejected you and 'twas one of the hardest things I have ever done. I want you more than anything. But I couldnae marry you believing I was cursed. But after listening to you at the cliffs, memories of my last night with Lilias came back to me in bits and pieces. You are right, Lilias kenned she was dying. She even had told me what her last wishes were for the bairns.

"But I also recall something else she said. She made me promise to move on and find new love. I do no' ken why I never remembered that until I talked to you. After our conversation at the cliffs, I spent the next two days thinking about Lilias and everything from that night returned to me. Mayhap I blocked it out because I did no' want to remember it.

"I also visited our old healer, Gunna, and she verified everything you said. She kenned I did no' kill Lilias and said she had told me so, but I wasnae ready to hear her. I was too distraught. I am sorry I did no' tell you where I was for those two days. I do go off by myself to think sometimes, and I apologize for that, too. But I needed to clear my head and I did. I was never with Iona or any other lass. After I settled with Lilias, I thought only of you and how much you mean to me."

He turned to her and wrapped his hands around hers. "I love only you. I want only you. I need only you." He knelt in front of her and held her hand in his. "Lady Brenna, will you marry me?"

Brenna could not believe what he had just said. She gazed into his eyes and saw the love she had hoped to see someday.

"Quade, I do no' ken what to say. I am so surprised."

Was he the lad for her? Would he love her and cherish her the way Alex loved Maddie? The way her father had loved her mother? She swiped at the tears gathering on her lashes.

The real question was—did she love him enough to say aye? Did she love him enough to leave her family and spend her life by his side? In her heart, there was only one possible answer she could give this man.

"Say aye, Brenna, and make me the happiest lad alive." He kissed the tender skin on the inside of her wrist and the heat spread up her arm like wildfire.

"Aye."

Quade let out a whoop and lifted her into the air. She gazed into his eyes and knew she had made the right decision. She loved him more than she'd thought possible. She would never have been able to walk away from him.

She threw her arms around his neck as soon as her feet touched the ground again. His lips found hers and she melted. He pulled back enough to gaze into her eyes. "I love you, Brenna, never forget that. I can be a horse's arse sometimes. But never forget that I love you."

"Aye. And I love you, Quade Ramsay. You make me daft sometimes, but I do love you. You have made me verra happy."

CHAPTER TWENTY

He took possession of her lips with a searing kiss, wanting to show her how much he loved her. Her response sparked a low growl in his throat. He lifted her and found a soft patch of grass to settle her. He started by kissing her cheeks, her lips, and then trailed a path of kisses down her throat to the tender spot at the base of her neck.

Her response fueled his. He ran his hand up from her waist until he cupped her breast, searching for her nipple through the soft cloth of her gown. He rubbed the soft nub until he felt her peak beneath him. He kissed her again, angling his mouth over hers to allow him a sweet taste of her luscious tongue.

She arched beneath his touch and he lost all control of his senses, thinking about how passionate she would be when he bedded her. He knew he shouldn't, but he found his way under the layers of cloth to the soft skin of her long legs. Brushing his hand across her creamy thighs, he sought the curls at the apex of her being, unable to control his own response when he discovered the wetness there.

Brenna jerked in response to his intrusion, but then opened her legs to allow him easier access.

He continued his assault on her mouth, ravaging her lips while he caressed her dewy mons. All he could think of was how much he wanted to bury himself in her wet sheath until he made her scream his name in satisfaction.

Just as quickly as she had opened for him, she clamped her legs closed.

She grabbed his biceps and held tight. "Quade, 'tis too fast."

He saw the confusion etched onto her features. He shouldn't have gone this far, not here where any of his men could find them. "Hush, beautiful one. I ken." He removed his hand and pulled her skirt back into place. She still clung to his arms.

"What are we doing? I do no' think I am ready yet. Please?"

"Forgive me, Brenna. You make me forget myself. You are so passionate." He gazed into her eyes and kissed her lips soundly. "I shouldnae have gone that far. But trust me when I say we will be wonderful together, and I will never do anything you do no' want me to do."

He stood and held his hands out to her, then helped her stand. He wanted to smile with satisfaction at the dazed expression on her face. They would be wonderful together.

Once he had them looking presentable again, he cupped her face with his hands. "Remember I love you. You make me verra happy, but I should have waited. We will wait until our wedding night. I promise."

A smile erupted on every face in the solar when Quade announced that Brenna had agreed to be his wife. Micheil, Lady Ramsay, and Avelina hugged them both.

Wee Lily ran over and wrapped her arms around Brenna's legs. "Does this mean you will stay with us, Lady Brenna?"

Brenna leaned down to pick her up. "Aye, this means I will stay with you, Torrian, and your da." She kissed her cheek.

"Forever?" Her hand rested on Brenna's shoulder as she peered into her eyes, her expectant gaze never leaving hers.

"Aye, lass, forever."

Lily yelled, "Aye!" Then she wrapped her arms around Brenna's neck and leaned her head on her shoulder. "I love you, Lady Brenna."

Brenna's heart melted. She walked over to the chair Torrian sat in and knelt down in front of him. She set Lily in the chair with him and gave them both a gentle hug. "I love you and Torrian, too."

Torrian spoke up "When are you getting married, Da? I want to come to the wedding. May Lily and I come?" They both peered up at their father waiting for a response.

Quade ruffled his hair. "Of course you are both coming, Torrian. We wouldnae get married without you. Would we, Brenna?"

"Of course no'. We will find something special for you and Lily to do so you can be a part of the wedding."

Lily clapped her hands in excitement, then whispered to her brother, "Torrian, we will have a mama again."

Lady Ramsay wiped the tears from her cheeks before speaking to her son and future daughter-in-law. "How soon? Do you ken when you will marry? We will need to arrange for a priest."

Quade hesitated before glancing at Brenna. "'Tis up to my betrothed. I would marry her tomorrow. But I am sure she would like her family here. Aye, Brenna?"

"Aye, we will need to send a messenger to Alex to see how long it will take them to get here. I want my sister, Jennie, and my other brothers here as well."

"I would guess a fortnight, Mother. I will send a messenger tomorrow. I think they can get here by then."

Torrian stood up, hanging onto the chair next to him. "Lady Brenna, do you think I will be able to walk on my own by then? I want to be strong for my da's wedding."

Brenna kneeled in front of him. "We will try our best, but if no', I have another plan."

Brenna and Lady Ramsay were in the great hall where bolts of cloth decorated the tables for their perusal.

"Aye, you are correct, Lady Ramsay. You have some beautiful bolts to choose from."

"'Tis your choice, lass. We will make whatever you choose. I am so excited to have you as a part of our family." Lady Ramsay gave her a quick hug.

They were still examining the fabric when Margaret and Aggie descended the stairs with Torrian and Lily. Aggie marched right over to Brenna. "I would be honored if you would allow me to stitch your dress, Lady Brenna."

"Aggie's stitchery is among the finest," Lady Ramsay said with a smile.

"Of course, if you would have the time," Brenna said. "But Lily needs a dress as well. Who could sew her frock?"

"Aye, my lady. I will do both," Margaret said as she helped Lily onto a stool.

After she settled Torrian on a nearby stool, Margaret joined them. "And Aggie's sister is wonderful with the thread as well."

Brenna clasped Aggie's hands in her own. "Thank you, I would love to have you make my gown."

Brenna wandered the room, searching for the right cloth. She came upon a pale blue. "Lady Ramsay, what do you think of this for Lily?"

"Aye, 'tis beautiful."

Lily ran over to see the cloth. "Aye, can I have that one, Grandmama? But I want to look like you, Lady Brenna. Will you wear it, too?"

Brenna stepped toward the end of the table. "Nay, I think we will be different, Lily. But what if we wear different shades of blue? I like this darker blue and it would match the blue in Quade's plaid." She ran the cloth through her fingers, thinking about what threading would look best. "Mayhap gold decorations and threading. Or gold in the sleeves?"

"Och, aye, 'twould be perfect!" Lady Ramsay stood at her side, glancing over her shoulder to survey her choice.

Margaret and Aggie both nodded in agreement.

"Aye, then I can look almost like you, Lady Brenna!" Lily's exuberance rubbed off, and they all joined in her laughter.

"What about me?" Torrian sat on the stool where Margaret had left him, still unable to walk on his own without support.

Brenna held her hand out to him and helped him walk to the door. His steps were slow and deliberate, but he persisted. "Your da will help you pick clothing for the wedding, but I have something special for you right now. Come, Mungo has a new friend for you."

She took Torrian out to the steps in front of the keep and whistled for Mungo.

"Send him, Mungo!" She yelled loud enough for Torrian to cover his ears.

"What are you talking about, Lady Brenna?" He peered up at her, his hands still covering his ears. When he turned his head back toward the gate, he yelled, "Och, nay! Brenna, help me! He will run me down." His hands reached for her as a huge deerhound ran their way.

"Nay, Torrian," she said with a laugh. "This is your new pet." Just as she finished his statement, the big dog lumbered up the steps and licked Torrian's face.

Torrian's hands covered his face in an attempt to block the slobber from the very large tongue that ran a line up his cheek. "Och, yuk. Sit!"

The dog promptly sat in front of him, awaiting his next command.

Brenna checked Torrian for his response. His eyes met hers, the gleam in them evident. "He listened to me. 'Tis true? Is he mine?"

"Och, aye!" Brenna laughed and helped Torrian turn back toward the door to the great hall, beckoning for the hound to follow them.

"Nay, Lady Brenna. Grandmama does not allow dogs in the great hall."

"Aye, but he is special. Grandmama agreed to let him in so he can help you."

"How will he do that?" His curiosity piqued, he petted the dog carefully.

Brenna picked Torrian up and carried him over to the chair near the hearth. The deerhound followed close behind. "Come with me and I will show you."

"What's his name?"

"Mungo said his name is Growley. They had four pups that lived from their most recent litter. He is just over a year old."

"Why did they name him Growley?"

"Because he likes to growl in his sleep. But he does no' hurt anyone. Mungo said he is very gentle, and I think he is the perfect height for you."

"Why? How can he help me?" He peered at the furry animal lumbering near his chair. The beast's coat was a beautiful gray with tufts of brown mixed in. The dog came over to him and settled his head on his lap. Torrian patted his head carefully and started to giggle. "Lady Brenna, his nose is cold! I like him, but he is verra big."

"'Tis why he is perfect for you." Brenna helped Torrian out of his chair. "Come. I will show you what Growley can do."

She noticed that everyone in the great hall had stopped to watch.

Torrian called out to his grandmother.

"Grandmama, may Growley stay in here with me?"

Brenna noticed that while Lady Ramsay nodded her head, she didn't speak. Her hands wiped at her eyes several times. Brenna returned her attention to the dog. She stood and patted her thigh. "Come, Growley." The dog padded over and stood at attention facing her. She stepped to his side and placed Torrian next to him.

"Now what do I do?" He looked up at her in confusion.

"Torrian, he is the perfect height for you. I want you to place your arm on his back so that he will support you while you walk."

Torrian gingerly placed his hand on Growley's back, and started to pet him. "Like this?"

"Aye, almost. You can pet him anytime, though, this is different. Come a wee bit closer to his head. I want you to place your hand near his neck. When you give Growley his command, he will start to walk with you. If you feel yourself falling, grab hold of the fur around his neck."

"But if I do that, I will hurt him and he will bite me, will he no'?"

"Nay, Mungo and I have both trained him. 'Tis how mama dogs pick up their pups, by the fur on their neck. 'Tis verra thick and willnae hurt him. Try it."

Torrian played with the fur on the dog's neck for a bit before he attempted a slight tug. Growley never budged. He turned to her with a big grin. "You are right. He did no' mind. How do I tell him to walk?"

"Place your hand near his neck and say, 'Go, Growley.' When you want him to stop, say, 'Stop.' Try it and see."

"Will you go with us to catch me if I fall?"

"Aye, but you willnae need me. Growley will take care of you." She nodded her head in encouragement, hoping the lad would try on his own. Mungo had worked with the dog for many hours, and she was confident the two would make a great pair.

Torrian held onto the dog's neck. Brenna stepped slightly back and when the boy glanced at her, she nodded. "Go ahead, Torrian. He will help you. He is verra gentle."

The boy looked around, as if searching for something, when he saw his grandmother standing nearby. He smiled, hung on, and said, "Go, Growley." Brenna could tell Lady Ramsay was holding her breath as she waited. Every eye in the great hall was on the wee lad and the big deerhound that was almost twice his size.

The dog took a few steps, Brenna following along at his side helping to set the pace. Torrian's face lit up as he walked. Every time he started to fall, he grabbed onto Growley's neck and righted himself. It wasn't long before the two made it over to Lady Ramsay, Brenna still by their side.

When they arrived, Brenna knelt in front of the hound, ruffled his ears and said, "Good dog, Growley."

Wrapping his arms around Growley, Torrian announced, "I love my new pet."

Brenna stood and smiled at Lady Ramsay.

"See, Grandmama, I can walk by myself now," the boy said. "I want to go back now. May I try again, Lady Brenna?"

Brenna was showing him how to get the dog to turn when Quade strode in the front door and halted at the bottom of the stairs.

Torrian yelled in delight. "Papa, watch me walk." He grabbed hold of his pet's thick fur and said, "Go, Growley."

The dog led him over to Quade. Torrian only faltered twice, but the hound kept him on his feet both times. Somehow, the creature knew just when to slow down and when to speed up. Brenna beamed as she watched the pride on Quade's face. Tears streamed down Lady Ramsay's cheeks as she took in the scene, too. Then she wrapped Brenna in her arms and said,

"You are such a blessing. Thank the Lord you came to us."

Quade's gaze caught Brenna's and the expression on his face almost caused her to tear up. But she was too happy to see the young lad and his new friend together to cry. When he made it over to his papa, Quade picked him up with a whoop and swung him in a circle.

Lily ran over and shouted, "Me, too, Papa! Me, too!"

A few days later, Brenna decided to take Torrian and Growley outside with her while she picked herbs from the garden. It was time for him to practice on uneven surfaces instead of the flat stone floor in the hall.

She filled her basket with her pickings while she kept an eye on Torrian. Getting down on her hands and knees, she tugged at a particularly deep clump of mint. She watched as the lad and his pet maneuvered around a group of trees until they were out of sight. She wasn't concerned, though, since she could hear them even if she couldn't see them. Torrian chattered non-stop to his new pet and Growley was a wonderful listener. Poor lad hadn't had many friends to talk to besides Margaret and Ennis for a long time.

A voice interrupted Torrian's chatter. "There you are, you fraud. Who do you think you are, pretending to be the laird's son? He died years ago."

Brenna stood up as soon as she heard Growley's low growl. The dog continued to issue his threat while she made her way to the group of trees.

"I am the only one who will be a mother to the laird's son. You are a phony and I will teach you not to lie anymore."

As she rounded the trees, she heard a scream, followed by a fierce bark. She smiled when she took in the scene in front of her. Torrian was sitting safely on the ground while Growley had Iona pinned to a tree, growling at her with bared teeth.

"Call him off, witch! He will kill me. Call this mad dog away from me!"

Brenna couldn't stifle her laugh as she looked at Torrian. "I guess we ken why he is called Growley, do we no'?"

CHAPTER TWENTY-ONE

A sennight and a half passed and excitement for the upcoming wedding grew each day at the Ramsay keep. Word had reached them that the Grant contingent would arrive within the planned timeline. Brenna and Quade sat in the great hall breaking their fast with Lily and Torrian when one of Quade's best guards, Seamus, barreled in the front door shouting for Quade.

"Chief, the Grants have been sighted a few hours away. Should be here by midday. Any special instructions?" The large hulk of a man stood in front of his laird, awaiting his orders. Micheil strode into the keep, chuckling as he came down the stairs into the great hall.

"Something amusing, Micheil?" Quade stared at his brother, an eyebrow arched in question.

"Aye, Lady Brenna said her brother fussed over his wife, but never have I seen such a contraption before."

Brenna's eyes lit up. "Och, my brother's wife is carrying. I can imagine he wouldnae allow her to ride a horse and has her plumped up on pillows. Am I correct, Micheil?"

Seamus guffawed and slapped his knee. "There are about two hundred guards spread in a circle around two wagons. But he has his wife on so many mounds of fluff to pad her ride that her head is almost above his own on the horse. 'Tis a sight to see. His sister and an old maid ride with her."

Brenna sprang out of her seat and clapped her hands in joy. "Aye, Maddie brought Jennie and Alice. I cannae wait to see them. I will get ready to ride out to greet them."

"Whoa, love of my life." Quade shot from his chair as fast as his betrothed.

"Aye, what is it?" she said, turning to look at him. "I would like to greet my family."

Quade wrapped his arms around her waist and pulled her to him. "I ken you do and you willnae like what I have to say, but do you ken how many strangers are outside the keep? We invited many guests to the wedding. Tents are scattered all over the meadow and not just for guests. Others have come to sell their wares even though they willnae attend the wedding. 'Tis no' safe for the laird's betrothed to chase across a meadow. Your family will be here in a few hours. I do no' want you riding your horse out to greet them."

"Are you telling me I am a prisoner in your keep?" Brenna's stare was all challenge.

"Nay, you ken 'tis no' what I meant, and 'tis *our* keep. Your safety is paramount to me. 'Tis no' wise for you to go outside unescorted."

"Well then, escort me, please." Her hands fisted on her hips as she awaited his response.

He kissed her cheek. "I would love to, but I need to check the surrounding area with my guards to make sure of your family's safe passage. 'Tis important there are no reivers or troublemakers of any kind in hiding. I willnae do a good job canvassing my lands if I have to worry about my betrothed. Will you do me this favor and wait until they arrive?"

He watched the thoughts dance through her quick mind. She had to realize he would not risk her life for any reason. After all he had been through, losing her would tear his insides out in a flash. He gazed into her eyes in the hopes she could read his thoughts without him having to vocalize them in front of his children. Her gaze softened a touch. For a moment, he thought he had her, but then the telltale gleam returned.

She wrapped her arms around his neck and kissed his cheek. "All right, I will follow your instructions. But if you will pardon me, I have much to do before they arrive. I must check the chambers. Aggie and Margaret can tend to the wee ones while I settle everything upstairs."

He waited until she was out of hearing before the three of them headed for the doorway. "Seamus, stand outside the gate with five guards and go with her when she leaves. Micheil and I will canvas with the rest of the guards."

Micheil grinned as he nodded toward the stairway. "You do no' think she will follow your instructions?"

"Nay. She is a stubborn lass. When she sets her mind to something, you cannae change it. Better for me to accept her as she is and adjust accordingly. Take care of her, Seamus. I willnae lose this wife." The trio stepped outside and headed for the stables.

Micheil slapped his brother on the back. "Wise lad. I was worried she would outsmart you, but you will make a good pair. By my sword, this will be an entertaining match."

Seamus bellowed out his agreement.

Brenna found a pair of trews she had borrowed from the stable lad. If she was going to ride fast, she had to get rid of her skirts. Her father had never minded because he'd considered it safer for a lass to ride in trews. Her mother had finally agreed after her father had explained all the various ways Brenna's skirt could get caught while she was riding.

She felt a trifle guilty for not doing as her husband-to-be wished, but she had found a way to justify her actions. She had promised to follow his instructions, and she would—she would find an escort.

As she rounded the corner of the barn at the stable, she stopped short. The lad stood there with her horse saddled and ready to go. Her eyes narrowed as she searched the area for her betrothed.

The lad helped her mount. "Thank you. I was surprised to see you had saddled my horse," she said. She had to find out why he'd prepared her horse for travel. Somehow, she didn't believe this was an instance of where her husband went, she would follow.

"Aye, my lady. Seamus awaits you outside the gate." He grinned innocently.

Saints above, she hoped Quade wasn't with him. She really did want him to canvas the area. If anything happened to her family because of her impatience, she would never forgive herself. She moved at a slow canter until she was just outside the gate. Seamus was waiting there with a smile on his face. Donald, Ennis and two other lads were with him, but not Quade. She let out a sigh of relief. She was sure she would have hell to pay later. First, she needed to see Jennie.

As she passed Seamus, she yelled, "See if you can keep up with me."

She let her horse set the pace, loving the feel of the wind in her hair. No matter how she tried to keep her hair back, the pins always fell out when she rode. She swung her head back and forth to release them all, reveling in the feeling. After all, her brothers were used to seeing her ride with her hair free. Alex wouldn't mind.

A few minutes later, Seamus slowed and barked an order for her to do the same. He pointed to the forest to their right and sent two of his men into the trees to investigate a strange reflection from the sun. The other riders closed in around her until the lads in the forest gave Seamus the all-clear sign.

As soon as they moved away to give her more space,

a sharp pain ricocheted through her right leg. Her horse bucked at the sudden change in his rider. She grabbed the reins, trying desperately to hang on as the horse ran wild. When she leaned over to grab his mane, she caught sight of the river of blood trailing down her leg. Seamus roared as her guards' horses attempted to surround her, but they couldn't get close enough to grab the reins.

Brenna watched the scenery fly by at a pace she had never experienced before. Sharp pain radiated up her leg in a delayed reaction, and when she instinctively put her hand to the wound, she felt an arrow protruding from her upper calf. Wrenching it free, she stared at it blankly while her other hand clutched her horse's mane in a death grip. Her vision blurred and her grip started to loosen just as she felt an arm lift her and slam her onto another horse.

Fighting to remain conscious, she turned her head to see Ennis holding her.

"I've got you, my lady. You are safe. I'm going to bring you back to the keep."

They traveled in a semi-circle and took off at a furious gallop, the four other horses surrounding them.

The last thing she heard was her betrothed's battle cry.

She was in deep trouble now. This was all her fault.

CHAPTER TWENTY-TWO

Quade had just finished canvassing the area with his guards and was riding beside Laird Alexander Grant when he saw Brenna heading toward them, surrounded by his guards. He'd known she wouldn't be able to stay away. At least he had checked the area first.

Alex glanced at him from the corner of his eye. "Would that be my sister in trews heading toward us?"

"Aye," Quade said with a smile. "She's a beauty on her horse, is she no'?"

"You allowed her out with all the strangers in the area?" Alex quirked an eyebrow at him.

"Nay, I told her to stay put. But I ken how stubborn she is, so I left five guards to follow her if she left."

"Aye, this marriage may work quite well, Ramsay. 'Twill be a challenge to stay a step ahead of my sister, but mayhap you are the one to do it."

The next second, Quade's world shattered. He watched, helpless, as her horse bucked and she almost fell off the animal. She grabbed the beast's mane and hung on as her horse ran wild.

He shouted his battle cry to pull in all his guards. The Grant bellowed next to him, too, and all his guards surrounded the Grant women in the center of the procession. Quade took off in a fury toward her, praying she could hang on until he reached her.

"Brenna, do no' let go. I will get you. Hang on, do

you hear me? Hang on!"

Everything flashed in front of his eyes as he watched her cling for life on the back of the wild horse. Did this mean he was cursed after all? Well, that did not matter. He would not lose her now. Under no circumstance would he lose this woman who had given hope and meaning to his life again.

He had almost reached her when she started to slip. Just in time, Ennis pulled up beside her and hoisted her onto his horse. Quade signaled for Ennis to return her to the keep and ordered Micheil to have his guards search the area.

They had almost reached the gate to the keep when he pulled up alongside Ennis and reached for her. When his guard handed her over, Quade held her so tight, she probably couldn't breathe. He pinned her against his chest with one arm, her head tilted to the side. She had not responded to him. Dark red blood ran down her leg. They crossed the bridge and the whole keep bore witness to his agony.

"Brenna, open your eyes, love. Please. You cannae leave me. Do you hear me? You willnae leave me." When he reached the stables, a guard reached for her.

"Nay, support me when I drop," he ordered. "I willnae let go of her." He dismounted, stumbled a bit, but righted himself and tore to the keep.

"Find Lady Ramsay. And someone bring Gunna to the hall," he barked as he entered the keep, bolting up the stairs two at a time. She still had not opened her eyes. When he arrived at her chamber, he sat in a chair by the hearth and held her there.

"Brenna, please. Open your eyes." His hands trembled as he caressed her back. He looked down and realized she still had a piece of an arrow clutched in her hand.

Shot by an arrow? Who in blazes would want to hurt his wife? Had they been trying to kill her, or were they after him? But they couldn't have wanted to kill him.

He hadn't been anywhere near.

He rocked her slowly on his lap. The maids came in with water and his mother followed close behind.

"Quade? What happened? Is she still alive? My heavens, this cannae be!"

Brenna's eyes cracked open for a second then closed. "Brenna? Please open your eyes for me." He cupped her cheek and kissed her forehead.

Her eyes fluttered open again and she stared at him. "What happened? Quade? What happened? Did I fall off the horse? The arrow. Someone shot my leg. 'Tis hurting. Quade, I am sorry. I shouldnae have gone out. You were right. Who would do this to me? I do no' understand."

Quade grinned when she started talking again. He kissed her brow and both eyelids. "You are all right? Hellfire, you scared me, lass. Do no' ever do that to me again. Do you hear me? You frightened the life out of me. Are you hurt anywhere else besides your leg?"

He ran his hands up and down her body until he found the wet stickiness of her wound.

His mother stood beside the bed. The maids had brought in the tub and were filling it with steaming water. "Quade, we need to clean her up," Lady Ramsay said. "There is blood all over. We must to see to her injuries. Gunna is on her way, hopefully."

Brenna attempted to sit. "Nay, 'tis just my leg. Who would shoot an arrow at me?"

"Quade, get out. We need to undress her and wash the blood away." His mother stood at his side, plucking at the trews on Brenna's waist.

"I am staying, Mother. She is to be my wife tomorrow. I'll hold her while you get her clothes off. You cannae lower her into the tub and she cannae walk. I willnae allow another lad in to hold her. No one else but Gunna is to enter the room."

"Lady Brenna, is this acceptable to you?" his mother asked. "Who do you want to tend you?"

The maids stood just inside the door, awaiting instructions.

"I am no' leaving," Quade barked again. "You may stay, Mother, to help me. Everyone else out. One of you wait outside the door to fetch healing supplies. Someone make sure that Margaret and Aggie are tending the bairns. They will be upset when they hear what happened. And knock when Gunna arrives."

Brenna nodded. "Bring me a clean shift and I will put that on." Lady Ramsay located a shift while Quade peeled off her trews. Blood trickled down his hand as soon as he pulled the cloth away from the wound.

His mother helped her with the rest of her clothes. He had sworn it would kill him if he had to wait until they married to see her beautiful body, but this was not how he'd envisioned it. He succumbed to her dignity and turned his head while his mother pulled the clean shift over her head. Then he lowered her into the steaming tub so they could assess her wound.

Quade's head spun a wee bit when the water in the tub turned pink from all the blood. He sat on a stool on the side and helped her wash her leg. He was so grateful she was here and able to talk to him.

"Tell me what you need me to do, Brenna. How can I help?"

"Where is the arrow that was in my leg? Did anyone see it?"

"You still had it in your hand when I brought you up here. You must have pulled it out yourself."

Brenna's head leaned back against the side of the tub, and she closed her eyes. "Was the tip on it? You ken why I am asking, aye?"

Quade's heart sunk into his belly. Hellfire, he hadn't thought of that. "Mother, I think we dropped it over there."

His mother located what was left of the arrow and brought it over. "No tip, lass. Why? What does that mean?" She glanced from Brenna to Quade.

"'Tis still in her leg. We will need to pull it out."

His mother's eyes widened. "Och, who? I couldnae do that! In fact, I am getting a bit dizzy just from looking at all the blood in the water."

"Lady Ramsay, why do you no' find my family and advise them I am fine. We can manage." Brenna's hand clutched Quade's each time a new wave of pain struck her.

"All right. I will be back in a wee bit. I think I need to sit down for a time." Lady Ramsay opened the door and stepped out, but then returned with a stack of clean linen strips. "You will need these when you finish." She set them on the chest and departed.

As soon as his mother left, Quade stood up. "I will find someone to pull out the arrow tip." He opened the door and stuck his head out, hoping to see Gunna, but she was nowhere in sight.

"Quade?"

He turned back to her at the door. "Aye?"

"I would like you to do it. Do no' run from me. I am no' going anywhere. I just have a small injury. I willnae desert you or leave you alone, but I would prefer for you to remove the tip. I do no' want another to touch my leg. I trust you."

Sweat gathered across his brow as he thought of what she asked him to do. Aye, he hated being around illness and stayed away whenever possible, particularly when the person in pain was someone he loved. Was she right? Was it because he was afraid of losing her?

"I would be happy to accommodate you, lass, but I do no' ken if I am able. Would you like me to get one of your kin?"

Her brothers had obviously arrived, and Alex was barking somewhere outside the door. "Alex, I am fine," she yelled, "but stay out, please. I am no' presentable." Turning to Quade, she said, "Nay, I do no' want my brothers here when I am in my shift. My sister-in-law is carrying and Jennie is too young yet. Will you please try? I will guide you. I would do it myself but 'tis toward the back of my leg and I do no' think I would be at the proper angle."

Quade nodded his head and made his way back to the tub. He gazed at the love of his life as he listened to her calm and composed instructions for removing the arrow tip from her tender flesh. He would have to insert his finger into her soft skin, probe for the piece of arrow, and yank it out. He did no' think he could do it. He sat on the stool next to the tub and stared at his betrothed.

"If I do no' do this, what will happen?" he whispered.

"Probably my leg will swell and I will get the fever. If 'tis still in me, 'twill no' be good."

"Could you die from it?"

"'Tis possible. Or I could lose my leg. 'Twould keep me from losing my life if someone amputated my leg."

All was quiet in the room as Quade thought on it.

"If I lose my leg, I will release you from the betrothal." Brenna stared at the water.

"What?" He couldn't believe he had heard her correctly.

"A laird shouldnae have a cripple for a wife. 'Twould no' be right. Besides, 'twas my fault this happened. I did no' follow your instructions. I was bull-headed. I cannae seem to remember I am marrying the laird." Tears gathered at her lashes, and her hand swiped at them as she fought to stay in control. She had always been the strong one for him, and he didn't like to see her this way. Defeated.

He grabbed a towel and set it on the side of the tub. His anger grew as he puttered. "Do no' ever talk like that again." His voice increased an octave. "You will marry me. You promised or have you already forgotten? You will be my wife, and you willnae be crippled. And 'twas no' your fault that some daft person shot you with an arrow." His bellow shook the rafters.

Dead silence settled between them as he lowered his face to hers. "Tell me what to do," he whispered. "I will do it."

She took his hand and held it next to the wound. "You need to insert your finger and see if you can feel the tip."

He positioned himself as best he could and said, "Tell me when you are ready."

She gripped both sides of the tub and nodded. "Go ahead."

As soon as he touched her wound, her entire body tensed. He could see it in her jaw, in her eyes, in the white knuckles on the side of the tub. He plunged ahead. He would do this for her; there was no way he would allow her to die. He hit something hard right away.

She hissed as soon as he touched it. "That's it. Can you get it, Quade? I usually ken when I see the patient writhe in pain. It hurts so much more when you touch it. 'Tis the tip, I ken it."

He pushed in a little further, forcing himself to ignore her gasp. Probing a bit more, he managed to slip his finger behind the tip and carefully pull it out. He refused to look at her as he worked, knowing that he would not be able to continue if he saw how much pain she was in. As soon as the tip landed on the floor, she shouted in relief. He put his hands under her arms and lifted her out of the tub, holding her close to him. He didn't want to let her go. He knew he was dripping water all over the floor, but it didn't bother him. He wouldn't let her go.

He didn't want her to see the tears in his eyes.

❧ ❧ ❧

'Twas the midday meal and Brenna was happy to be seated at the dais with all her family. After everyone got past the hugging and the crying over her injury, they spent at least an hour reminiscing while they ate. Jennie and Avelina got along wonderfully, and just as she'd suspected, Lily spent most of the time on Alex's lap. Madeline was as beautiful and regal as always, and her belly was nicely rounded. Alice fussed over her terribly and loved every minute of it. The twins were presently running circles around their uncles, Brodie and Robbie, and Micheil. After being on a horse for so long, they had an abundance of energy to burn off. Torrian and Growley walked the outside of the hall, trying to keep track of the twins but keeping a safe distance from the melee.

After the meal, the topic of her injury was finally broached.

Alex was the one who first brought it up. "Who is your primary suspect as the archer, Ramsay?"

"We have naught at the moment. Seamus thought he saw something in the woods before it happened. He sent two men to check, but they turned up naught. A moment later, the arrow came from that same spot."

"Did they ken enough to check the trees?" Brodie asked.

"Aye, my lads checked the trees." Quade held his betrothed's hand in his as he spoke.

Brenna knew how much of a fright the whole incident had given Quade, and she was sorry for it. He had held one wife in his arms while she died and he wasn't about to let the same thing happen with her. He hadn't left her side since the incident.

Alex directed his next question to her. "Lass, do you ken anyone who would want to hurt you?" He turned to Quade. "And I have to ask you if there is someone in your clan that would have been particularly upset about your betrothal to my sister?"

Brenna glanced at Quade before she answered. "Aye, there is one person."

"Lass, I do no' think it could have been Iona," Quade said. "She cannae shoot arrows. She has never worked a day in her life. She has nae skills."

Alex spoke up. "And who would Iona be?"

"Iona is the only one who has been blatantly nasty to me. She threatened Torrian and me and tried to convince many of his clan that I was a witch. She has also threatened Lily."

"Aye, true. But she did no' get verra far. No one believed her. She is no' capable of shooting you, so she would have needed to find someone to do it for her." Quade squeezed her hand. "I am sorry, love, but I do no' think she would attempt to kill someone. She is jealous, aye. But a murderer? I do no' believe it. The arrow traveled a good distance. 'Twould have to be from a man's bow."

Lily leaned over to whisper something in Alex's ear. His face contorted instantly and he turned to her. "You come to me if it happens again, Lily, if your papa is no' around to protect you."

"What are you telling the laird, Lily?" Quade asked.

"Papa, I do no' like Iona. She tried to hit me. Lady Brenna stopped her before you came. She is mean." Her head dropped as everyone around them quieted. Her last statement came out in a whisper. "I do no' like her."

"I think we need to look elsewhere and consider other possibilities," Quade said. "There are so many strangers around for the wedding. I have my men out asking questions and canvassing the area for any clues. That arrow could have been meant for any of my men. We have to consider all the possibilities." Quade kissed her forehead. "You look tired, sweetness. Would you like to rest for a bit? Mayhap Lily would go with you while I talk to your brothers."

Brenna nodded her head and decided it was probably a good idea. She was exhausted. Quade carried her up to her room with Jennie, Avelina, Lily, Alice, and Maddie right behind him. They all gathered around her on the bed, asking what they could do for her.

She didn't have any idea what she needed, so she closed her eyes while still holding Lily and Jennie's hands. There was only one thing on her mind.

Tomorrow was her wedding day.

CHAPTER TWENTY-THREE

Brenna stood just outside the chapel and peered up at her brother, wondering if this was all real. The weather had turned out glorious. Aggie and her sister had sewn the most beautiful dress for her. Running her trembling hands down the full skirt, she felt every bit the princess she had once dreamed of being as a little girl. The blue velvet hugged her curves, and the gold bell sleeves and the gold threading gave the dress a regal appearance that had taken her completely by surprise. She was still coming to terms with the fact that she was actually taking this step away from her family and her clan. She fought tears as she stared at Alex, the laird of the Highlands with the fierce reputation and the soft heart, and felt proud to be his sister.

"Are you ready, lass? Tell me this is what you want before you walk down the aisle."

"Aye, Alex. I love him so. He has had a verra difficult life, but I am hoping things will improve for us." She stepped on her tip-toes to kiss his cheek. "Thank you for worrying about me, but he will make me verra happy. And I love his bairns as well."

"I couldnae believe how improved they both are, Brenna. You are truly gifted."

Alex stepped through the doorway with Brenna limping at his side. "I still think I should carry you to the Ramsay. Your injury pains you. What difference does it make if you actually walk with me? 'Twas Maddie who convinced me to leave you to make your own steps."

She squeezed her brother's hand to thank him for allowing her to walk beside him. Her wound had healed much, but not completely. Still, she had to be part of her own wedding, did she not?

As soon as they stepped inside the doorway to the chapel, Torrian joined them with Growley, his face beaming. Quade rushed down the aisle and stopped directly in front of them. Brenna couldn't take her eyes off her handsome fiancé in full dress. His blue and black plaid contrasted with the Grant red plaid, which was beautiful in its own right. He shook Alex's hand and said, "My thanks, but I will assist my bride the rest of the way." He promptly scooped Brenna up in his arms and carried her to the altar, where Father MacGregor stood waiting.

After Quade put her down, Brenna took a moment to smile at her loved ones, who were gathered throughout the church. Glancing over Quade's shoulder, she beamed at a very proud Torrian, who was dressed exactly like his papa, Growley by his side. Micheil waited at the front next to Father MacGregor, accompanied by Lily in her pastel blue dress. Lady Ramsay was there, too, wiping tears from her face. It was a large gathering at the front of the church, but a joyous one.

Micheil leaned over before Father MacGregor started. "Just couldnae wait to get your hands on her? Or were you afraid she would turn and run?"

The officiant chuckled and Brenna beamed at her favorite priest. She had been shocked and pleased to learn that Quade had located him for their wedding. He had married Alex and Maddie and she had so hoped he would be available.

Father MacGregor began the service by taking Quade's plaid and wrapping it over both of their wrists. Brenna gazed at Quade the whole time, still unable to believe she was actually marrying him. One glance was all it took to set her heart aflutter, especially when he stood in his full clan dress. He finally realized she was staring at him and flashed her that boyish grin she so loved.

When the ceremony came to an end, Quade carried her outside and set her on his horse. He mounted behind her, to the cheers of the crowd, and cantered in the courtyard a wee bit before bringing her to the great hall. After what had happened, he had told her he would not risk taking her outside the keep walls.

He stood on the stone steps to his keep and held her hand high for all to see. "Welcome my wife, Lady Brenna Ramsay." She blushed at the cheers and applause that came from the gathered crowd. In keeping with tradition, his guards lined up to swear fealty to her. Quade brought a chair for her to sit in due to her injury and sent the wee ones inside for the duration of the ceremony.

Almost an hour passed before they finished. When the last guard stood, another cheer went up from the crowd. Quade helped his wife to stand, but a strange hush descended on the gatherers.

Brenna whispered to her husband, "Quade, what is happening? I thought the guards were finished swearing fealty."

"Hush, sweetness. I do no' ken what is happening. I will check." He nodded to Micheil, who entered the crowd with two guards behind him and worked his way to the back of the group. A few minutes later, the crowd parted again, and Micheil and his guards marched back toward their laird, followed by a lone lad in full Ramsay plaid. Whispers were exchanged fast and furious among the group as they made their way to the front.

Micheil had a smug look when he showed the loner up the steps to his laird. The lad stopped in front of them, placed his sword on the ground in front of Brenna, and knelt. After a lengthy pause, he finally spoke loud enough for all to hear. "I, Logan Ramsay, vow to lay my life for you, Lady Brenna Grant Ramsay, for the rest of my days. I will guard your life as if it were my own. I am, now, and forever will be, grateful for all you have done for my clan and my family, especially my brother and his bairns."

Brenna peered up at her husband, tears in her eyes, as Logan swore fealty to his laird again. When he was done, the brothers embraced and the crowd cheered wildly. After a long moment, Logan broke away and turned to her. He reached inside a sack, pulled out a familiar book and handed it to her. "My lady, I believe this belongs to you. My pardon for taking it without your permission." He winked at her. "I owe you a favor for my transgression."

Tears flowed freely down her cheeks as Brenna stared at her mother's book. She caressed the pages carefully. She looked up at Logan. "Thank you for taking such good care of my treasure."

Quade put his arm around her and assisted her inside the great hall. Logan stood at the top of the steps with them, searching the group that had already gathered inside. As soon as they entered, Torrian yelled, "Uncle Logan!"

Logan was about to rush toward Torrian, but Quade pulled him back. "Allow him to come to you."

"He can walk again?" Logan whispered, his eyes wide.

Quade nodded but never took his eyes off his son. "Aye. With help."

"Watch me, Uncle Logan! I can walk. Lady Brenna gave me Growley and he helps me walk."

The entire crowd turned to watch as Torrian made his way over to his uncle with the deerhound, only stumbling once.

"Your idea, my lady?" Logan asked Brenna.

She nodded. "Aye, with Mungo's assistance. And Growley is wonderful with him."

When he made it to his uncle's side, Torrian was promptly scooped up by Logan and set on his shoulders with a Ramsay war whoop that made Brenna cover her ears. Hanging onto his nephew, Logan leaned over and kissed Brenna's cheek. "Well done."

Due to the size of the crowd, a feast table sat in the middle of the courtyard as well as inside the great hall. Pheasant, fish, boar meat, and duck graced both tables. Meatpies were plentiful along with various apple confections and pear tarts. A roasted pig sat on the table inside for the wedding party. Ale and mead flowed freely both inside and out. Guests brought little cakes and stacked them on tables as gifts for the couple.

The marriage contract was signed inside the solar, then the bride and groom rejoined the gathering.

As soon as Quade and Brenna stepped back into the hall, Lily ran up to Brenna and tugged on her skirt. "Lady Brenna, may I have some pear tart or a pastry cake. Please?"

Leaving Quade with his brother, Brenna took her by the hand and walked back into the kitchens, "Nay, you cannae have the pastry or the tarts, Lily, but Cook has fashioned something special for you."

"Aye?" Lily scampered over to Cook's side. "What did you make for me, Cook? Is there enough for Torrian?"

Cook brushed the flour from her hands onto her apron. "Och, wee one. I think you will like this."

Lily's eyes lit up as she grinned at the head of the kitchens. "What is it? What did you make me?"

Cook helped Lily up on a tall stool and set her sweet delicacy in front of her. "I cut up your apples and pears, then covered it with a mixture of sugar and oats with a touch of spice and baked it just for you. You take a test and let me ken what you think." Cook gave her a spoon.

Lily took a small taste and squealed. "Cook, 'tis so good. I cannae wait to share this with Torrian."

Cook beamed. "I am glad you like it, lass. But I have a separate one for Torrian. You tell the lad to come get his when he is ready."

Lily ate a few more bites, and then climbed off the stool. "Cook, will you save it for me? I want to tell Papa and Torrian."

"Aye, wee one. Go have your fun. I will save it for you." Cook chuckled.

Lily headed for the door, but Brenna stopped her. "Lily? Did you forget your manners?"

The wee lass stopped, turned around, and curtsied. "Forgive me, Lady Brenna. Thank you, Cook, for my special treat."

"That's a good lass," Brenna said as Lily spun around and ran into the hall.

Quade greeted her as soon as she stepped outside the kitchens. "How is your leg, love?"

"'Tis a bit sore. I think I should like to sit for a bit, if you do no' mind."

He kissed her cheek. "Naught would please me more." He helped her to the dais, and sat next to her. "Shall I get a plate of food for us?"

Before he was able to move, Logan set a full plate down in front of them. "Thought you might need something to eat in order to make it through the night's festivities." He winked at Brenna.

Brenna blushed straight to her toes. She was excited about the day's activities, but dreaded the bedding ceremony. How could one small tradition make her so nervous?

Quade glared at his brother. "My thanks, brother. I think that wench in the corner has her eyes on you."

Logan grinned and sailed off in her direction.

"Forgive my brother's crudeness. He likes to have his fun. Did you check your book? He did no' ruin it?"

"Nay, 'tis in perfect shape. Did he tell you why he took it?" Brenna searched his face as she awaited an answer. What a fine-looking lad she married. She hated to be caught just staring at Quade, but she couldnae stop herself.

"Nay, we will find out someday. Let's no' worry today, just enjoy the festivities."

"Aye, I am grateful to have it back."

Lady Ramsay came to the table with Lily and Torrian. Quade's mother fussed over her grandchildren. She had told Brenna several times how happy she was to have her as a daughter-in-law, and she all but beamed as she sat at the table. The rest of their family slowly made their way to the dais.

"It has been a long time since I have seen my family so happy," Lady Ramsay said, picking up the linen square she had been keeping for all the tears that had been spent that day.

Avelina kissed her cheek. "Mama, please stop your crying and be happy. 'Tis a wedding." She wrapped her arm around her mother's shoulder. "You have cried so much since Lady Brenna arrived, 'tis time to stop now."

"I ken. You are right, daughter. I will try to stop. I am too emotional."

Brenna ate until she was stuffed. Quade gave her more than she could manage. The minstrels and musicians began their songs, hoping to get the crowd dancing.

A loud voice interrupted them as a lad made his way over to Alex Grant. "Laird, I would like permission to dance with your youngest sister." The young lad stared at his toes as he stood in front of Alex Grant.

"Nay!" Alex's bellow shook the rafters and the lad

scurried away with a sheepish glance at Jennie.

"Alex, how can I enjoy myself if you bark at everyone?" Jennie was close to tears as she looked back and forth between him and her other brothers, Robbie and Brodie. "There must be someone I can dance with besides my own brothers. I am no' a bairn anymore."

Brenna elbowed Quade at the dais to be sure he was watching the show her brother was putting on for all to see.

"Your brother is jesting?" Quade peered at her.

"Nay, he loves to scare off all the lads. He did the same for me. No one dared to come near me."

He kissed her cheek. "Och, I will be sure and thank him. Otherwise, you may have swooned for another and I want you for myself."

She swatted his arm affectionately. "I was never interested in another. It does not mean he has to spoil the special night for her. 'Tis her only sister's wedding." She squeezed his hand before yelling at her brother. "Alex!"

Alex made his way over to her with narrowed eyes. "'Tis only due to your injury and your wedding that I answer your beck and call."

Madeline followed her husband and took the seat beside Brenna's. "Alex, love, you need to ease up and allow your sister to dance a wee bit. There must be someone she could dance with this night."

Alex scanned the room. "Nay, 'tis no one."

Jennie's face fell and her arms dropped to her sides, her lids blinking back tears.

"There is one solution I can propose. Why do you not dance with your sister?" Madeline gave her husband her sweetest smile.

Brenna stifled her laughter as she glanced at her husband, who choked on his ale. Logan stood a few steps away grinning, and Brenna's other brothers were laughing so hard they started to choke. Avelina came over when she noticed the sudden family grouping.

"'Tis impossible, wife, and you ken that. I do no' dance."

"Alex, I know it is not your favorite thing to do, but you are quite capable. Sorry, Jennie, but if he dances, it will be with me." Maddie smiled at her husband. "Besides, if I carry a wee lass and we dance, it will be like rocking her to sleep." Brenna noticed how quickly he softened his demeanor. Apparently, his feelings for his wee wife had not diminished one bit.

Quade spoke up. "May I make a suggestion?" He gave Logan a pointed glance.

Alex barked. "Aye, please!"

"I do no' want any randy lads dancing with my sister either." Avelina's face fell, as though she were imagining an evening empty of dances.

Logan broke through the gathering and held his hand out to Jennie. "Would you care to dance, my lady?" He gave her his best courtly bow.

The girl's face beamed as she waited for her brother's approval.

Quade interrupted. "Seems like a perfect solution to me, Alex. I have two brothers to dance with Jennie and you have two brothers who can take turns dancing with Avelina. It should suit everyone."

Alex searched the group of faces before giving a gruff, "Aye."

His wife stood up from her chair, and stood on her tiptoes to kiss his cheek. "Very wise decision, dearest. Now would you care to escort your wife for one dance?"

Brenna squeezed Quade's arm as her brother's chest puffed out a wee bit more, if that were possible. "I so enjoy watching my brother tamed by a wee lass. He would do anything for Maddie."

The floor filled with dancers, and even Avelina and Jennie seemed to enjoy dancing with their partners. All the lasses at the gathering loved Logan, however, which took the attention off the newly married couple at times. Brenna did not mind at all.

As they sat at the dais, Quade entwined his fingers with hers before running a trail of kisses up her wrist, causing her to shiver. A gleam entered her husband's eye. "Cold, lass?"

"Nay, and you ken it. 'Tis your touch." She blushed and turned away to watch the revelry.

"Och, you always smell like lavender. 'Tis your scent to me now."

"Aye, I like lavender oil in my bath."

"I can tell. Are you happy, lass? I am sorry you cannae dance with your injury."

She leaned her head on his shoulder. "Never happier. 'Tis nice to have my family here with yours. Jennie and Avelina have become fast friends. 'Tis fun just to watch everyone enjoy themselves. Torrian and Lily are having the time of their lives." She noticed the two were presently dancing in a circle around Growley. The dog, patient as ever, stayed still while Torrian hung on to him.

"Aye, they are, thanks to your healing powers."

"'Tis so nice to see them grow. You have raised two strong bairns, my laird."

"I hope you are right and they continue to improve."

"As long as everyone helps them follow their diet, they will be fine. They are children, so it's inevitable that they will someday try something they shouldn't, but they will learn the hard way."

Quade dropped her hand and wrapped his arm over her shoulder, kissing her forehead. "Are you nervous, lass?"

She peeked up at him. "Aye... Nay."

He chuckled.

"I will take that as an 'aye.'"

"Aye, because of the unknown. I have delivered bairns, so I ken what happens, but it has never happened to me before. Nay, because I trust you, and every time you touch me, I melt. I have faith in us,

Quade."

"You ken I cannae wait to get you upstairs to our chamber. Do you wish to ready yourself first or will you give me the pleasure of carrying you up the stairs myself?"

"I would prefer to go with you. I admit I am afraid of the bedding ceremony." She whispered so as not to be overheard discussing such an embarrassing topic.

"You have three strong brothers here. My guess is they willnae allow it. But I will instruct my guards to protect the staircase if you wish." He ran his hand down through her thick brown curls, stopping to caress her neck.

"Nay, I am too embarrassed to ask my brothers. Will you ask the guards when I am no' next to you?"

"Och, I have the perfect solution, and I will need to speak to only one. Can you handle one person?"

She nodded, but still could not bring herself to look at the crowd while they discussed such a humiliating topic.

Quade gave a short whistle. Logan flew over. "Aye, my laird?"

"Nae bedding ceremony. I need you to keep them all down here."

"Och, are you daft, Quade? They'll run me down. Besides, you will be taking all our entertainment away."

"As your laird, I am telling you to stand guard at the stairs. As your brother, I am asking you to do a favor for your new sister-in-law. My wife does no' need all these lads pawing at her injured leg. She has three verra large brothers who would be glad to assist you, I am sure. Along with Micheil, I trust you can handle this."

"I will try, but 'twill no' be easy. The crowd is a wee bit rowdy. You should move soon if that is your wish."

Brenna's gaze dropped to her lap. "My laird, may I speak?"

"Of course, Brenna. You do no' ever need to 'my laird' me. You are my wife. Speak your mind, please."

She brought her gaze up to Logan's. She could feel the heat in her cheeks, but she plundered on. "Logan, you said you owed me one favor for borrowing my mother's book."

"Aye, lass, I did. I do no' go back on my word."

"Then I am asking you to do this for me." Her head turned into her husband's shoulder. How could she have said such a thing to her brother-in-law?

Logan stood back, bowed to her, and said, "Consider it done. My gift to you as my new sister-in-law." He glanced at his brother. "Give me five minutes to find Micheil and rally her brothers." He turned and disappeared into the crowd.

"Quade, I hope he can do this for us. And I hope I never have to be this embarrassed again for the rest of my life."

"Logan said he would. I have never seen him no' uphold a promise. 'Twas a verra wise choice calling in your favor for his transgression with your mother's book. He willnae fail you, I promise. Logan can be an animal, especially if 'tis for a lass he respects as much as you."

Her brow furrowed. "He respects me? How do you ken such a thing?"

"I can see it in his eyes, and I ken my brother. You saved his niece and nephew. He adores them. You have his fealty for life. He meant what he said."

"I wonder why he took my mother's book."

"I havenae had the chance to ask him yet, but we will find out, believe me. I am just happy you have it back safely in your possession."

They waited a few more moments before Quade stood and held his hand out to her. "'Tis time, lass. I cannae wait any longer. 'Tis sheer torture to no' have you alone and in my arms." He grinned and gave her a sound kiss for the crowd. The guards erupted in cheers and graphic shouts that she tried to ignore.

Quade carried her over to the staircase as the crowd followed them. The vulgarities made her want to cover her ears. Her color had to be the deepest shade of red. *Please, Logan and Alex, save me from this humiliation.*

As Quade started up the stairs, a loud whistle shrieked through the air that left her momentarily deaf. She glanced over Quade's shoulder and watched as Logan made a flying leap, landing at the base of the staircase behind them. Alex, Brodie, Robbie, and Micheil joined him with their claymores drawn at their sides. The crowd halted in shock.

Logan peered at his guards, crossed his arms, and announced, "No' tonight, laddies."

Brenna smiled and buried her face in her husband's chest.

CHAPTER TWENTY-FOUR

Quade set his wee wife down inside the chamber. "How is your leg, lass? 'Tis paining you much?" He strode to the door and bolted it behind them.

"Nay, 'tis fine." She stood in front of him, rubbing her hands first on the dark blue of her dress, then together. He could tell how anxious she was.

"Sit by the fire. I had some spiced wine sent up. Allow me to pour you a glass." He assisted her over to the bench near the fire. He would lose his mind if he had to wait much longer to get his beautiful wife in his bed, but he reminded himself he needed to be patient. He poured a goblet and offered it to her, then poured one for himself.

"Have I told you how beautiful you are today?"

"Aye, several times, in fact." She smiled. "I do feel beautiful. Aggie did a wonderful job with my dress. Is the door bolted?"

"Aye, naught will get past Logan or the door. The crowd seems to have calmed. I believe Logan and your brothers have handled the bedding ceremony."

Brenna's shoulders dropped in relief.

"Now you can relax, sweetness?"

"Aye, I did no' want to go through that. 'Tis a terrible custom for lasses."

He pulled a stool over in front of the bench. "Why no' let me take the flowers from your hair? I would love to brush it if you will allow me."

She nodded and Quade got her settled. He ran his hands through her thick sable waves, releasing the flowers and their pins. "Your hair is lovely. I ache to see you with naught but your hair flowing over your shoulders."

Brenna blushed but said nothing.

"Close your eyes, lass."

She did and he ran the brush through the thick locks slowly, reverently. He could feel the tension leave her body as he continued his ministrations. He wanted this night to be the most memorable for her. His first wedding night had not gone well. He had been overexcited and clumsy as could be. His wife had been a virgin, and he had rushed things, much as a young laddie would.

Somehow, he knew his relationship with Brenna would be different. He had tasted her passion, but he also believed she was intelligent and willing to try new things. It pleased him to know they would both work to satisfy the other. He believed this with his whole heart—that she loved him as much as he loved her. There wasn't much he wouldn't do to make her happy and he believed she felt the same way.

He wanted this night to be perfect. She swigged the wine down a bit too fast. A little bit would help her relax, but he did not want his wee wife drunk, so he didn't refill her glass. Her brow was dotted with beads of sweat, so he plunged ahead, hoping he wasn't going too fast.

"Mayhap I can undo your ties and help you out of this dress? 'Tis warm for you, no?" His fingers started at the top and she moved her hair to the side to give him better access. As each tie parted, he kissed her spine tenderly.

"Your skin is flawless, love. I fear I will wish to taste you often." When he finished untying her dress, he helped her to stand and said, "May I?" She hadn't said much and he wasn't sure what his next step should be.

She turned to him, reached up to grab the gown off her shoulders, dropped her dress to the floor and stood in front of him in just her shift. He could see her full breasts, her brown nipples peeking at him through the thin material. Her brown thatch of curls caused him to turn hard instantly. He forced his gaze back to hers and sighed in wonder. "Perfect. You are absolutely perfect, lass."

Brenna smiled at him, and then surprised him by tugging him close. "Kiss me, husband."

Quade emitted a low growl as he wrapped his arms around her and pulled her close, possessing her lush mouth with his. His lips met hers in a crushing kiss, and he swept his tongue over hers, plunging in and out until she panted.

Her hands tugged at his shirt. "Off, please, take it off."

"Easy, sweet, we have all night. We do no' need to rush."

When his shirt was off, she licked her lips and grabbed his biceps. "Och, but I have waited too long for of this. We always had to stop before. Now we finish, husband, please!"

Quade grinned and removed the rest of his clothes while watching his wife. The passion in her eyes fueled his own. "You still have a piece to remove yourself, wife."

Brenna lowered her shift to the floor and hoped she would see satisfaction in her husband's eyes when he saw her nude body. His eyes gleamed as she dropped the thin material. She hoped that was a good sign.

"I am acceptable to you, husband?"

His face broke out in a huge grin. "Acceptable? Nay. Beautiful beyond words? Aye."

He started with his boots, removing his clothing so fast that she almost laughed. He was in as much of a hurry as she was, apparently. When he was completely nude, she couldn't help but stare at his very large member jutting toward her. She moved closer and grasped him carefully in one hand.

"Och, are you trying to kill me, lass?" His eyes closed, either in pain or rapture, she could not tell.

"Am I hurting you?" She grinned as she awaited his answer.

"Nay, it feels too good." He pulled her hand away and lifted her up and carried her to the bed. She giggled as she writhed against him. "You will make me lose myself like a laddie if you do no' stop." He kissed her soundly and said, "Brenna, I want this to be perfect for you. Tell me whenever I am hurting you."

She gazed into his green eyes smoldering with lust and cupped his cheek. "I do no' think you could ever hurt me, Quade. You are too gentle."

"Aye, lass, but this is your first time. You ken 'twill hurt. I have to hurt you, but I will wait for it to subside before we move on."

"'Tis fine. I ken what will happen, but I want to feel it for myself." She smiled at him and pulled his lips back to hers. He kissed her deeply, passionately, like he never wanted it to end. His hand caressed her breast and he brushed his thumb across her nipple. She tensed against him, shocked by the decadent sensation. His tongue ran a path down her shoulder and through the valley of her breasts all while his hand continued to fondle her breast. When his tongue replaced his thumb, she jolted. He ravished her nipple to a taut peak and ran his hand down her hip, kindling a fire in her she had never before experienced.

"Do you like this, lass? Do you want me to stop?"

"Aye ...nay ...do no' stop."

She arched her back to give him better access. He took the pearl of her nipple in his mouth and suckled until she squirmed in his arms. She reached for his hardness and he pushed her hand away. "No' yet, lass."

"But Quade, I want, nay, I need you. I need..."

"I ken what you need, lass, trust me."

He trailed kisses down her to her navel and she cried out, grabbing his hair as he moved lower. He kissed the tender skin on the inside of her thigh, and then touched her tender nub with his tongue. She cried out as he tasted her, shock and embarrassment overpowered by the delicious sensations swirling through her core.

"Quade, what are you doing? I do no' understand..."

"Quiet, love, relax and enjoy. I will help you understand." He took her tiny bud in his mouth and suckled until she bucked against him. A fevered frenzy overtook her as her legs opened for him. Close to losing control, she fisted the sheets in her hand. A decadent thrill pulsed through her, begging for release. He continued to stroke her, then plunged his tongue inside of her. She exploded and wave after wave of pleasure whorled around her as she gave in to the needs of her body.

When she was finally able to think again, she gazed at her husband in astonishment. "I had nae idea."

"I ken it and it makes me verra happy to be your first and to watch you while I pleasure you." He kissed her cheek and smiled at her.

She ran her hand down his powerful biceps, still savoring the after effects of her first climax. "But what about you? I need to do the same for you."

"Do no' worry, we are no' done, but I wanted to make it easier for you."

"Aye, tell me what to do next."

⁂

Quade settled himself between her thighs and teased her entrance. Taking her mouth in his again, he tantalized her tongue, swirling it with hers. He had wanted this for so long, wanted her, more than he had ever wanted anyone. He focused his attention on her breasts again, tasting the soft brown pebble. She made velvety throaty sounds that went right to his groin, making him so hard he thought he would lose everything before he even entered her.

Quade's fingers teased her crease and he felt her liquid heat melt around him. Och, she was so ready for him. He removed his hand and braced his manhood at her passage, teasing her to sense her reaction. As soon as the head of his member crossed her juncture, he groaned. She was so tight, so wet, her juices welcoming him and wrapping around him. Then he felt her barrier.

"Love." He kissed her forehead as he steeled himself. "Here is where it will hurt."

"It does no' hurt, Quade. Go ahead."

The trust in her eyes humbled him. "Aye, but 'twill hurt when I push ahead. I am so sorry I have to hurt you."

She opened her legs wide for him, not realizing this one small movement would put him over the edge. He pulled back and plunged ahead, breaking through her barrier and hating himself all the while for hurting her. He stopped, panting, when he felt her tense beneath him. "Brenna, are you all right? I am sorry, but the worst is over now."

"Och, stings a wee bit, but I think I will be all right. Give me a moment to get used to you again."

He braced himself on his arms and held himself in place. It was probably one of the toughest things he had ever needed to do. His member throbbed with the need to finish, but he would not continue without her agreement. He would not hurt her anymore. His love for her was so strong, it frightened him. He gazed down into her golden brown eyes, kissed her brow, and held his breath, waiting for her to accept him.

Suddenly her legs opened wide and she grabbed his bum. "Och, Quade, you feel so good inside me. Finish this, please!"

Quade was happy to oblige her. With a shout, his hands cradled her hips and he plunged inside her, burying himself so deep he groaned with pleasure. He had known they would be great together, but he never would have imagined this. He pulled out and buried himself again and again, reaching a frenzy that caused him to grab onto her with all his might, his muscles bunching with tension. She met his rhythm with her own thrusts; their panting, sweating bodies both screaming for release as they reached their peak. She wrapped her legs around him and he plunged even deeper, thrusting over and over again until she shattered, wrapping her hand around his neck as she quivered with her release. Her orgasm was so powerful, it sent him over the edge and he roared her name as he convulsed in spasm after spasm, sending his seed into her core.

He had been right. He had known all along they would be fabulous together and he had been right. His orgasm had been beyond even his expectations. He savored the last spasm of his climax, reveling in the feel of still being inside her. He kissed her lips, her cheeks. "Are you all right, lass?"

"Aye." He barely heard her response through her panting. He finally pulled out, rolled to his side and tugged her with him, resting her head on his shoulder. She settled her hand across his hard belly, playing with the coarse hairs below his navel.

Neither spoke for a few moments, their sweat mingling from their entwined limbs. When she was finally able to speak, the first thing his wife said made him chuckle.

"I think I would like to do that again. How long must we wait?"

CHAPTER TWENTY-FIVE

When they entered the great hall the following morn, the hoots and whistles forced a blush from her at first, but then she laughed with everyone when she saw the happiness in her husband's eyes. She'd lost count of how many times they had made love, and it had been Quade who had finally refused her advances, claiming to be the only sane mind in their chamber. He convinced her that if they didn't stop, she wouldn't be able to walk on the morrow and she would blush deeper than ever before.

As she crossed the great hall to greet her family, she was thankful he had convinced her to stop. She had to admit to being a bit tender in a place she hadn't noticed before. Well, it had been worth every moment of ecstasy.

"'Tis a wee bit late, brother. Too busy to greet your guests?" Micheil grinned from ear to ear.

Quade glared at his brother. "I must admit what I had to look at in my chamber was much more appealing than your sorry face." He leaned over and kissed his wife's cheek.

Brenna scanned the area for Torrian and Lily, but did no' see them. "Good morn to all."The front door banged open and Logan entered with wee Lily on his shoulders and Torrian by his side, his hand wrapped in Growley's fur. Logan had to duck to get through the opening. His face beamed with pleasure; his joy with the wee ones was evident.

"Papa!" Torrian yelled and raced toward them as fast as he could with his treasured pet.

Logan set Lily down and she tore over to her hug her father, and then wrapped her arms around Brenna's good leg.

"Careful, lass. Remember Lady Brenna's sore leg." Quade assisted Brenna to a chair at the table with their family.

Lily followed her to her seat and leaned down to kiss her injury. "There! 'Twill be all better now." She giggled and moved over to tug on Alex's arm. He scooped her up and deposited her onto his oversized lap. "Och, wait, Laird Grant, I need to ask Lady Brenna something." She slid off his lap and ran to Brenna's side, pulling her down so she could say something in her ear.

Everyone quieted, curiosity getting the best of them as they waited to hear Lily's request. The wee lass didn't seem to notice.

"Lady Brenna," she said in a stage whisper that could be heard throughout the room, "since you are my new mama, may I call you 'Mama' now?"

Brenna didn't quite know how to answer. She gaped at the golden-haired lass she loved. "Oh my, Lily. I think 'tis up to your papa."

She fought the tears threatening to drench her face as she turned to look at her new husband for guidance. Quade smiled, but didn't say anything. She knew he would form his answer carefully since the lass's feelings were so tender. How would he feel about his daughter's request? Would he object? Would it remind him of his first wife every time Lily spoke to her? If so, mayhap it was not a good idea. She awaited his answer, as did everyone at the table.

Torrian spoke up first. "Papa?"

Quade put his hand on his son's back. "Aye?"

"If you do no' mind, I think we should both call her

'Mama'...that is, if Lady Brenna agrees."

"Are you sure about that, Torrian? I do no' want you to forget your mama."

"Aye, I ken. But I think we should do it because Lily has never had anyone to call 'Mama' before. 'Tis only right that she has a mama, too. Our mama would be okay with that. She told me so." He whispered to his father. "She worries about Lily."

They all sat with bated breath. Brenna noticed the tears running down Madeline's cheek as she watched the wee angel stare up at her father, her grip tight on Brenna's hand. The only sound in the hall was a quenched sob from Lady Ramsay.

Quade turned to his daughter. "Aye, Lily, if 'tis acceptable to Lady Brenna, then 'tis acceptable to me."

The cherubic face turned to her. Brenna nodded and said, "I would like that, lass. I would like that verra much."

Lily jumped on her lap and held her face between her tiny hands. "I love you, Mama." Then she scooted off her lap and ran over to Alex, pulling on his arm until he settled her onto his lap again. She patted the big laird's arm and said, "There, you cannae take my mama away. Is that no' right?"

"Nay, lass. I willnae take your new mama away." Alex stared at the rafters for several moments, though Brenna couldn't guess what he stared at. Had Lily gotten to her brother again?

Lily climbed down Alex's long legs and scampered over to Lady Ramsay's lap."See, Grammy," she said, "you do no' need to cry anymore. We are all happy." Then she pointed to her belly. "And so is my tummy."

She hopped off and ran over to Logan. "Up, Uncle Logan?" When she was sitting comfortably on Logan's lap, she scanned the room and announced, "I love everyone in my new family."

The servants brought in apples, bread, and more porridge just as the door banged open again. This time

Brodie and Jennie flew in with the twins, Jake and Jamie. The lads tore across the hall and headed straight for Uncle Robbie.

Jennie managed to squeeze in next to Brenna. Her head hung low. "Brenna, I will miss you. 'Tis too far to visit often."

Brenna wrapped her arm around her sister. "Aye, lass, I ken. I have spoken to Alex and my husband about you. I will miss you most of all. We decided we would split your time between our clans if you are agreeable. You can spend six moons with us and six moons at home. How does that sound? I am just no' ready to lose my sister yet either." Brenna rubbed the lass's arm as she spoke.

"Truly? You will allow me to stay here for awhile?"

"Aye and nay. Alex would like you to stay and help Maddie until her time comes. Then he will escort you here when she is up and about again. There are plenty in the village who can help with the new bairn, but Maddie needs you before the birth. We thought that would work well. What do you think?"

"Aye, I ken Maddie needs me now. I will stay. But I would like to spend more time with you."

"And our brother wants me to train you in healing."

Jennie's eyes lit up at the mention of healing. "Aye, I would like that, too."

"Good, because I feel bad leaving my clan without a healer. You will have to learn quickly, but I think you will do a great job. Alice can train you as well. She can act in my stead for a bit until you gain more knowledge."

Jennie threw her arms around her sister. "Thank you, Brenna. I was happy for you because you were happy, but I was sad for me. Now I do no' feel like I am losing you completely."

"I also expect you to write to me, to show me that you are keeping up with your letters."

"Aye, I promise."

"I'm sorry I am leaving you, lass. But you have Maddie."

"And in a way, I am gaining a new sister, Avelina. We will have fun when I come to stay."

❧ ❧ ❧

Quade and his brothers sat in the solar with Alex and his brothers.

Alex paced the room. "Have you discovered anything, Ramsay? I need to take my family home, but no' if we are needed here to protect my sister."

"My guards have swarmed the area without finding any sign. We have no idea who shot Brenna. We have had many theories, but none have proven fruitful."

"What about that jealous lass?"

"Iona? She is in a cottage with another guard. Claims they are madly in love and have handfasted. I have spoken to her and she does appear to care for the lad."

Micheil spoke up. "There were plenty of strangers in the area. There was no sign of anyone when our two men searched the area where the arrow came from. We hadnae started feeding anyone and the ones who came that early were on their own for food. There had to be several out hunting. It could have been a complete accident. "

Robbie nodded. "Aye, 'tis possible."

"I hope you are correct. Otherwise, I wouldnae dare risk my sister's life." Alex stopped his pacing. "How many guards have you?"

"Around one hundred and fifty. I can take care of my wife. We will spend more time in the lists and I will send a group out daily to search the area."

"Aye, I believe you," Alex said with a nod. "We will take our leave on the morrow."

Quade stood and met the Grant's eyes. "I promise you, by my arrow, I willnae lose this wife. I love your sister. I will protect her with my life."

Alex brought his sister up to the parapets that night. "Lass, I have to ken if the lad treats you right."

"Aye, Alex. He is a wonderful husband. You were right when you told me that we would make a good match."

"Och, you are happy then?"

Brenna hugged her brother. "Aye, I am verra happy. Go home and take care of your wife and your weans. I will be fine. Quade will protect me well."

Alex kissed her cheek. "I hate to lose our healer, but Jennie will learn well. If you ever need me, you ken we will be here as soon as possible. Just send word."

"Aye, I ken you will always be there for me, but I will be fine, Alex." She hugged him tight, marveling at how it was impossible to wrap her arms around her eldest brother.

Would the stupid Grants ever take their leave? How much patience was a person to have? Brenna Grant needed to die and die soon.

The plan had been in place for a fortnight, but they couldn't move ahead with it until the Grant left and took his guards with him. It wouldn't be hard to get past the Ramsay laird. He hadn't been thinking straight ever since the whore had joined him in his bed.

Logan was the only possible problem, but he would run off shortly after the Grants left. He always did.

The plan was perfect. Soon everything would be as they wanted it.

Patience. Just a bit more patience and the bitch would be dead.

CHAPTER TWENTY-SIX

Brenna didn't think she could be any happier. Her husband had made glorious love to her before leaving a few moments ago. She tried to sway him into staying with her, but he continued to carry on in the lists as if her life was in danger. He scouted many morns or sent Logan out to search the area. 'Twas foolish of him to fear that something would happen to her, especially since it seemed certain that the arrow wound had been accidental, but she tried to be patient with him. After all he had been through, it made sense for him to be careful.

As she stepped out of her bed, she couldn't help but smile. Her husband did spoil her so. He had sent the lads up with a tub and steaming water so she could languish in a bath. After she added a few drops of lavender oil, she climbed in with a sigh, luxuriating in the warm water. No wonder Alex and Maddie were so happy. She had never guessed the marriage bed would be so enjoyable. Quade came up with new ideas all the time, and she had even come up with a few of her own.

When she finished, she plaited her hair, then headed down the stairs to break her fast.

"Mama!" She smiled as Lily ran toward her and jumped into her arms. What better greeting could she have in the morn?

"Did you eat your porridge?"

"Aye, and I had a piece of cheese, Mama."

"Good lass, you will be big and strong like Papa verra soon."

"Nay, Mama."

"Och, nay?" Brenna grinned at her step-daughter.

"Nay, Mama, big and strong like you. You are a lass, so I want to be like you, not Papa. He is a lad like Torrian." She giggled and stared at Brenna.

"Aye, wee one?"

"I like calling you 'Mama.'"

Brenna waved at one of the servants, who rushed into the kitchens to grab some porridge for her. She sat at the dais and Lily hopped down.

"Aye, I must hide my stones for Torrian, Mama! He said he was well enough to find them now." Off she went.

A few moments later, the servant set a steaming bowl of porridge in front of her. Her stomach rumbled at the pleasant aroma. Aggie joined her since Lily was so busy, and Torrian had gone with his father. Her appetite seemed to be particularly voracious lately. She glanced at Lily over in the corner when the door opened and a new stable lad rushed in.

"My lady, she is sick. In the path in the village, she is so sick. Can you no' help her?"

She turned to Aggie, "Stay with Lily, please, I must go." Brenna grabbed her cape and satchel and headed out the door. "Who is it, lad? Who is sick?"

"I do no' ken her, but she told me to get you."

Brenna followed him out. As soon as they reached the village, the lad stopped. "Where did she go? I do no' see her anymore. Forgive me, my lady. She must be better now."

Brenna searched up one path and down another, to no avail. There was no one in the area at all, certainly not a patient. She shook her head and sent the lad on his way.

She was on her way back to the keep when she heard moaning. She followed the sound, which took her around a corner and off the path. As soon as she rounded the corner, she was struck in the head and her whole world went black.

***

The sun had almost set when Quade strode through the courtyard on his way back to the keep. He couldn't wait to see his bride. Even in his wildest dreams, he had never guessed he and Brenna would be this happy. He even missed her while he was in the lists. Had it not been for the arrow in her leg, he wouldn't have to worry so. But he had to make sure his family was safe.

How his bairns had changed in the short time since Brenna's arrival. Torrian was almost strong enough to walk without Growley. Fact of the matter was, he probably already was, he just liked having the big dog nearby. Lily loved having a new mama and used the word at least fifty times a day. He hadn't realized how much she wanted another woman in her life.

And his wife? Saints above, what a passionate woman. He had smiled half the day away just recalling their previous night's adventures. What would she think up next? Some day he would take a sword in his belly because of his wandering thoughts.

Micheil caught up with him. "Are you still grinning? Must have been some night."

"Aye, 'twas something else," Quade said, running a hand across the back of his neck, "but I willnae say another word out of respect for the love of my life."

His brother guffawed and slapped him on the back. "Good to see you so happy. You deserve it. Has been a long time coming." Nodding his head, Quade pushed open the door to the great hall. He sniffed and thought his wee wife would probably prefer it if he took a bath. He would have to order a tub later, as it was getting too cold to jump in the loch. Snow was in the air; he could always smell it before it started.

As soon as his eyes adjusted to the dimness of the great hall, he searched for Brenna, but she was nowhere to be seen. He took the stairs two at a time, hoping he would catch her just getting up from a nap. She didn't normally take naps, but she had been up late last night. He tiptoed into his chamber, but she was nowhere to be seen.

When he returned to the great hall, he noticed her cape was gone from the wall. Her satchel was missing as well. Puzzled, he wandered into the kitchens where his mother was chatting with Cook about the night's meal.

"Greetings, Mother. Have you seen my wife?"

"Nay, I havenae seen her since this morn. Margaret told me she left to help a sick woman in the village. I do no' think she has returned."

Quade went off in search of Margaret and found Aggie and Lily instead. "Lily, where is Mama?"

"My laird," Aggie said, "she left this morn to help a woman in the village who had fallen sick."

Quade's stomach churned. Something was wrong; he could feel it. "What woman?"

"I do no' ken. One of the new stable lads fetched her and she went right away."

"Papa, what's wrong?" Lily waited patiently for his response.

Logan and Micheil strolled in the front door and immediately caught his concern. "Micheil, fetch Seamus and a few other guards and bring them here.

"I do no' like the look on your face, brother. What is it?" Logan's voice was stern.

Not wanting to alarm his daughter, Quade leaned over to kiss her cheek. "Naught is wrong, Lilykins. I will fetch your new mama right now. Come, lads. Let's take our leave."

They stepped outside into the cold night. Quade turned to Logan. "Brenna is missing. According to Aggie, she left to tend a sick one in the village this morn. A stable lad came up to fetch her and she went with him. Something is no' right. She wouldnae be gone this long without us hearing more about the illness in the village."

Micheil arrived with Seamus and Ennis. Logan caught them up on the situation.

Quade could feel his hand start to tremble. This could nae be happening. "Micheil, take whatever guards you need and knock on all the cottages and find out where she is or if anyone has seen her today. Logan, stay with me."

Micheil, Seamus, and Ennis saddled their horses and headed for the village.

Clapping a hand on his brother's shoulder, Logan said, "We will find her. No stone will go unturned."

"I was right all along," Quade said quietly. "I am cursed. I kenned it and I shouldnae have married her. Look what has happened. Her life could be in jeopardy."

"We do no' ken anything yet. She could be delivering a bairn. Mayhap someone passed and she is comforting their family. She has a big heart. She could be helping any number of clan members."

"It does no' feel right, Logan. And you ken it, too. We have always had the same sense. Something has happened to her, I know it." His hands trembled as he ran them through his hair. "What do I do? You need to help me. I love her so much, I cannae think straight. I cannae lose her, do you understand?" He shouted the words. His mother always said the lord only gives you what you can handle. Well, enough was enough! He could not handle losing Brenna. His head threatened to explode at the very thought.

"Aye, I agree. This does no' feel right. I ken it. We will wait for the lads to return before we extend our search. But I will start getting the guards together. Come with me, we will head to the stables. Get your horse ready."

"I shouldnae have let the Grants go. We could use their help now. We need to find her fast. What if she is lying near death somewhere? What if she was attacked by a wild animal? What if she was kidnapped? How will I find her?" Quade's thoughts raged in ten different directions.

Logan glared at his brother. "I ken you are scared, but get yourself together. You ken these lands better than anyone. If she is missing, and we do no' ken that yet, you need to be strong."

Logan was right. He needed to pull it together. He would not lose her. He would fight for her to the bitter end. He would kill for her.

Someone had made their last mistake if they had harmed his wife.

Their search of the village turned up nothing. No one knew anything about a sick person in the village, and they had been unable to locate the stable lad.

Quade and his guards headed outside the village to search the immediate area for any sign of Brenna or anything unusual. After several unproductive hours of searching in the woods and meadows around the perimeter of his keep, they returned to the stables, where more guards awaited his orders.

He stood outside the stable and questioned everyone.

"Lads, are there any horses missing?"

The stable lads rushed to check. "Nay, they are all here, my laird."

"Where is the new lad that was here this morning? Who is he?"

Duncan, the lad in charge of the stables, sauntered over. "Chief, 'tis my fault, no' theirs. I let the new lad help out this morn. His da was a guard, died a few years ago. He was young and has been hanging around, hoping to help. He isnae old enough yet, but I let him help a wee bit."

"Duncan, I just need his name." Quade wanted to throttle him but kept his temper.

Duncan hung his head. "That be the problem, my laird. I do no' recall. I have tried and I haven't seen him since this morn. When I see him, I will send him to you."

"Nay! Keep him here. Do no' let him out of your sight. Just send for me or Logan."

"Been so busy with the wedding and the Grants, my laird. I just needed a bit of help to get things in line again."

"I ken, Duncan." Quade rubbed his forehead. "Try to locate the lad." He turned to the leaders of his guard. "We will meet in the great hall to plan our next move. Mayhap someone has learned something there."

He trudged up the hill to the great hall, thinking of all the possible circumstances that might have pulled his wife away. He didn't like some of the thoughts that traveled through his mind.

He greeted his mother at the entrance to the great hall and discovered that naught new had happened in their absence. He turned to his guards. "Here is the plan. I want every clan member in the village brought here for questioning. And I want you to find the lad who talked Brenna into leaving with him. He is our only connection to her right now. Do it and do it fast." Quade stood on the dais and barked his orders. Naught would stop him until he found his wee wife.

Brenna awoke to find herself tied up in a dark spot, a dirty rag stuffed in her mouth. Rolling as best she could, she discovered she was in a large rectangular wooden crate. It was completely dark, which almost caused her to panic, but she forced herself to stay calm. She had to, for now there were people counting on her to stay strong—Quade, Lily, and Torrian—

three wonderful reasons to maintain control until she found a way out of this situation.

Much as she tried to stay awake, she dozed frequently. The potion they had given her must have been powerful. Quite a bit later, a door slammed shut and the sound of heavy boots moved closer to her prison. The top of the box popped up and she closed her eyes at the shock of candlelight.

"Och, you are awake. That is no' helpful. I will have to put you to sleep again."

Brenna stared at her captor in shock.

"Sorry, my lady. I willnae hurt you, but I must continue with our plan." He tugged her gag down and held her nose to force her to drink a foul tasting liquid. Though she spat out as much as she could, Brenna couldn't help but swallow a bit. They had some knowledge of a healer's work, she realized. The draught she drank was strong and just a wee bit would have done the job.

"Please, do no' do this." Darkness threatened her world again. She fought to stay awake, but to no avail.

Quade stood at the steps in front of the great hall and surveyed the gathering before him. The faces of his clan members were twisted in confusion and fear. He had not called a group meeting such as this one in a very long time.

His brother let out his famous whistle and everyone instantly quieted.

"My wife has been kidnapped." Quade waited for the gasps and whisperings from the crowd to subside before speaking again. "I ask your help. A new stable lad came into the keep and told my wife a sick woman in the village needed her. Does anyone ken aught about this? If you do, I need you to come forward and speak."

He waited as he scanned the crowd for anyone who

was acting suspicious or anyone who looked like they might know anything. Naught. Not one person stepped forward. He was losing his patience. "Does anyone ken who the lad was? Do you no' remember a lad running to the keep around midday? Does anyone recall someone being struck ill around that time?"

He searched their faces. He saw concern, worry, and furrowed brows, but no one came forward.

"Och, my laird, we wouldnae harm your wee wife," someone said. "She has saved your bairns. The clan has come to life again. We wouldnae do such a thing."

Quade sighed. "Aye, I ken what you are saying. Yet someone has taken her."

Another spoke. "Och, tell us what we can do to help. We will search with you, Chief."

Quade's mind churned in with all his choices, but he forced himself to be logical. "You force me to do something I did no' wish to do." He paused as he looked at his brothers for support. "All lasses are to move inside the great hall. All lads under ten and five are to move inside as well."

He nodded to Micheil and sent him inside. "Get them organized and send for Aggie. She should recognize the lad."

As soon as the women and boys were inside, he spoke to the clansmen who remained. "My guards are to commence a search of all your homes. I apologize for the intrusion, but I must find my wife. Whatever you can do to assist us will be greatly appreciated. Follow Logan to the courtyard."

"Logan," he said, turning to his brother, "organize a search party for the village cottages. We have searched outside, now we will search inside. I am going to go and aid Micheil."

Logan nodded. "Aye. Good plan, brother. Now you are acting like our laird."

⁂

Brenna was face down on a horse, hidden under a blanket. They rode so fast, she was sure she would spew any moment. With a gag in her mouth, she could end up choking so she did everything she could to prevent heaving.

When they finally arrived at their destination, her captor carried her inside the cottage and tossed her on a small pallet. How could this be happening? She prayed her captor would remove her gag. This was someone with whom she could reason. She could convince him to let her go; she was sure of it.

He peered out the window, wiping the grime away with his sleeve. "Aye, 'tis a beautiful clear night."

He left the cottage and returned with wood for the hearth. He glanced at her. "Och, lass, 'twill no' be much longer."

Until what? Her death?

CHAPTER TWENTY-SEVEN

Quade stood on the dais, scanning the faces of the lads in front of him. Some were fighting tears; others just looked confused.

"Aye, lads, one of you came to the keep to fetch my wife to assist a sick lass. You need to come forward and let me ken what happened. You willnae be in trouble if you help me now. I ken that you were doing what you thought best, but I need your help now."

Naught. No one moved.

A woman in the back shouted. "Och, Laird, mayhap wasnae one of our lads."

He needed Aggie. Now. He glanced at Micheil and said, "Do no' let anyone leave. I will be back in a moment."

He headed up the stairs and then raced down the corridor to Lily's chamber. He froze at the sounds he heard as he was passing Torrian's room. He fell back and stuck his head in the doorway. "Margaret? What goes on here?" He froze as he absorbed the scene in front of him.

Margaret was holding a bowl in front of Torrian as he retched. She had her arm around him, holding him upright.

"Papa!" He heaved again into the bowl.

Paralyzed, he could not believe what his eyes told him was true. Could his son be sick again? He had not retched in a fortnight.

"Margaret!" his son yelled as he heaved again.

"Never mind, Margaret. I must find Aggie."

He closed the door and headed to Lily's room, still stunned. His world was caving around him. How could that be? He hated to leave his son, but he would survive the sickness. His wife's life could be in jeopardy. He forced himself to focus on her, promising himself to return and help his son as soon as possible.

Aggie must have heard him because she and Lily came toward him before he even entered the room. "Do you need me, my laird?"

"Aye, Aggie, will you come to the hall and help us identify the lad who came for my wife?"

"Of course, but what about sweet Lily? Shall I leave her with someone?"

"Nay, just bring her to the hall. Margaret is busy with Torrian."

"Papa, did you find my mama yet?"

He reached for his daughter to carry her down the stairway. "Nay, lass. We havenae found her yet. Will you be quiet in the hall for Aggie? We need her help. It will just take a few moments."

"Aye, Papa." He set her down next to him and walked over in front of the group. Aggie followed.

"Aggie, I want you to look carefully at all the lads here and tell us which one came for my wife." He nodded as he scanned the rows of lads in front of him, hoping to notice a particularly anxious face among them. Naught. He would have to depend on Aggie.

He took a step back and held Lily's hand. He needed help. How could he have any idea where she was without some direction? Frustration tore at his insides. No clues, no information, absolutely naught had been uncovered about Brenna's disappearance. How could that be? Someone had to know something.

Aggie took a quick glance around the hall. "I do no' see him, Laird."

"Take your time. Move up closer to the lads and look

more carefully. 'Tis verra important." She had to recognize one of the lads. Where else would he have come from? *Think! Think! Who would want to hurt my wife?*

She nodded and began to move up and down the rows of lads. At the back row, she turned to him and shook her head. "I am sorry, but I do no' see him. I do no' remember very well, though, my eyes arenae what they used to be."

Aggie seemed flustered, so he waved her back to the front of the room. Lily let go of his hand for a moment while he listened to the older servant, who was wiping tears from her eyes. "I am so sorry, my laird. I would no' ever want anything to happen to your wife. We need her. Look what she has done for our Lily. Who would want to hurt the lass? 'Tis awful."

"'Tis all right, Aggie. Why do you no' take Lily up to Torrian's room. I think Margaret could use your help."

Quade turned to locate his daughter and found her standing in front of a lad in the second row with Micheil, who turned and nodded to him, a smug look across his face.

She tugged on the lad's sleeve, peered up at him and said, "Where's my new mama?"

Quade ran over, scooped her up and said, "Good lass, Lily." He took one look at the lad in front of him and the boy burst into tears. He handed Lily over to Aggie and said, "Come with me, lad."

Logan kneed his horse again to pick up speed. He had a task to complete and he would do it, distasteful though it was. He noticed the beginning of the first snowfall as the flakes danced around his face. He smiled knowing the snow would make his job much easier.

Quade had dismissed all the lads except for the one

who had been identified by Lily. Every lass in the clan gathered in front of them.

"Quiet! Nae one will speak until the lad has passed each of you."

The lad moved past each of the lasses and shook his head. About halfway through, Seamus strode in from outside.

"Naught, Chief. We have checked each of the huts. Nae sign of your wife or any struggles. We have interviewed many. No one recalls anything."

Quade sighed, realizing his best hope was in a lad of mayhap ten summers. "Keep moving, lad. Search carefully for the correct lass. Do you no' see her here?"

The lad turned, tears streaming down his face. "My laird, she gave me a coin and she was in a dirty old cape with her hood up. I did no' see her well." He stopped to hiccup. "My mama needed the coin, my laird. Ever since my da died, I try to help her. I thought the lass was sick. I did no' ken she was fooling or that she wanted to hurt your wife."

Quade stared at the lad. His papa had been a loyal guard for Quade. His life was ended when he was gored by a boar, just as Quade had been.

"Does this mean I cannae be a guard for you when I get bigger? My da wanted me to be a guard like he was. Please, Laird. I never saw her before."

He pulled the lad in front of one of the remaining lasses. "How about this lass, lad?"

Iona stood with her hand on her hip, her chin jutted forward.

"He wouldnae dare. I had naught to do with this." Iona glared at Quade.

The venom she spewed was enough to send the lad scampering behind him.

Quade grabbed Iona's arm and pulled her into the kitchens.

"What have you done with my wife? You are the only one we ken who hates her."

"I havenae touched her, Quade. I was foolish for thinking there was something between us. Now I am with a lad who makes me happy, and I do no' need you. I tell you, 'twas no' me." Her stare never wavered and for some reason, he believed her.

"Aye, I believe you. Now go."

Quade strode back into the hall, feeling as though his last hope had let him down. The lad stood beside his brother, Micheil. "'Tis all for now, lad. You may go."

"Your pardon, my laird. Please forgive me." His voice hitched twice while he delivered his apology.

Quade ruffled his hair. "'Tis enough tears for now, lad. I ken you did your best. If you wish to be in my guard, then head home and help your mama."

The lad sniffled. "Aye, my laird. Thank ye." He ran as fast as his legs would carry him.

After sending the remaining lasses home, Quade and Micheil followed them and made their way out to the front steps of the keep. Quade searched the area for his brother, but could not find him. "Seamus, where is Logan?"

"He was here a bit ago. I do no' ken where he went. He's a loner, aye?"

Quade turned to look at Micheil.

"Do no' even think it," Micheil said. "Our brother has naught to do with this. He may be searching on his own, but he wouldnae hurt Brenna."

He would never have thought it possible, but there had been that argument before Logan took off and left him and Brenna at the old hut. They had fought over *her.* Logan had said he wanted her. He shared this privately with Micheil.

"Do no' even think it, Quade. You and Logan have fought over many lasses. He wouldnae do this to you."

Quade slapped his brother on the back. "Nay, you are correct, Micheil. He was verra happy for me and for Brenna. I believed that with all my heart. But he is a loner, so he is probably chasing his own hunches. I hope he uncovers something we are missing."

The door slammed open and the newcomer stalked over to the pallet and kicked Brenna in the side. "You foolish bitch! You ruined everything for me." Her hand slapped one of Brenna's cheeks, then the other.

Brenna steeled herself not to scream. The lass was clearly daft. Brenna's hands and feet were tied, so there was naught she could do. Her captor had just stepped outside.

The lass stalked over to the hearth and picked up a piece of wood that had been set to the side. She strode over to Brenna and swung it, connecting with her flesh over and over again. "Look what you have done, you rotten whore. You have ruined everything. My life is ruined. Everything was fine until you showed up."

Brenna rolled in a ball in an attempt to protect her inner organs from the lass's wild battering. The attacker was so daft in her head that some of her swings only connected with the air, fortunately. Her face, bathed in tears as she circled Brenna, was full of rage and hate and madness. The lass had lost all touch with reality. This did not bode well. She screamed through her gag, hoping to bring the man back into the room. She had not seen the madness in his face.

"Bitch, bitch, I will kill you for ruining my life. How could he believe you? You are naught but a witch. I would have fixed everything."

Every word brought more anger down upon her. Blow after blow pummeled her body.

The door slammed open. "Och, lass, stop this. What are you about? You cannae beat the laird's wife."

"Leave me be, fool! I will kill her. You will help me. Kill her! Kill her now or I will!"

"What's our next step, Quade? Where do we go from

here? Seamus is waiting outside."

The chief stared at the stars in the sky, hoping for guidance. "Give me a few minutes to think, Micheil. I need to go check on Torrian. He is sick again."

"What? Cannae be!"

"Eh, but it is. Will you come?"

Quade made his way to the staircase with his brother following directly behind him. He took the stairs two at a time, anxious to see Margaret.

Quade burst through the door and saw his son on the bed, sound asleep from exhaustion. Aggie sat to the side with Lily on her lap, playing with her stones. He sat next to him and brushed his hair back off his forehead.

He searched the room for Margaret, but she was nowhere to be found. "Aggie, where is Margaret?"

"She left as soon as Lily and I came in. She said you needed to see her. You havenae?"

"Nay."Quade glanced at Micheil. "Have you seen her?"

"Och, nay."

His son opened his eyes and tugged on his sleeve, still weak. "Papa, I tried to tell you, but I couldnae stop heaving."

"What, Torrian?" He waited, anxious to hear what his son knew.

"Papa. 'Tis Margaret. She made me eat from a trencher. Mama told me I couldnae ever eat from a trencher. There's wheat in the trenchers and 'twill make me sick. Margaret was here when Mama told me, but she still made me eat it. I told her I did no' want to and she hit me. She told me to be quiet and do as I was told."

Quade was stunned. The woman he had trusted to care for his bairn was the cause of this? She had kidnapped his wife? He hid his reaction for the sake of his children. "Good lad, many thanks." He leaned over and kissed his forehead.

A small voice came from his side. Lily pulled on his leather trews. "Papa, find my new mama. Do no' let anyone hurt her."

He ruffled her hair and ran out the door, Micheil already behind him. "Your uncles and I are going to get your new mama back."

Quade and his brother hurried out into the courtyard, where they came upon Seamus. "Where's Ennis?" Quade asked him.

Seamus searched the area. "I do no' ken. I havenae seen him since he went to check his house and the cottages next to his."

Quade strapped his bow to his back and jumped on his horse. "Micheil, do you have your broadsword?"

"Aye, let's go."

They flew to Ennis's house with twenty guards behind him. He left the rest to watch the keep. He would not lose his children either. He pulled on the reins in front of Ennis's cottage, but noticed all was quiet. He, Micheil, and Seamus dismounted and went inside.

"Naught here, Quade."

Quade searched the small hut. Something was not right. He sniffed the air, then ran over to the large bench that doubled as storage for the couple. He recalled when Ennis had built it for the lads. They used to hide inside together. He stuck his nose inside and turned his head to Micheil.

"Lavender."

His brother looked at him as if he was daft. "What?"

"Lavender. 'Tis my wife's scent. She was here." He charged back out the door and ordered his men to follow.

With renewed energy, he yelled to his brother. "Now we ken who our enemy is. Margaret and Ennis are in deep trouble."

CHAPTER TWENTY-EIGHT

Ennis held his wife high up in the air. "Och, lass, stop! You willnae hurt the laird's wife. I never agreed to kill her. Are you daft? How can you even consider such a thing?"

Margaret kicked and screamed. "Leave me be, Ennis! She took our son away. Can you no' see she must die? Otherwise, we will no' ever see our son again."

Ennis struggled with her but managed to wrap his brawny arms around her upper body. "Nay, wife. She had naught to do with our son dying. Todd had the red throat. He passed on long before she came here."

"Torrian, our son's name is Torrian, Ennis. What is wrong with you? And she did take him away."

"Margaret. Torrian is no' our son. He is the laird's son. Remember Lilias? Lilias was his mother, just like she was Lily's mother. Lily and Torrian are brother and sister."

"Nay, Lilias's son died, our son lives. I am so happy that Torrian is doing better, but he lived with us until she came along and took him back to the keep. Tell her she cannae have him. Torrian needs to be returned to us. The lad needs to be with his mama. If I have to kill her to get my son back, I will."

"Killing her willnae give us our son back. *Todd* is our son. Todd is in heaven and willnae come back. Leave her be, Margaret. Please. They will hang you for killing the laird's wife. And she is a healer. She helps so many. All the clan loves Lady Brenna. Cease, lass. You need to get your head straight."

Brenna could see the tension leave Margaret's body as Ennis spoke to her. Tears flooded her cheeks. How Brenna prayed he would be able to reach his wife. She had heard of many women turning daft after losing a child. Aye, 'twas certainly what befell this poor lass from losing her only son. Now Margaret thought Torrian was hers and she blamed Brenna for removing him from her house. How could this be set to rights?

Ennis set Margaret on a chair and turned her to face him. "Margaret, I agreed to hold her here so you could make Torrian sick again and then heal him. I ken you wanted the laird to appreciate all you have done for his lad. 'Twould have brought Torrian back to our house for a brief time, perhaps, but no' forever. We cannae keep him forever. Remember? I agreed to do this, but only if we set Lady Brenna free after you fixed him again.

"Iona gave us bad advice. This draught did no' keep her asleep as we had hoped. Now she kens 'twas us who kidnapped her. I do no' ken what to do other than bring her back and accept whate'ver the laird deems justice for us. This has nae gone as we planned. I ne'er meant to hit her in her leg. I only wanted to hit her horse to draw suspicion away from us."

"Nay, Ennis. Please! Do no' bring her back. The laird willnae return our son to us if she returns to the keep. Iona said she is a witch. Remember? Tell me you ken it, too." She grabbed hold of her husband's big hands as she pleaded with him.

"Nay, love, she is a healer. She saved Torrian. Why, if nae for her, he might be dead now. And you would never see him again. Do you no' remember how thin he was? He couldnae lift his head from the pillow. He couldnae walk. We should thank Lady Brenna. She saved Torrian's life. I ken you and Iona planned to make her look bad by calling her a witch, but she isnae. She is wonderful for our clan. Even now, you should be able to see the good she has done."

Margaret's sobs continued, growing louder with each minute.

"Nay, I want my Torrian back. He belongs with us at our cottage. Leave her outside for the wolves, Ennis. Then we can have Torrian back. The laird will never ken 'twas us if the wolves eat her. Please. I need my son back. I miss him so."

Ennis sat on a stool and pulled Margaret onto his lap, cradling her like a bairn. He kissed her forehead. "Margaret, you ken how I love you. I will do most anything for you, but nae this. We must return her to the laird. Do you no' see what is right here? I should never have gone along with this daft idea of yours, and I should never have allowed Iona in our home. Now we must stop before 'tis too late. Come, lass. Allow me to take her back to the keep."

Margaret hung her head and wrapped her arms around Ennis's waist. "Aye, you are right, love. Kiss me, please. One kiss before we return."

Ennis cupped her face in his big paws and kissed her. He pulled back and attempted to comfort her. "We will keep trying to have another bairn, lass." He kissed her again.

Brenna screamed as soon as she saw the dirk, but it was too late. Margaret swung her arm out with all her might and plunged the knife deep into his back. The dirk had sunk near his left kidney, and his eyes stared at his wife in horror before he slumped to the ground.

"Nay, Ennis. I do no' want another, I want my son, Torrian." Margaret patted his cheek.

Brenna was horrified. How could she kill her own husband?

As soon as Ennis fell to the floor, Margaret pulled the knife out, wiped the blood off and turned to face Brenna. She sauntered toward her, a wicked smile on her face, and held the blade in front of her eyes. "I could kill you now, but I have something even better planned for you. The cliffs. I will throw you over the cliff so you can see what it feels like to have your life pulled out from under you. Just as I did when you had my son moved out of our home."

She stepped back and put the dirk in the pocket sewn into the folds of her skirt.

Then she turned and scanned the hut.

"Aye, 'tis a perfect finish. I will send you over the cliffs and then come back to the cottage and blame Ennis for your death. I will tell them he tried to kill me, too, so I stabbed him." She turned again to Brenna. "He is daft, you heard him. How could he say Torrian isnae our son? I have loved that lad since the day he was born. I carried him in my womb, and now I will fight for him. I will die for him. Of course, I willnae die." She straightened and grinned.

"'Twill be you who dies. 'Tis all your fault. The laird will thank me when you are gone. Lilias is the one he loves, Lilias gave him that beautiful lad, Todd." She gazed out the window. "'Twas so sad when the red throat got Todd. I protected my Torrian from it. I am a good mother and my son needs me." She spun and faced Brenna. "I have a few things to do before I take you away."

She moved to the door and opened it, staring into the night sky. "Aye, the weather is perfect. Just enough snow for me to drag you on the sled. I will pull you for a bit, and then I'll have my horse pull you right over the side of the cliff. The horse is too daft to ken where he goes in the dark. He willnae disobey me. 'Twill be much easier to move you in the snow. I will just need to wait a wee bit until enough has fallen."

Margaret hummed as she puttered around the cottage. She kissed Ennis, and then emptied his pockets. She removed his coat and wrapped it around Brenna. "I will leave this on you to incriminate Ennis even more, if they ever find you, that is. I am so smart, and you are no'."

Her head bounced from side to side as she hummed. "Torrian loves Mama, Mama loves Torrian. Torrian will be so glad to have his mama by his side again. Sorry, Ennis," she said, stooping to stroke his cheek, "but we do no' need you anymore. I do no' want any other bairns. Torrian is my first and will live with me forever more."

Brenna prayed that Quade was on his way.

He would find her, wouldn't he?

Shortly after Quade gave his orders and his guards fanned out, he heard Logan's whistle, and answered with his own. Quade called out to Micheil and Seamus. They were heading in Logan's direction.

Quade almost launched himself at his brother when they reached him. "Aye, what have you found?"

"I found the cottage. At least, I believe she must be inside."

"Where?" Quade bellowed.

"Mungo's old cottage. Ennis and Margaret are in there arguing. I did no' see Brenna, but she must be inside. They must have her."

"But why? Why would Ennis kidnap her? He is one of my best guards and has been with me for years. They welcomed Torrian into their home."

"From what I overheard, Margaret is daft from losing Todd. She wants Torrian back in her home, and she blames Brenna for taking him away."

They were still quite a distance from the cottage, so Quade sounded his battle cry as he sent his horse into a gallop. His guardsmen flanked him, pulling in from the surrounding area.

Logan whistled as they neared the cottage, and they reined in a short distance away. "Quade, we need to take them by surprise," he said. "I do no' ken what weapons Ennis has. He may have his bow, and you ken what a marksman he is. 'Tis the only reason I did no' try to take him alone. I kenned you were near. We need to surround the cottage. Send some guards to the other side with me and await my whistle."

A few minutes later, Quade heard the lad's bird call from the other side of the cabin. They dismounted and crept up to the cottage silently. No sounds came from within. His gut churned as he began to imagine what they would find inside the cottage. *'Twas too quiet.*

When he and Logan finally stormed the small hut, his guard was lying face down on the floor.

He was the only one in the cabin. Brenna was nowhere to be seen.

Margaret continued her incessant humming, up and down, over and over, while she carted Brenna out the door on the sled. It was the tune of a mad woman. She had brought the small sled inside the cottage and forced Brenna onto it. Brenna had rolled off a couple of times, but Margaret had kicked her enough to convince her to go along. She planned on trying to roll off later.

Of course, once she was on the sled, she regretted that decision because Margaret decided to tie her onto it after covering her with Ennis's coat. Once they were outside, she gleefully hooked the sled up to the back of the horse. Brenna attempted to get her attention several different ways, but Margaret ignored her, truly daft at this point.

The ride was rough, but enough snow had fallen to guarantee a swift journey through the meadow. Margaret's cackling occasionally reached her ears, but it did not matter one way or the other. The lass would not change her plan.

Brenna rocked and rocked on the sled as best she could, but she could not loosen the ties that bound her so well. She wanted to give up, but Quade's face was burned into her mind. She could hear him fresh in her mind telling her he was cursed and could not marry her. She must survive for him.

CHAPTER TWENTY-NINE

Quade and Logan stepped inside the small hut and stared at their fallen comrade. Quade rolled him over to be sure he was indeed dead.

"Hellfire! What was that?" Logan yelled. Ennis's eyelids had flickered open for a second.

The brothers stared at each other, spooked by the slight movement. There was no visible breath leaving the lad's body. His eyes fluttered again. A very weak voice drifted up to them. Quade bent down and placed his ear next to Ennis's mouth.

"The cliffs. She is daft, so sorry, my laird. 'Tis my fault. She took her by sled. Wants to send her over the cliff." Ennis's eyes fluttered shut.

Quade grasped his guard's arm, then stood and rushed out the door. He shouted his orders as he mounted his horse and rode hard for the cliffs. His heart threatened to explode from his chest, but he would not stop.

Near an hour later, they crested the ridge near the cliff, just in time to see Margaret driving her horse madly toward the edge. An eerie sound reached Quade's ears as he feverishly pushed his horse onward.

Quade watched the events as if they were happening in slow motion. Margaret neared the cliff, her horse moving fast, though not as fast as his. All their shouts were ignored by Margaret, who never turned to acknowledge them. The small sled on the back bounced with a dark form on it. It had to be his wee wife.

He would not lose her. She had brought such meaning to his life by saving his bairns and making each day a joy. He pictured the way her brown eyes had beamed at him on the day of their wedding, the look on her face whenever he held her close, how beautiful she was the first night he had made love to her. Nay, he would not lose her.

Logan broke into his thoughts. "Shoot her! We willnae make it in time. Get up and shoot her! My sword is useless. She will be over the cliffs by the time we catch her."

Quade gauged the distance, and pulled the bow from his back. He took an arrow in his teeth and made sure several were still in the quiver. He then drove his horse closer and climbed onto her back. He and Star became one when he stood on her back; he could sense her every move, just as she could sense his.

A little closer. He didn't think he could hit her from this distance. Just a wee bit closer.

Logan's shouts echoed in his ears. "Now! Get her now, Quade."

Not yet. A bit closer.

Seamus screamed out, "Do no' wait forever, Ramsay!"

Logan and Seamus continued to bellow at him, but he had to wait until the time was just right. He had practiced this many, many times. He knew when he could hit a target and when he couldn't. He trusted Star to get him a wee bit closer.

When he thought he was where he needed to be, he signaled his mare to slow. He knew exactly how long it took her to come to a complete stop.

As soon as she did, he pulled back his bow, aimed, and released his arrow.

He refilled again, shot again. And again. He couldn't

see Margaret anymore, but he kept the arrows flying. Why couldn't he see her anymore? Where was she?

Hearing his brother's whoop, he fell back down on his horse. Crossing the meadow, he spurred Star closer, hoping he would find what he so needed to find. He reached the edge and looked over. Margaret's horse was rearing and bucking as if injured, but Seamus was calming him. There was no sign of Margaret or his wife. He stumbled around the horse. If felt like a stake was being driven into his heart when he saw the sled.

It was empty.

Quade swore he would never be able to take another breath. The stake went clear through his heart and into his gut.

He heard his brother yelling for him. "Over here, you daft lad. Why do you no' ever listen to your brother?"

Logan was laughing when he whirled around to look at him. His brother was standing next to a lump on the ground, holding Ennis's empty jacket.

The lump moved and Brenna turned her face to him. Tears poured down her cheeks, but a small grin erupted on her face when Logan bent down to untie her arms.

"What took you so long?" she asked as she peered up at him from her spot in the snow.

Quade scooped her up in his arms and held on tight, swearing he would never let her go.

⁂

Brenna's heart had burst several times since she had arrived home. Aye, she was a bit beat up, but it was naught she could not handle. When Margaret had pulled her across a rock, she had landed with such force that the ties pinning her to the sled had loosened. After much wriggling around, she had managed to roll off without Margaret noticing.

The instant Quade carried her into the great hall,

Lily screamed and ran over to her. She could tell the wee lass had been crying while she was gone. Quade sat Brenna in a chair by the hearth and his daughter climbed onto her lap and clung to her, kissing her several times.

His mother came out, said several prayers, and allowed the tears to flow freely. Logan, Micheil, and Seamus were there, too, all of them grateful that the incident had ended happily for their chief. Quade had sent some guards back to bury Ennis and to see if the horse, injured by an arrow, could be saved.

There were so many people talking excitedly that Lady Ramsay finally put to use the famous whistling ability that her son, Logan, had inherited from her. As silence descended on the hall, she spoke. "Would someone please tell me exactly what transpired from start to finish? I cannae listen to all of you at once."

Quade smiled, lifted his wife and daughter, and settled into the chair with both of them on his lap. Lily was now fast asleep. Torrian reclined on the floor beside them, his head resting on Growley, almost asleep.

"Mother, please, have a seat and I will explain what I ken." After she settled across from them, he began. "Margaret had taken care of Torrian for so long that when she lost her own son, she started to believe Torrian was hers. She was verra upset when Brenna came, and cured Lily and Torrian both. She became even more upset when I brought her and Torrian to the keep. My son did so well that Margaret feared she would not be needed anymore. The world she had created was being threatened."

Brenna nodded. "Aye, Lady Ramsay. If you think about it, since naught kenned Torrian was alive, Margaret, in essence, lived alone in her cottage with Torrian and Ennis. Torrian was completely dependent on her and no one came to see him except his father, you and his close family. She truly lived with the belief that he was her son."

Logan interjected, "And it was Margaret who paid the wee lad the coin to come and get Brenna this morning. Since Margaret had hidden herself under the hood, no one recognized her."

"All right, I understand why a woman might become daft after losing her only child at such a young age, but how did she convince Ennis to go along with her?"

"I do no' ken the answer to that," Quade said. "When he spoke to us in the cottage, he seemed genuinely sorry for his part. I do no' believe he realized how daft Margaret was."

"I can answer to that," Brenna said. "I heard them discussing the situation." Brenna swiped at her eyes before continuing. "Poor Ennis. All he did was agree to help her get Torrian back to her house." Brenna said. "When she arrived at the old cottage in the forest, she attacked me and said she would kill me for ruining her life. Ennis stopped her and said he had not agreed to hurt me, only to help her make Torrian sick again so he would have to return to their cottage."

Torrian rubbed his eyes and sat up. "Aye, and she made me eat from the trencher. I told her Lady Brenna had said we couldnae eat from them because they were full of wheat, but she made me." Growley licked his face and he giggled, swinging his hands at the dog. "Stop it, Growley."

As soon as he was able to continue, he said, "And when you came upstairs to fetch Margaret to help, Da, I tried to tell you, but I couldnae talk because I was heaving so much."

Quade continued. "Margaret got away in the confusion while we were interviewing people in the great hall. There were so many lads and lasses about that no one noticed her leave."

"If Ennis said he would no' do aught to hurt you, then who shot you?" Quade asked.

Seamus spoke up. "Ennis must have shot the arrow

in your leg. He is one of the two I sent to check the woods when I thought I saw something. He gave me the all-clear sign so we would fan out from you, but then he must have shot you quick."

Brenna pondered this. "But Ennis was the one who pulled me onto his horse. I do no' understand how he could have shot me."

"Your horse ran wild right toward the woods," Quade said. "Ennis was actually closer because he was hiding there."

"Aye, I ken 'twas Ennis who shot me. He admitted it in the cottage, but he had only intended to hit the horse. He hit me by accident. His purpose was to throw suspicion onto someone at the wedding."

"But how did Ennis end up dead?" Logan asked. "Margaret did no' kill her own husband, did she?"

"Aye, she did, and I witnessed it," Brenna said. "The hardest part was when Ennis tried to convince her no' to hurt me. I could see in his eyes that he still loved her, but he kenned she was no longer thinking clearly. He pulled her away from me and talked to her, but she finally broke down weeping. He held her for a long while. Then she kissed him and pulled her dirk out and stabbed him. I tried to scream and warn Ennis, but it was too late. You should have seen the look in his eyes when she stabbed him. 'Twas a horrible sight to see."

"Amazing he was still alive when we arrived." Logan stared at the flames in the hearth, mesmerized. "Quade, I believe he clung to life as long as he did to warn you."

"Aye, you could be correct." No one spoke for quite a while. Quade pulled his wife closer so he could kiss her cheek. "'Tis true you gave me the fright of my life, lass."

"I wish I could have seen you on your horse, husband." She gazed into his green eyes and was humbled by the love she saw there.

Lady Ramsay jumped in again. "So you explained how Ennis died, but where is Margaret? Who stopped her?"

They all turned to stare at Quade.

Logan spoke first. "'Tis quite a sight to see you riding Star the way you do. And the way she responds to you is beautiful. I am glad you did no' listen to me when I told you to shoot. You called it right, brother."

"Quade, what is he talking about?" Lady Ramsay said, glaring at her eldest.

"Aye, Mother, Margaret rode her horse to the cliffs pulling Brenna on a sled behind her. She intended to send the sled over the cliffs. All the riding Star and I have done together finally paid off."

"Never seen anything like it, Mama," Micheil said. "Quade stood up on Star's back, just like he always does. Logan and Seamus kept yelling at him to shoot, but he waited."

Seamus cut in. "Aye, he waited until we were about ready to strangle him. He was cool as could be atop his horse, waiting for the right time. Then he pulled out his bow and arrow, aimed her perfect and shot the instant Star stopped. Margaret's horse stopped short and Quade hit Margaret sending her over his neck and over the cliff."

Micheil guffawed. "'Except my brother couldnae tell he knocked her off, so he just fired and fired and fired. Poor horse took one in his right flank. He'll be fine."

"Saddest part was when Quade stood there staring at the empty sled on the back of the horse while Logan was unwrapping his wife behind him." Seamus nodded to Brenna. "In case you ever want to ken it, I will tell you that your husband loves you. Do no' think I have ever seen a sadder face than his at that moment."

"And my brother was laughing at me behind my back," Quade shouted.

Micheil looked at them cuddled in the chair. "'Tis a wonder you can still take a breath, lass, he hugged you so hard. We had to yell at him to let you go."

"Och, aye, but I have one more question, since we are clearing things up and we are all family now." Brenna stared at her new family to see if they had any objections.

"Aye," Quade answered. "Ask your question and I will try to answer."

"'Tis no' you I ask, husband, but my new brother-in-law."

Quade chuckled. "Och, good luck getting an answer, but you have the right to ask."

All those present looked back and forth between Logan and Micheil. She finally peered at Logan. "Why did you take my mother's healing book?"

Lady Ramsay shot up from her chair and moved toward her son. "You took her book? Without her permission? I did no' raise you to do such a thing. And what would you want with it?"

"Och, Mama, calm down. I had my reasons at the time." Logan stared at Quade, a grin breaking out across his face.

"'Twas a book my mother kept as a type of diary," Brenna said, addressing her words to Lady Ramsay. "It had all the healer's poultices and potions in it as well as her favored treatments. There were other things written in there from mother to daughter for my sister and me, so I was heartbroken when he took it. It disappeared after Logan argued with Quade and left us."

Lady Ramsay peered at her middle son, her demeanor much calmer now. "May I answer, Logan? I believe I ken why."

"Go ahead. I do no' think you will be right, but go ahead." Logan crossed his arms as he leaned against the wall, a sly grin on his face.

"He took it because he wanted to make sure the healing poultices would be available for his niece and nephew. He does no' like to let on how much he loves

Lily and Torrian, but I ken how much he does. He brought it here to help them in case you wouldnae." She glanced at the two heads of her grandchildren, Lily asleep on Brenna's lap and Torrian on Growley's belly.

"No' bad, Mother, but no' quite." Logan smiled. "Assurance."

Brenna shook her head. "I do no' understand."

"Och, Sis, you will come to understand what a bull head my brother is. You are aware of the curse he thought he had on him, aye?"

She nodded.

Logan continued, "I ken how stubborn my brother is. I also kenned right away that you were meant for each other. My fear was he would take you back to your clan to keep from falling in love with you. He believed he did no' deserve you."

"Och, nay. You were the one who said you would take me back to my clan, no' Quade."

"Aye, because we are brothers and we are close. Have you no' ever noticed the same with your own brothers? He does the opposite of whatever I say. If I say stay, he goes. If I told him to take you to your clan, I kenned he would take you to *our* clan. And you were much needed here, as you now ken."

"Och, you have me verra confused, Logan." Brenna stared at him wide-eyed. "I still do no' understand."

"Simple, lass. Wherever your book went, you would go. I could see it in your eyes how much that book meant to you, so I knew you would never leave without getting it back. I had to be sure that if my brother was foolish enough to take you back to your clan, you would insist on coming here first."

"True." Brenna still wasn't quite sure she understood.

"My niece and nephew needed you, so the book came with me to make sure you would follow.

Quade nodded his head, a sheepish look on his face,

and kissed his wife's forehead.

Brenna stared at him, still confused.

"Aye, I needed you here, lass. And my brother kenned it better than I did."

Logan smiled.

Brenna kissed her husband on the lips and smiled. "Laird Ramsay, your curse is over. I am never leaving you."

EPILOGUE

Lady Brenna Ramsay stood at the base of the stairs in her brother's great hall, a sense of happiness and peace suffusing her body. She and her sister, Jennie, had delivered her brother's wee daughter the previous night. She had just checked on Maddie and she was sound asleep in her chamber with her maid, Alice, fussing over her.

The scene that greeted her eyes was beautiful. Thanks to the snow storm raging outside, practically the whole family was gathered together. Jennie and Avelina sat at the table planning the garments they would sew for the wee lass while Brenna's two nephews ran circles around the perimeter of the hall. Lily, Torrian, and Growley scrambled at the boys' heels, their combined laughter bouncing off the rafters.

Brenna's brother, Alex, pumped up like a peacock after the birth of his daughter, paced the hall with his wee one, who was strapped to his chest with his plaid, cooing in the softest voice she had ever heard him use. She couldn't help but giggle. Alex had stayed by his wife's side during the birth, and he was so excited to finally have a daughter to love that he wasn't even disappointed that the lass had arrived with a shock of dark hair instead of Maddie's beautiful blonde curls.

She glanced toward the hearth and smiled when she saw that her husband had just left Robbie and Brodie and was striding toward her. He pulled her up into his embrace, and then turned her around to face the family gathering. He rubbed the small mound of her belly lovingly.

"I hope you willnae be upset if I do no' sit in the birthing room with you when your time comes. I am nae like your brother."

She peeked at him over her shoulder. "Nay, Quade. I ken 'twould no' be right for you. My brother is a bit different than most, as you can see." She nodded toward the cooing giant.

He kissed her neck before whispering in her ear. "Do you ken, this scene reminds me of the dream I had when I first met you."

Brenna turned to face him. "What dream?"

"'Twas when I had the fever from the boar wound. I dreamed I was standing in a great hall and my wee ones were healthy and running the hall, just like now, their laughter music to my ears. Even now, I cannae explain the feeling it gave me. But there was one thing not right."

"What?"

"You were not there, my love." He kissed her.

"And now you are where you belong, at my side."

THE END

AUTHOR'S NOTE

APPENDICITIS - Hopefully, you were able to recognize the illness that affected Quade Ramsay enough to slow his movements and cause him to be a victim of the boar. The symptoms of appendicitis are often frequent vomiting and weakness as he experienced on his trip through the Highlands to find a healer. A ruptured appendix can have devastating consequences, and was often fatal prior to the advent of antibiotics. Brenna's decision to remove it was most likely a life saving measure.

CELIAC DISEASE - Lily and Torrian both suffered from celiac disease. Celiac disease is a common affliction today and is easily recognized by physicians. The first reference I found to it dates back to the second century. Eating a gluten-free diet is the recommendation to prevent the recurrence of symptoms. Here is the definition of celiac disease as found on www.celiaccentral.org.

"Celiac disease is an autoimmune digestive disease that damages the villi of the small intestine and interferes with absorption of nutrients from food. What does this mean? Essentially the body is attacking itself every time a person with celiac consumes gluten."

The disease is treated primarily by avoiding foods with gluten-wheat, barley, and rye. Some people will have problems digesting oats as well, but not Torrian or Lily. Oats were a great alternative in the medieval times. Rice, potatoes and corn are other great carbs for celiac patients today but not found in medieval Scotland.

Celiac disease is a genetic disorder so it is not uncommon to have 2 or more siblings affected. It also has up to 300 symptoms which may or may not affect each person. Diarrhea, abdominal pain, and foul smelling stools are all common symptoms. The blisters and sores (dermatitis herpetiformis) that Torrian suffered are usually found in advanced cases. Fortunately, celiac disease is easy to diagnose and treat today, so such symptoms are rare. Before the discovery of the disease, I suspect these symptoms were much more common.

Since the disease affects the body's ability to absorb nutrients, patients were often thin and suffered from poor weight gain and delayed growth. Once the body is given gluten-free foods, the weight and growth can return to normal.

THE SCOTTISH DEERHOUND - The idea of using Growley, the Scottish deerhound, to assist Torrian in walking came from current practices in physical therapy. I have seen dogs such as Golden Retrievers used to assist pediatric patients in rehab. I love dogs and couldn't resist using this in my novel. Besides, all young boys should have a dog to love!

If you go to my Pinterest page, you will find my idea of Growley under my *Healing a Highlander's Heart* board. The Scottish Deerhound is a beautiful animal close in size to what Torrian required.

BLOODLETTING - Medieval Medicine was based on the four humors: wind, water, earth, and fire. In the body, the humorism is as follows: blood—air, yellow bile—fire, black bile—gall bladder, phlegm—water. Since microorganisms were not discovered until the age of the microscope, the idea of diseases being "in the air" was common. Since it was believed that air was related to blood, bloodletting was common practice used by many healers. It would definitely have been dreaded by any child who had experienced it.

Today, bloodletting (or cutting the body in places to allow the bad blood to bleed out) seems a barbaric practice but it was stilled used well into the 1800s. Of course, now we know it causes weakness. While to us it seems a ridiculous premise, I can see why an infected wound full of pus (white blood cells) would be cut open to allow it to bleed the poisons out. We still do this today in surgery when a large abscess is treated. We just have the benefit of antibiotics to clear up the infection.

CHILDBED FEVER - Lilias did not deliver her placenta after her second child, Lily, was born. This condition is referred to as RETAINED PLACENTA, and it can happen if the placenta remains attached to the uterine wall. Staying inside the mother's body would cause a severe infection. In the 1200s, this affliction might have been considered to be the same as childbed or puerperal infection (basically an infection of the uterus that spreads into the blood). Not uncommon, and again, now treatable with antibiotics, childbed fever took the lives of many young mothers.

RED THROAT- This is also known as strep throat or the infection of the upper respiratory tract by streptococcus bacteria. Easily cured with antibiotics, most of us have experienced it either ourselves or with our children. What if we had no antibiotics to cure it?

IN CONCLUSION - Overall, it may appear to you that I included too many medical tragedies in this. I would like you to think about it. If you or your family did not have any antibiotics for all your sicknesses, injuries, and surgeries, how many of you would not be here today?

Medieval times were full of death. Sad, but true.

Thanks for reading!

Keira Montclair

ABOUT THE AUTHOR

Keira Montclair is the pen name for an author that lives in Florida with her husband. An Amazon best-selling author, she brings you the second novel in her Clan Grant Series, Brenna and Quade's story. Also a Registered Nurse, Keira enjoys adding medical issues to her novels and loved writing the story of Brenna Grant as a healer.

Keira loves to hear from her readers. Stop by her website at www.keiramontclair.com to sign up for her newsletter. She also has a Facebook page at Keira Montclair, Author.

See her view of her characters and the settings for this novel at her Pinterest page-the *Healing a Highlander's Heart* board.

Feel free to contact her at keiramontclair@gmail.com. She promises to respond to all emails and comments on her web page.

Printed in Great Britain
by Amazon

72335542R00158